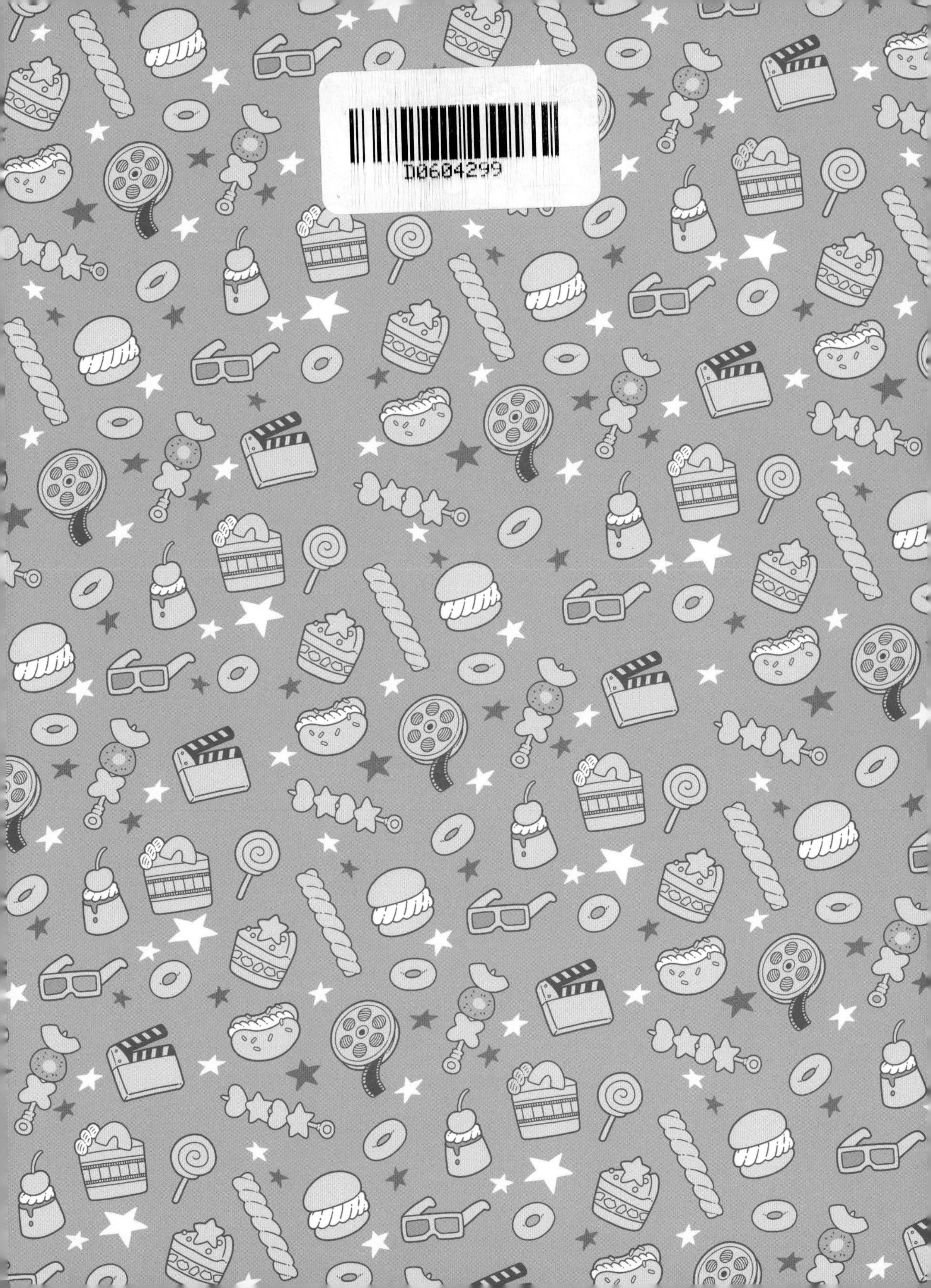

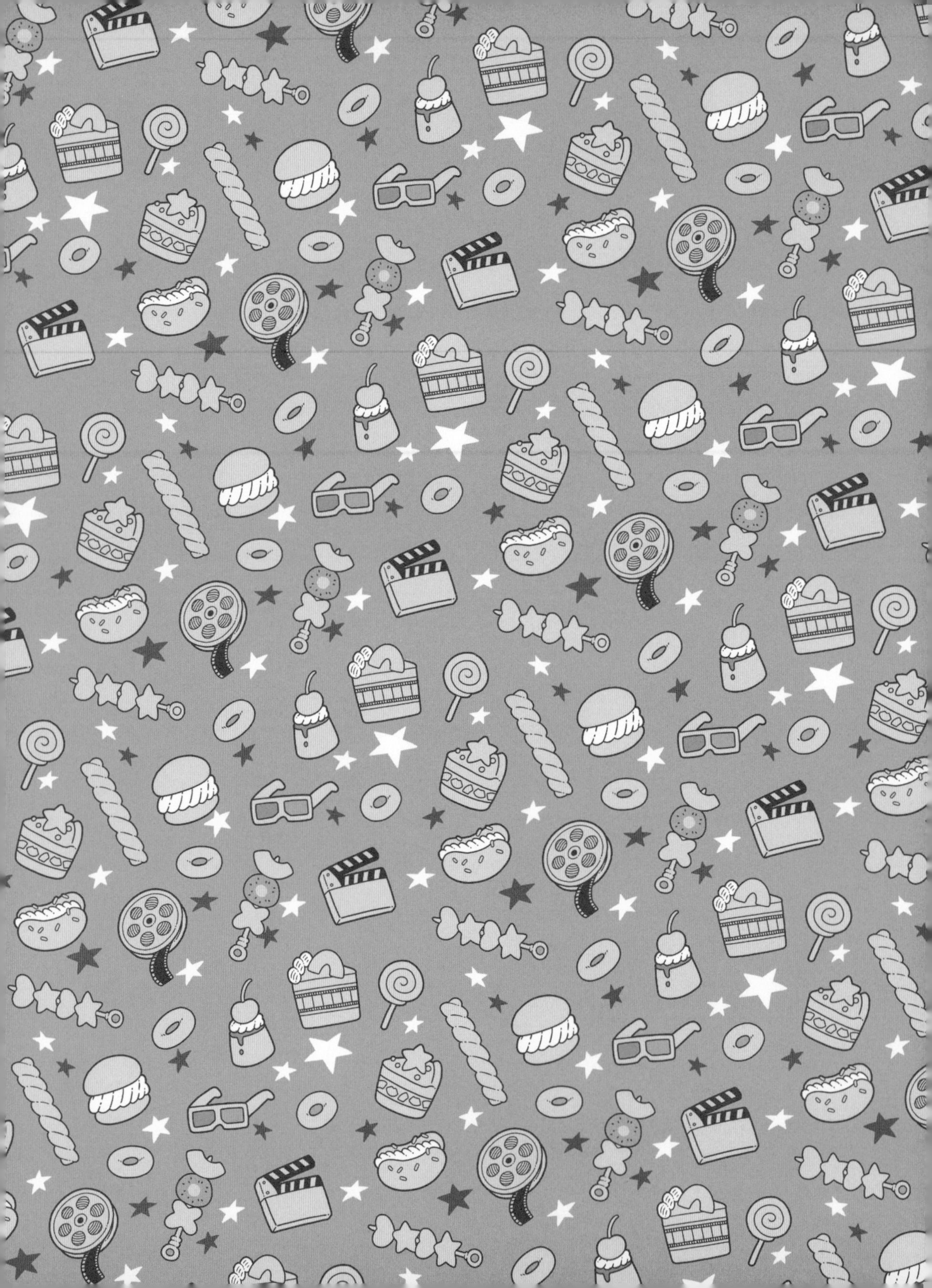

Kitty Sweet Tooth

Written by
ABBY DENSON

Art by
UTOMARU

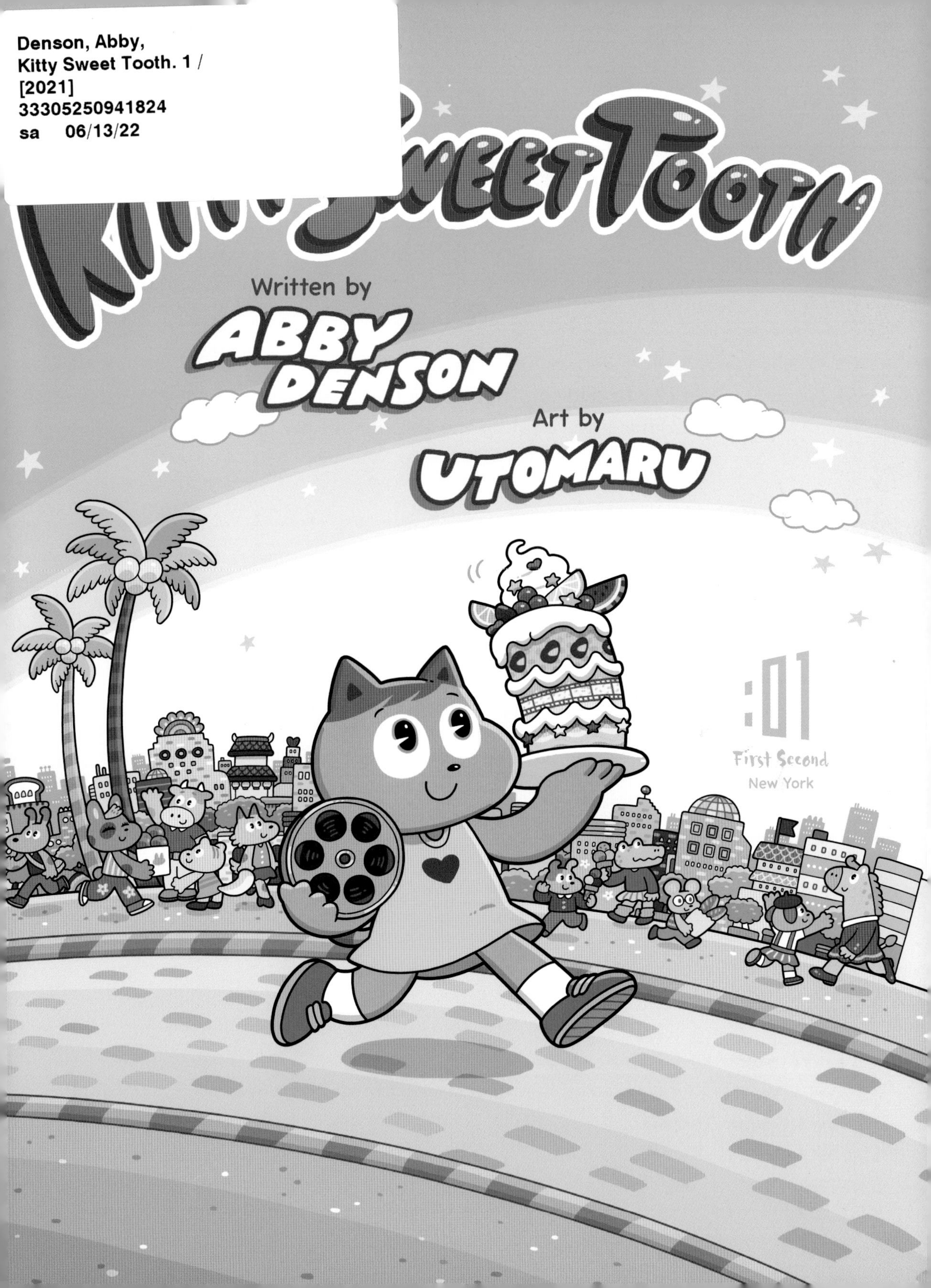

:01
First Second
New York

Dedicated to my Pop-Pop,
known for his sweet tooth and even sweeter heart.
–Abby Denson

I would like to dedicate this book to all the amazing movies
that have inspired me throughout my life.
–Utomaru

First Second

Text copyright © 2021 by Abby Denson
Illustrations copyright © 2021 by Utomaru

Published by First Second
First Second is an imprint of Roaring Brook Press,
a division of Holtzbrinck Publishing Holdings Limited Partnership
120 Broadway, New York, NY 10271

Don't miss your next favorite book from First Second! For the latest updates
go to firstsecondnewsletter.com and sign up for our enewsletter.

Library of Congress Control Number: 2020911253
ISBN: 978-1-250-19677-4

Our books may be purchased in bulk for promotional, educational, or business use.
Please contact your local bookseller or the Macmillan Corporate and Premium Sales Department
at (800) 221-7945 ext. 5442 or by email at MacmillanSpecialMarkets@macmillan.com.

First edition, 2021

Edited by Robyn Chapman
Cover and interior book design by Molly Johanson
Lettering assistance by Nadim Silverman and Samia Fakih
Printed in China by RR Donnelley Asia Printing Solutions Ltd., Dongguan City, Guangdong Province

Interior art created in Photoshop

10 9 8 7 6 5 4 3 2

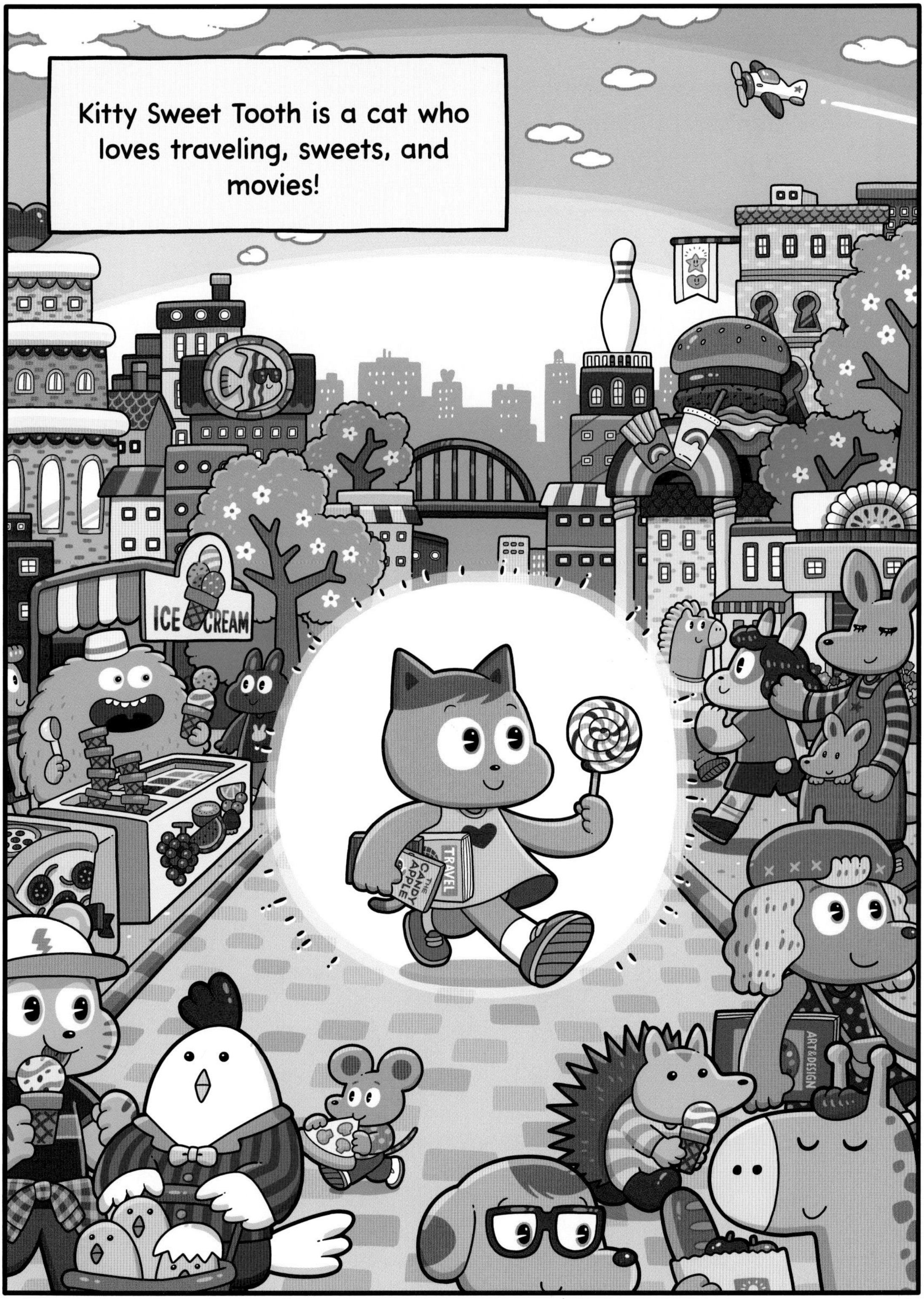
Kitty Sweet Tooth is a cat who loves traveling, sweets, and movies!
ICE CREAM
THE CANDY APPLE
TRAVEL
ART&DESIGN

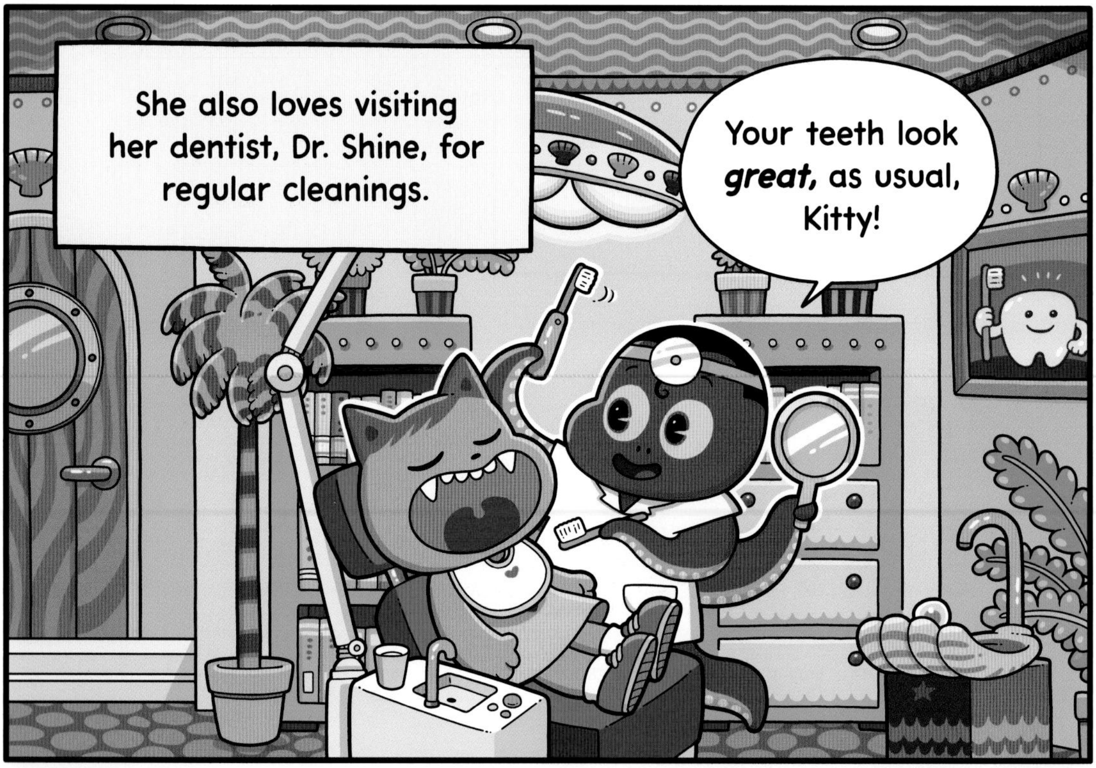
She also loves visiting her dentist, Dr. Shine, for regular cleanings.
Your teeth look *great,* as usual, Kitty!

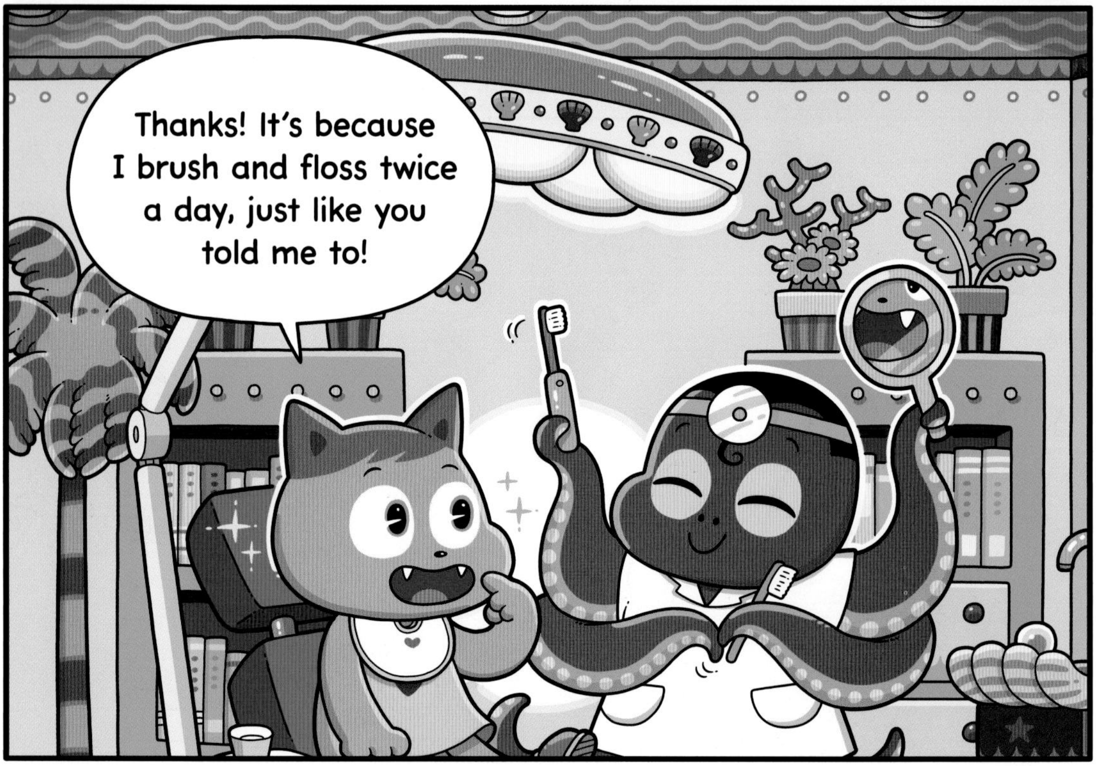
Thanks! It's because I brush and floss twice a day, just like you told me to!

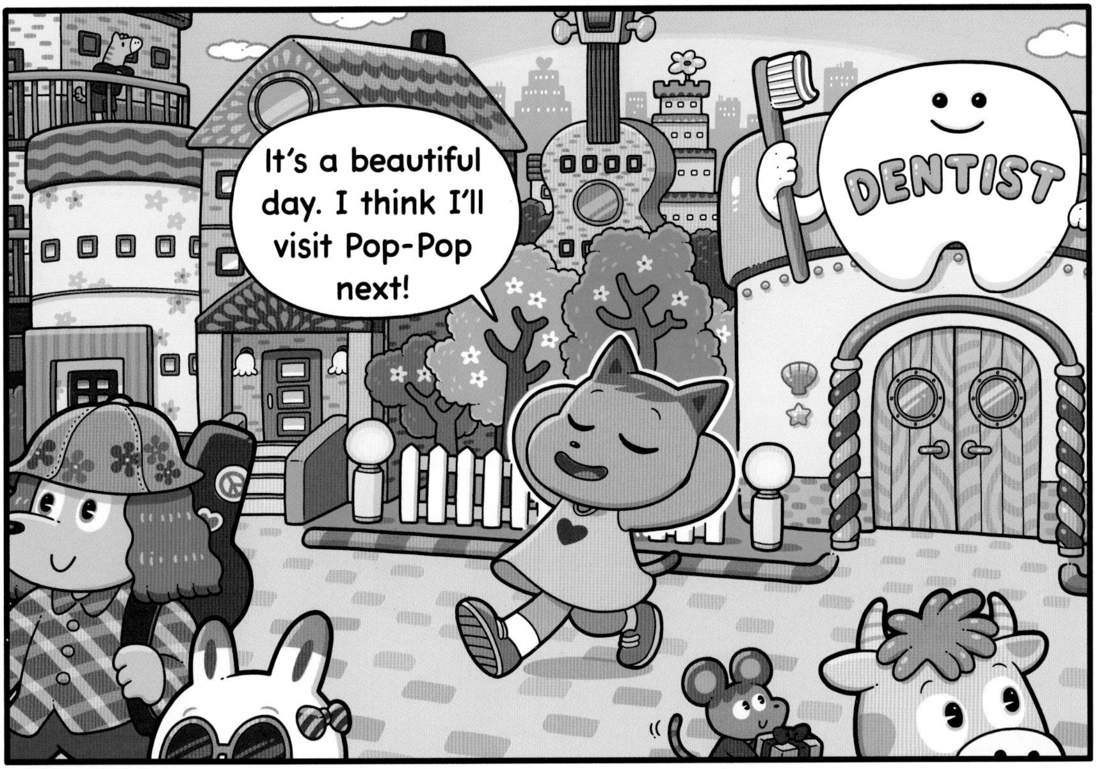
It's a beautiful day. I think I'll visit Pop-Pop next!
DENTIST

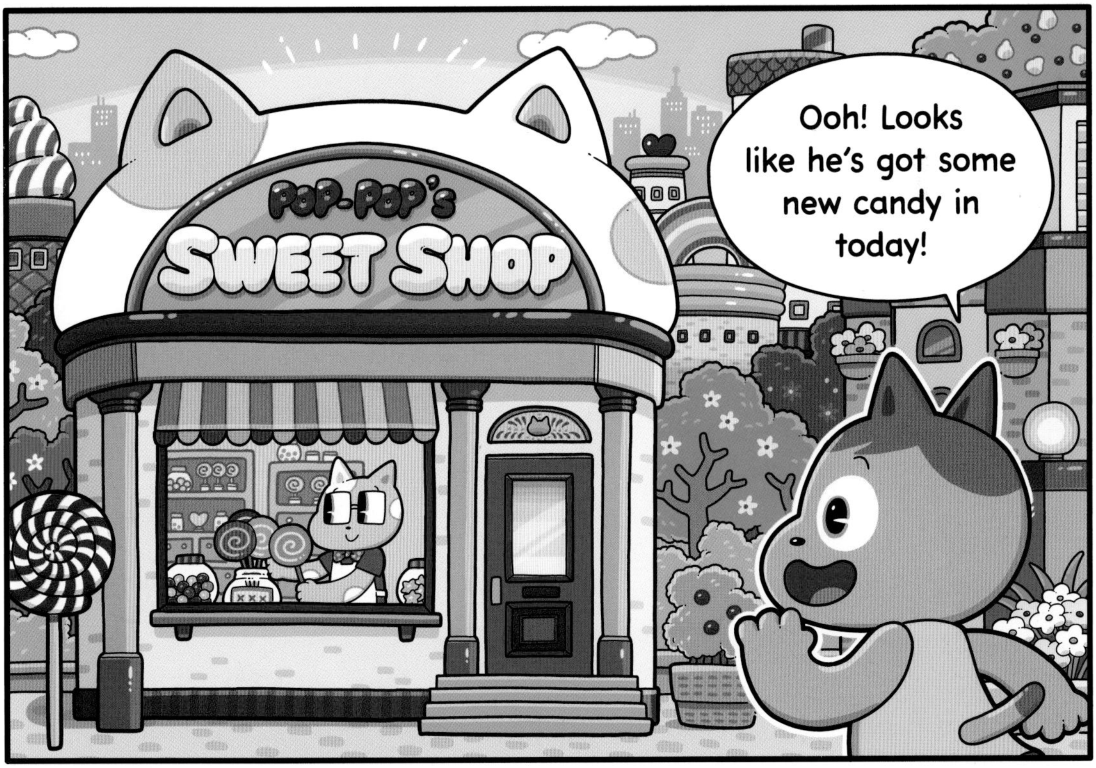
POP-POP'S
SWEET SHOP
Ooh! Looks like he's got some new candy in today!

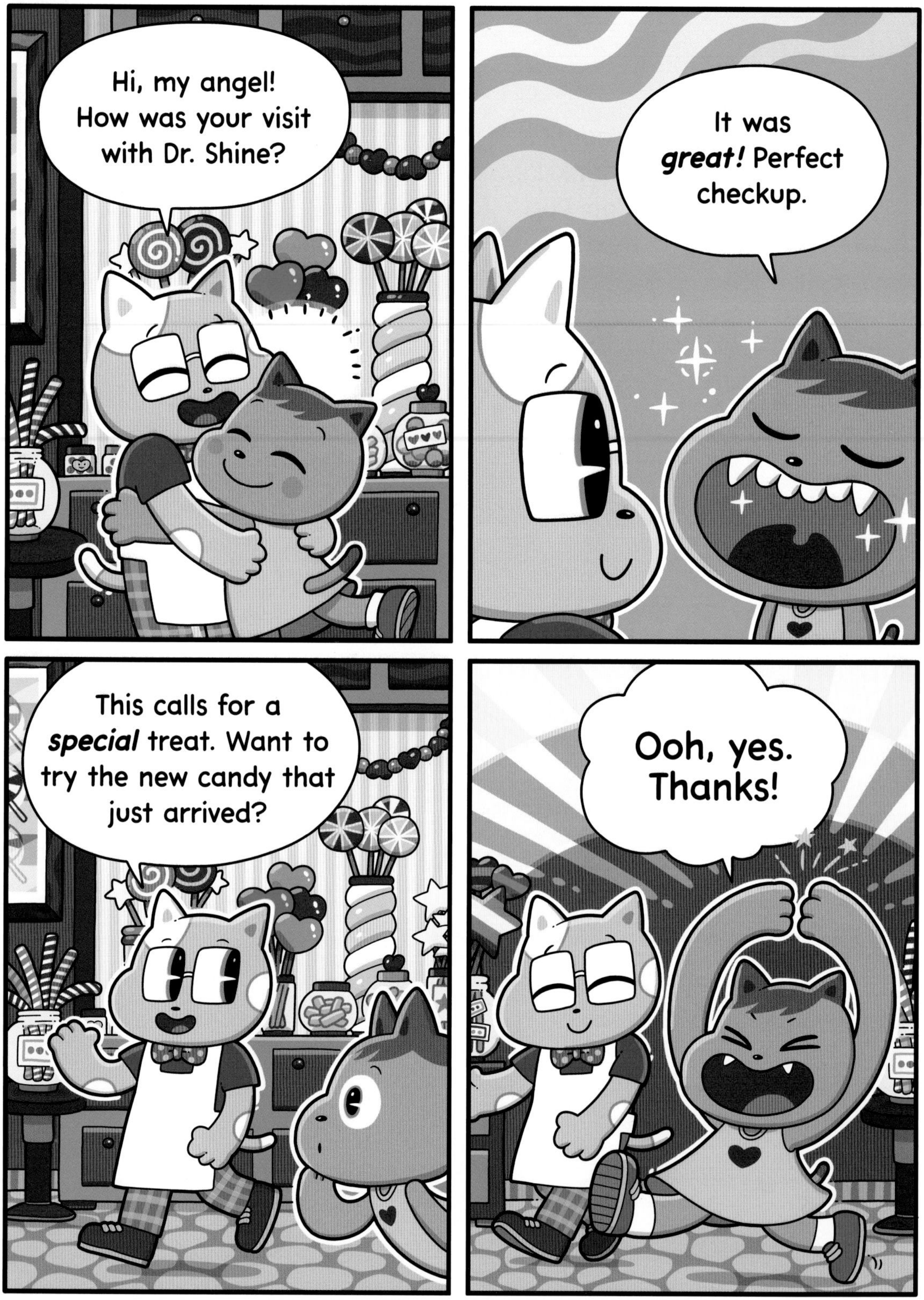
Hi, my angel! How was your visit with Dr. Shine?
It was *great!* Perfect checkup.
This calls for a *special* treat. Want to try the new candy that just arrived?
Ooh, yes. Thanks!

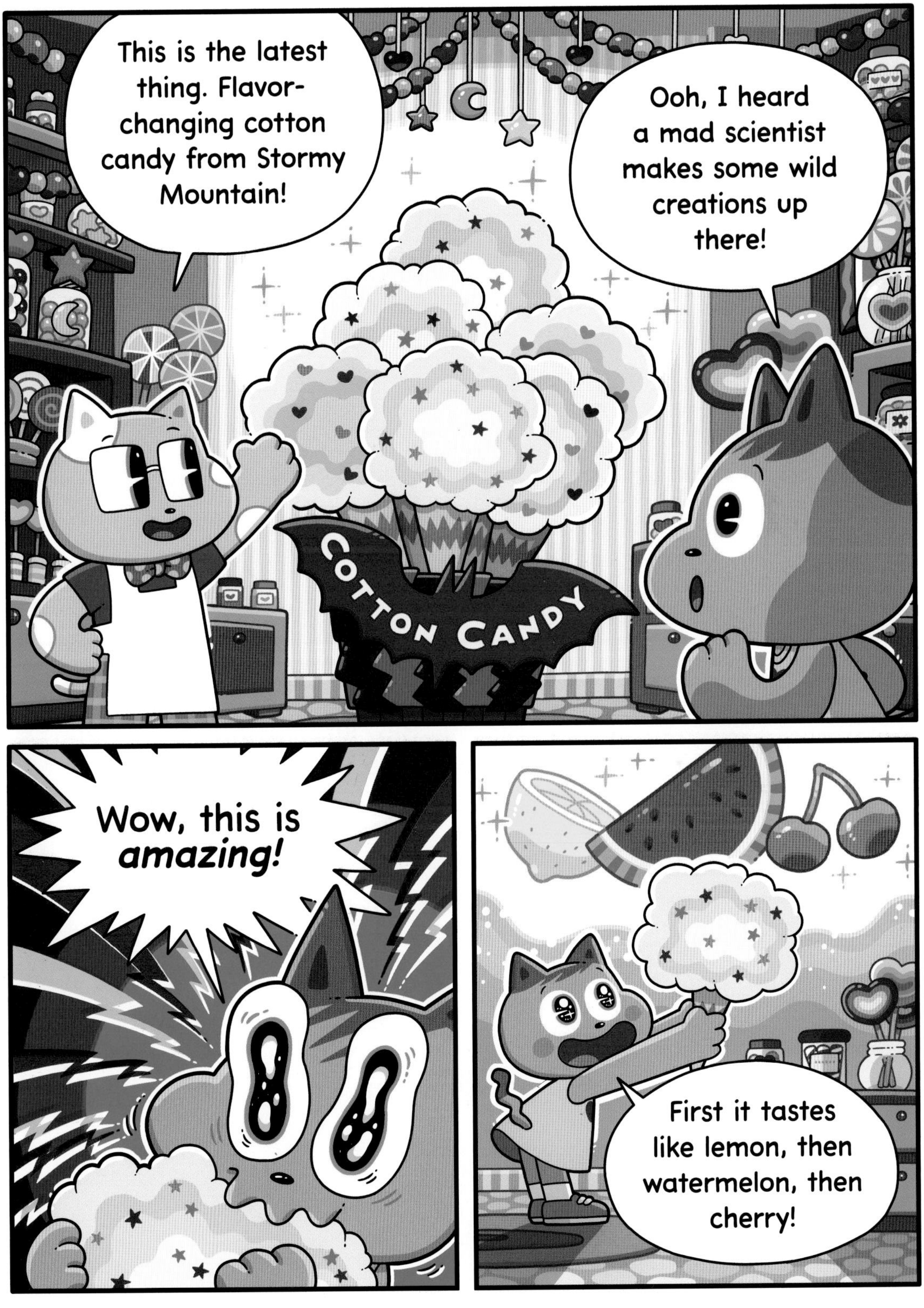
This is the latest thing. Flavor-changing cotton candy from Stormy Mountain!
Ooh, I heard a mad scientist makes some wild creations up there!
COTTON CANDY
Wow, this is *amazing!*
First it tastes like lemon, then watermelon, then cherry!

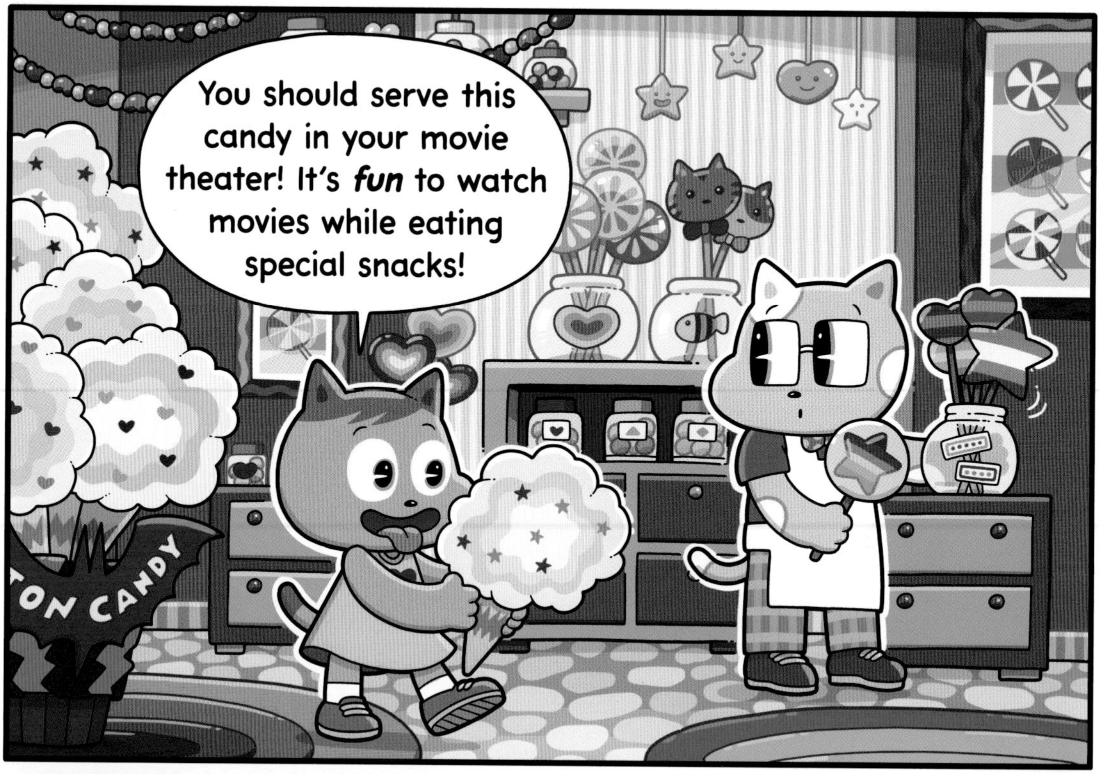
You should serve this candy in your movie theater! It's *fun* to watch movies while eating special snacks!
TON CANDY

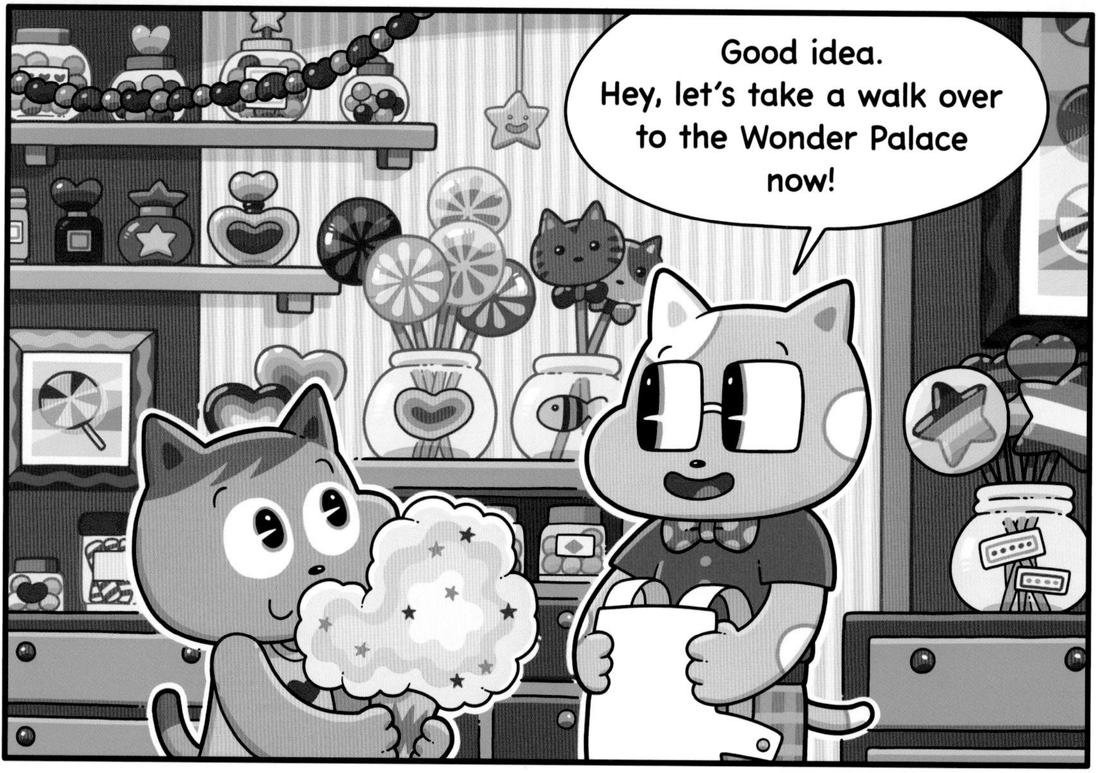
Good idea.
Hey, let's take a walk over to the Wonder Palace now!

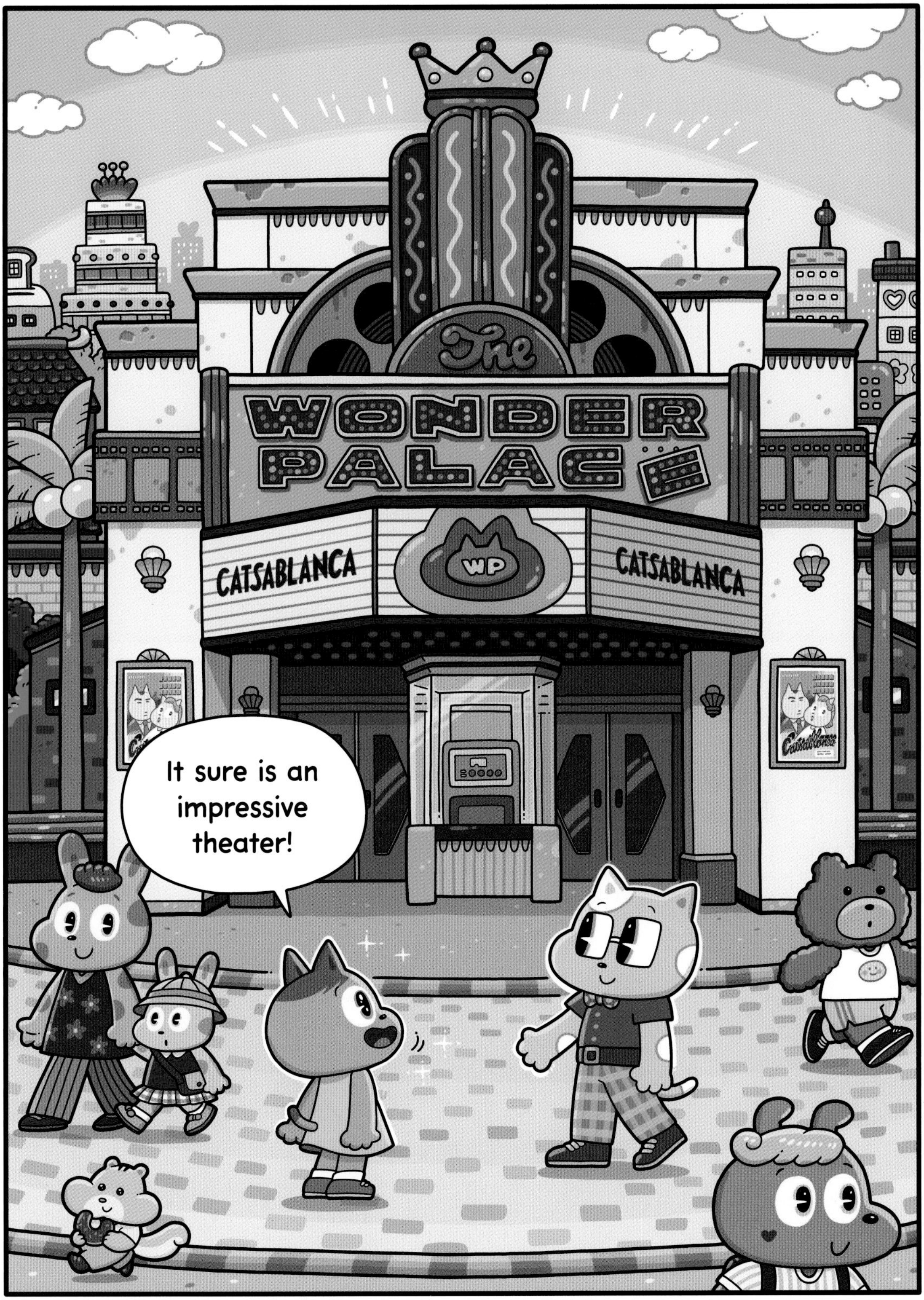
The
WONDER PALACE
CATSABLANCA
WP
CATSABLANCA
It sure is an impressive theater!

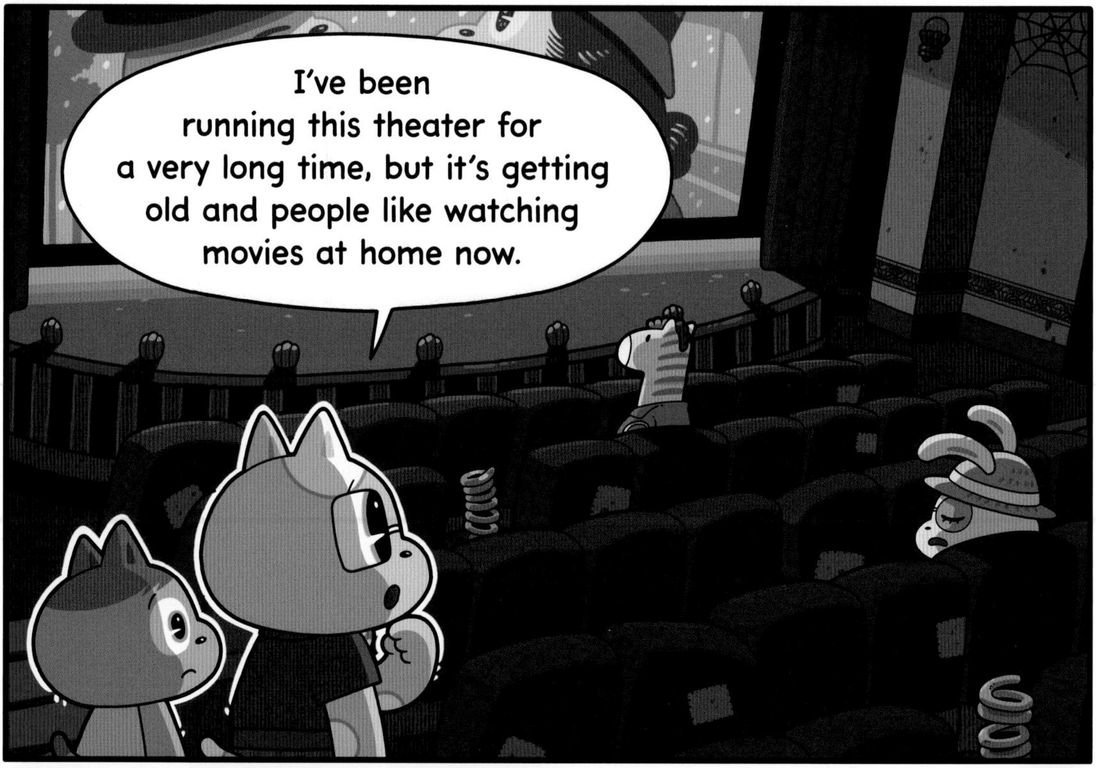
I've been running this theater for a very long time, but it's getting old and people like watching movies at home now.

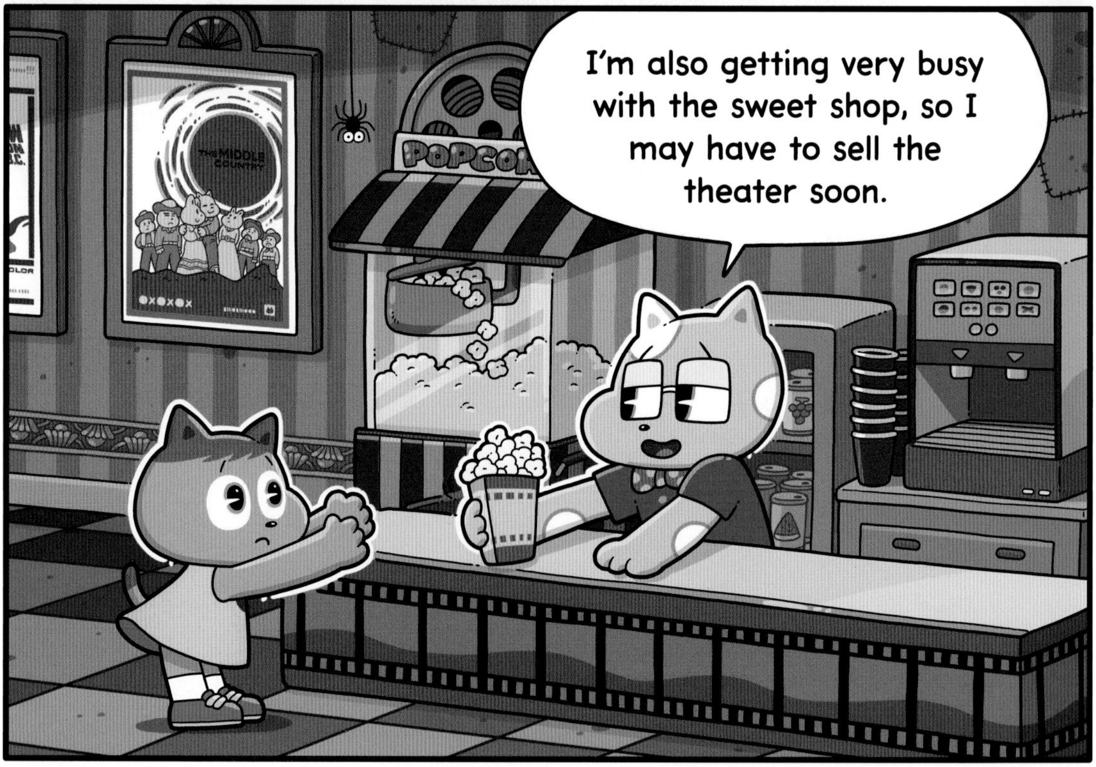
I'm also getting very busy with the sweet shop, so I may have to sell the theater soon.

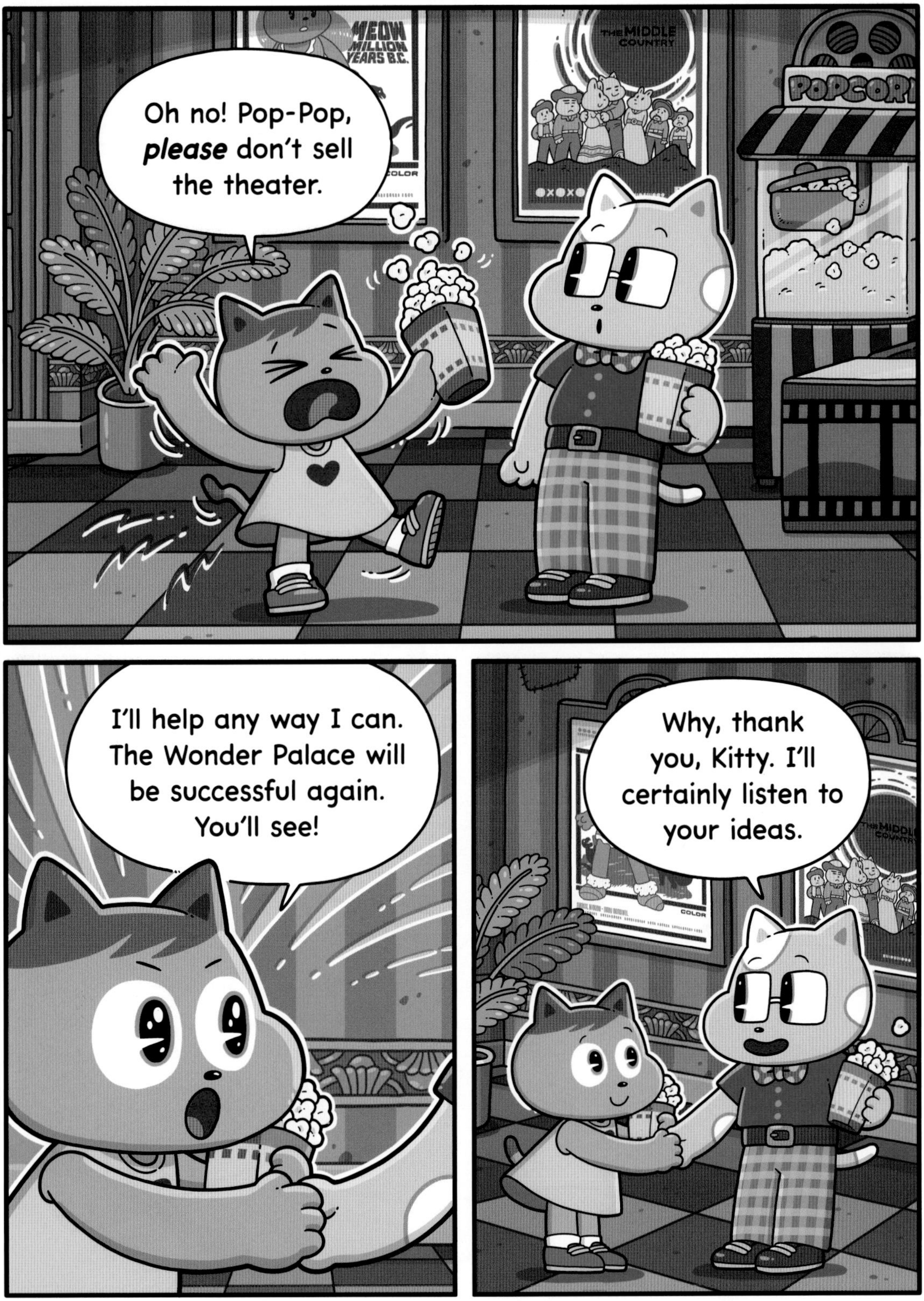
Oh no! Pop-Pop, *please* don't sell the theater.
I'll help any way I can. The Wonder Palace will be successful again. You'll see!
Why, thank you, Kitty. I'll certainly listen to your ideas.

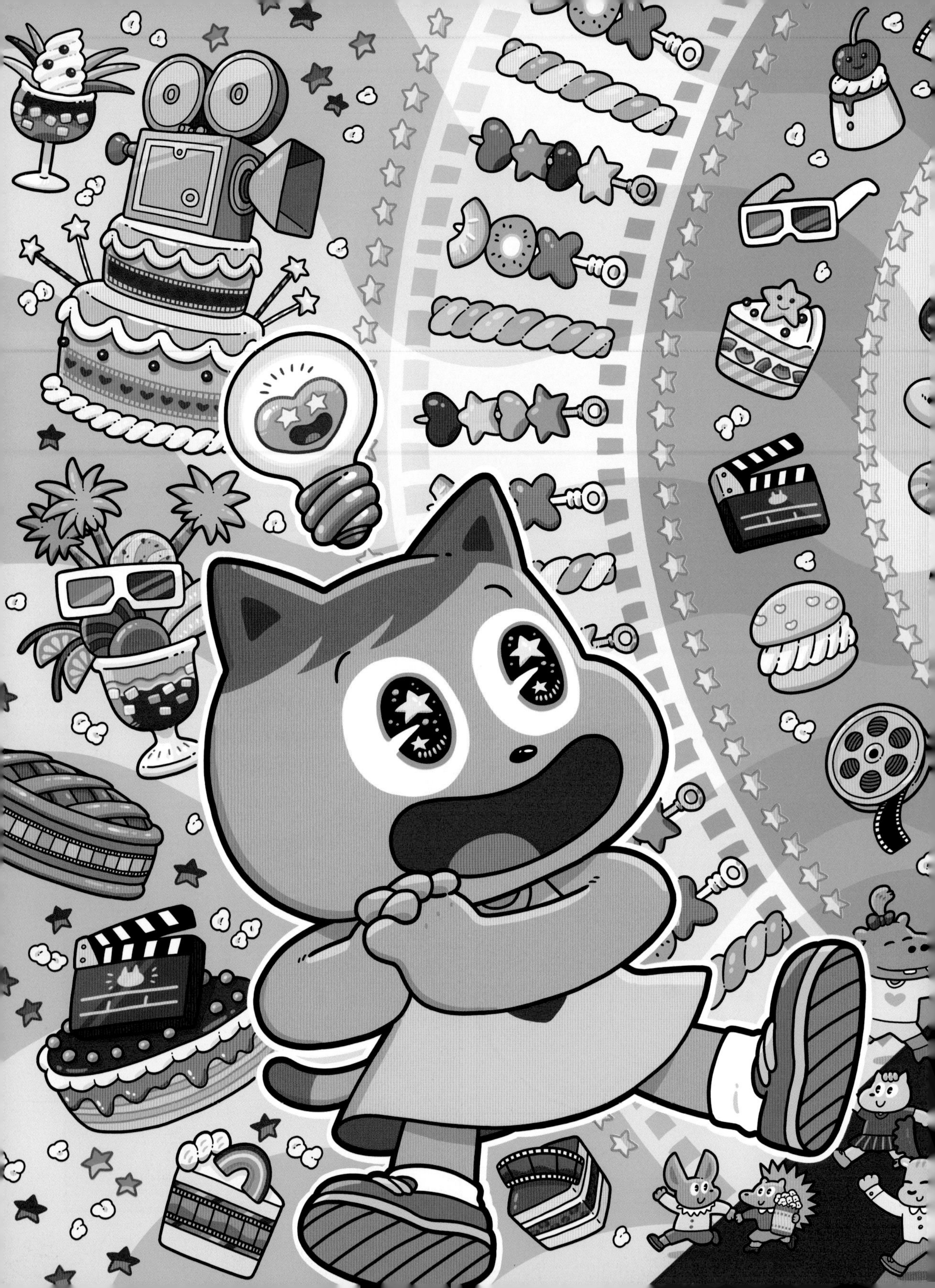

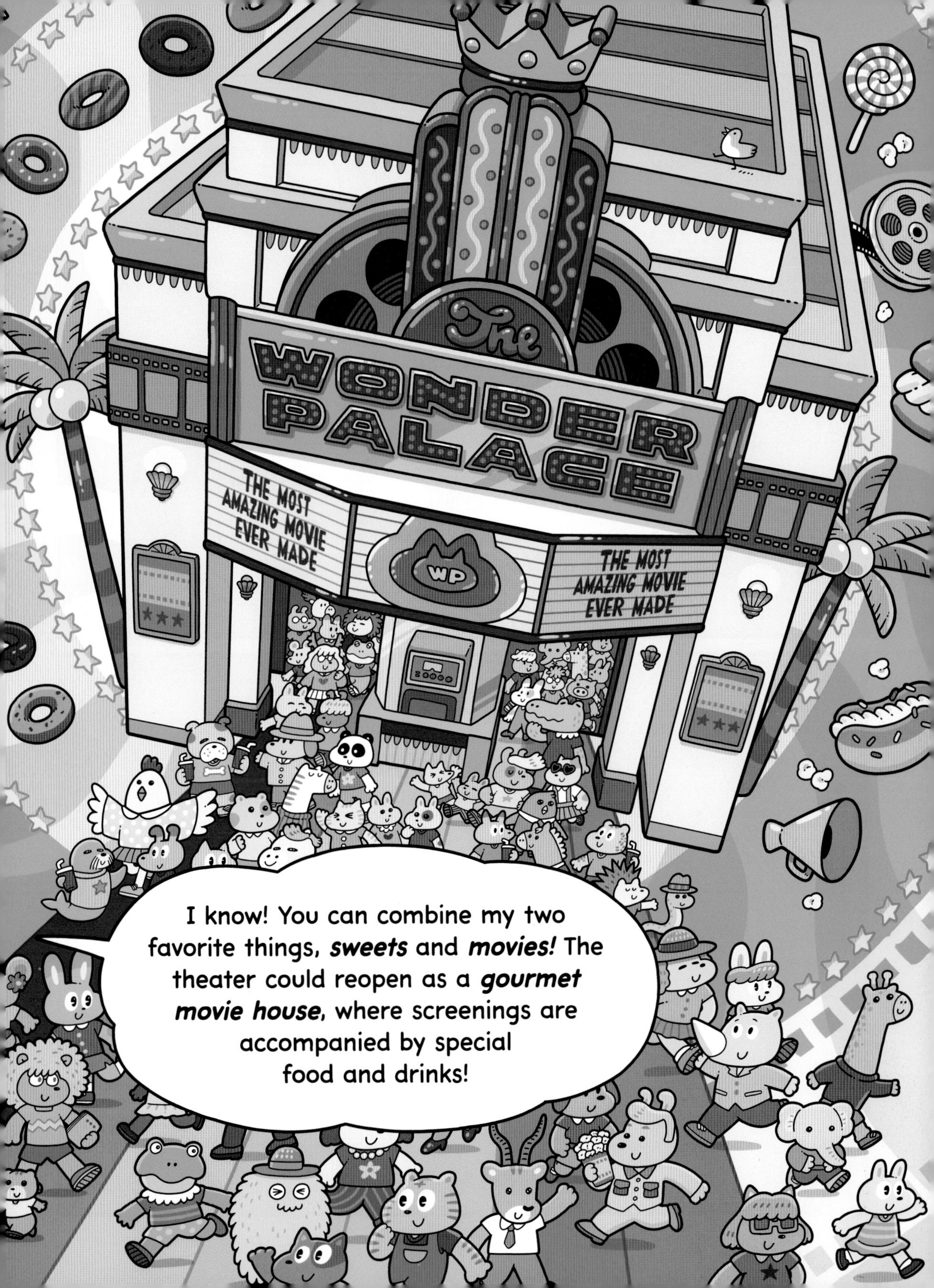
The
WONDER PALACE
THE MOST AMAZING MOVIE EVER MADE
WP
THE MOST AMAZING MOVIE EVER MADE
I know! You can combine my two favorite things, ***sweets*** and ***movies!*** The theater could reopen as a ***gourmet movie house,*** where screenings are accompanied by special food and drinks!

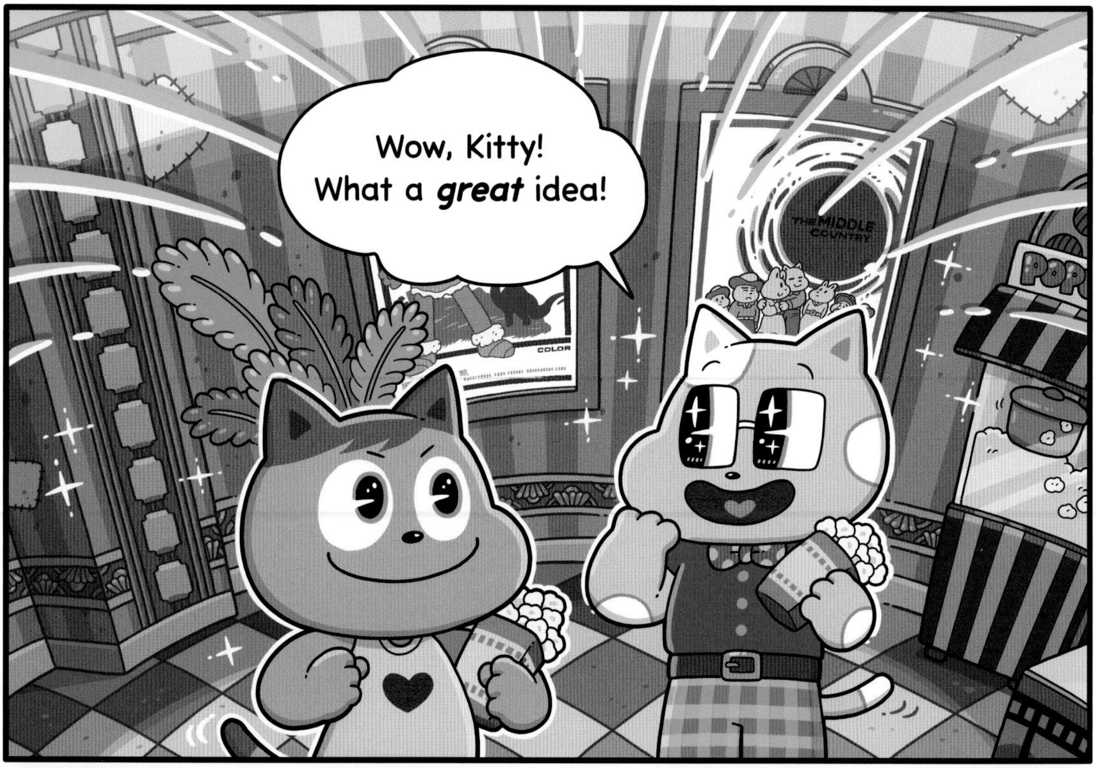
Wow, Kitty!
What a *great* idea!
THE MIDDLE COUNTRY
COLOR

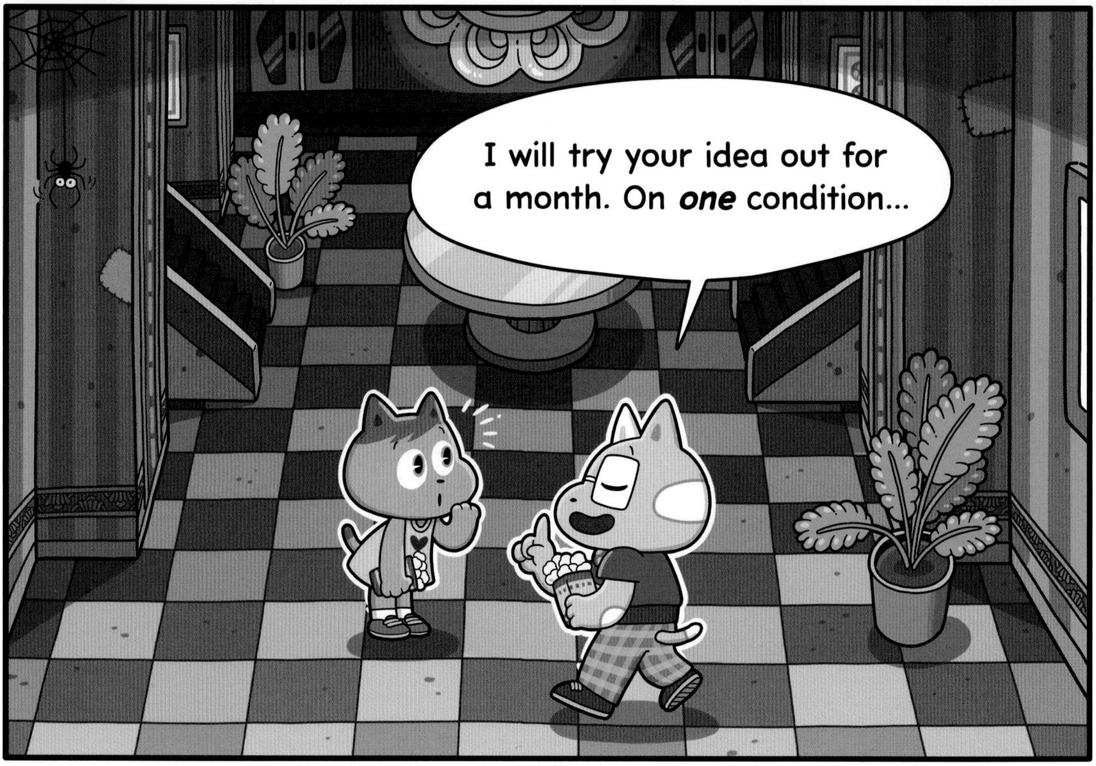
I will try your idea out for
a month. On *one* condition...

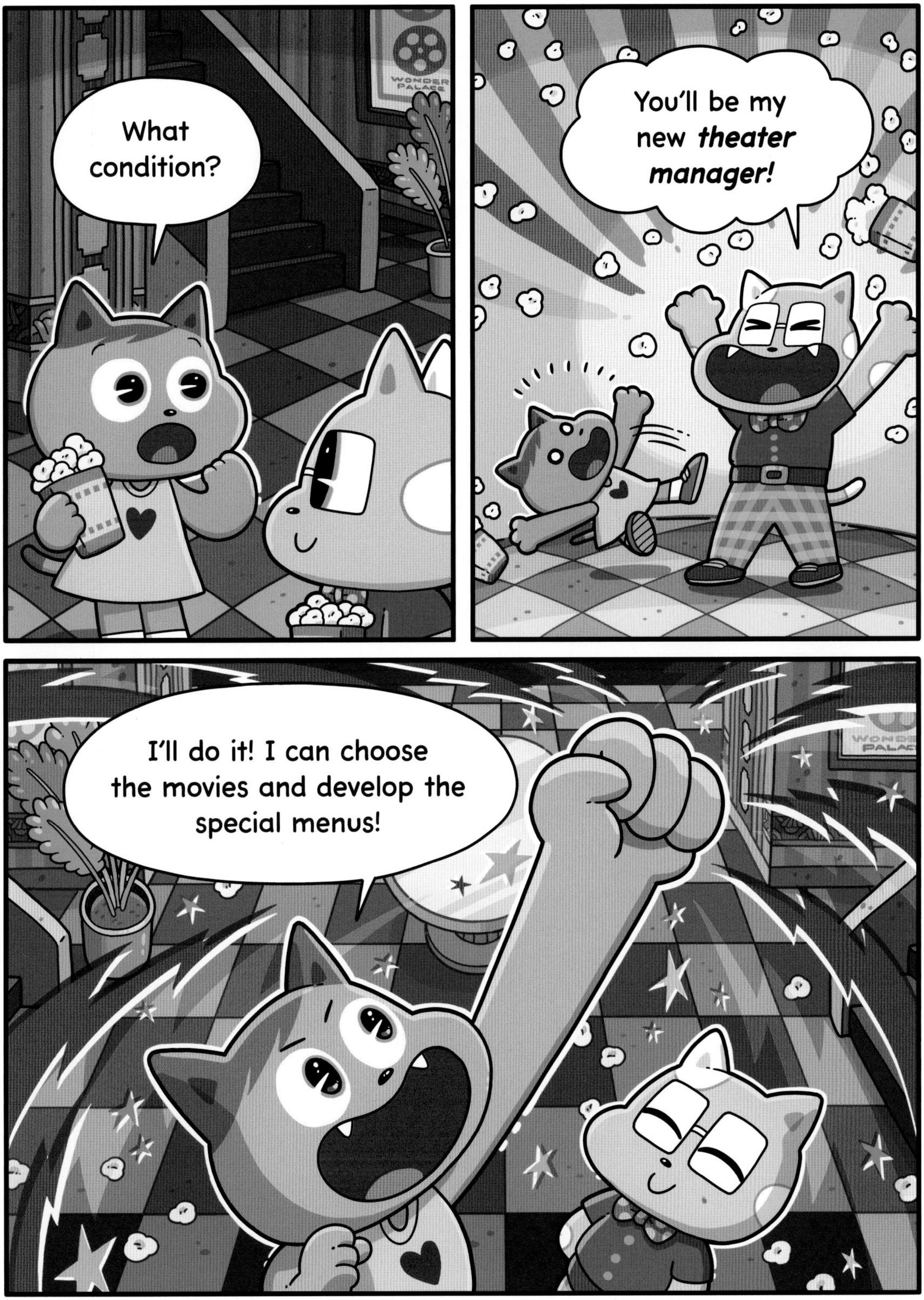
WONDER PALACE
What condition?
You'll be my new *theater manager!*
I'll do it! I can choose the movies and develop the special menus!
WONDER PALACE

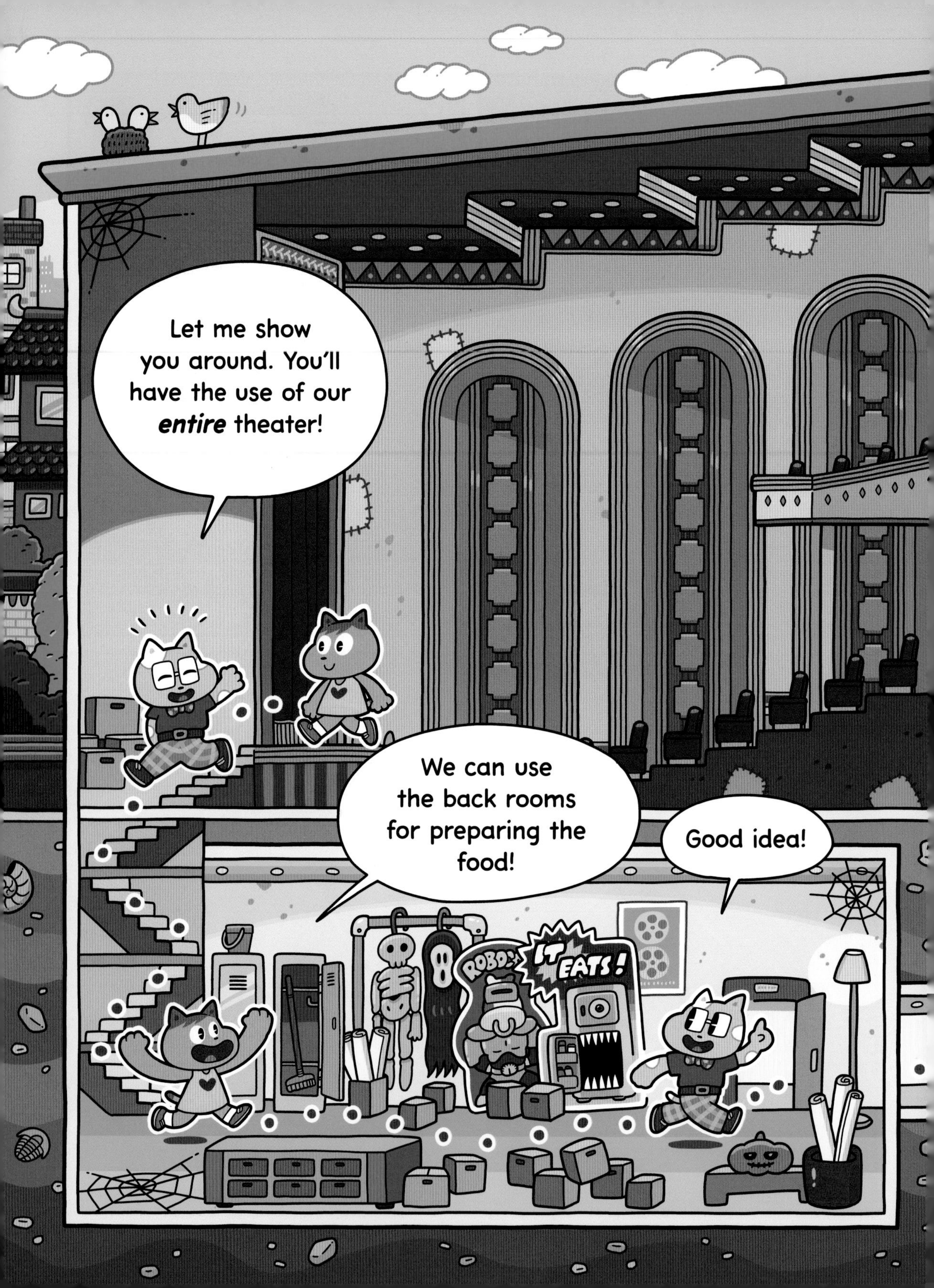
Let me show you around. You'll have the use of our *entire* theater!
We can use the back rooms for preparing the food!
Good idea!
ROBOT
IT EATS!

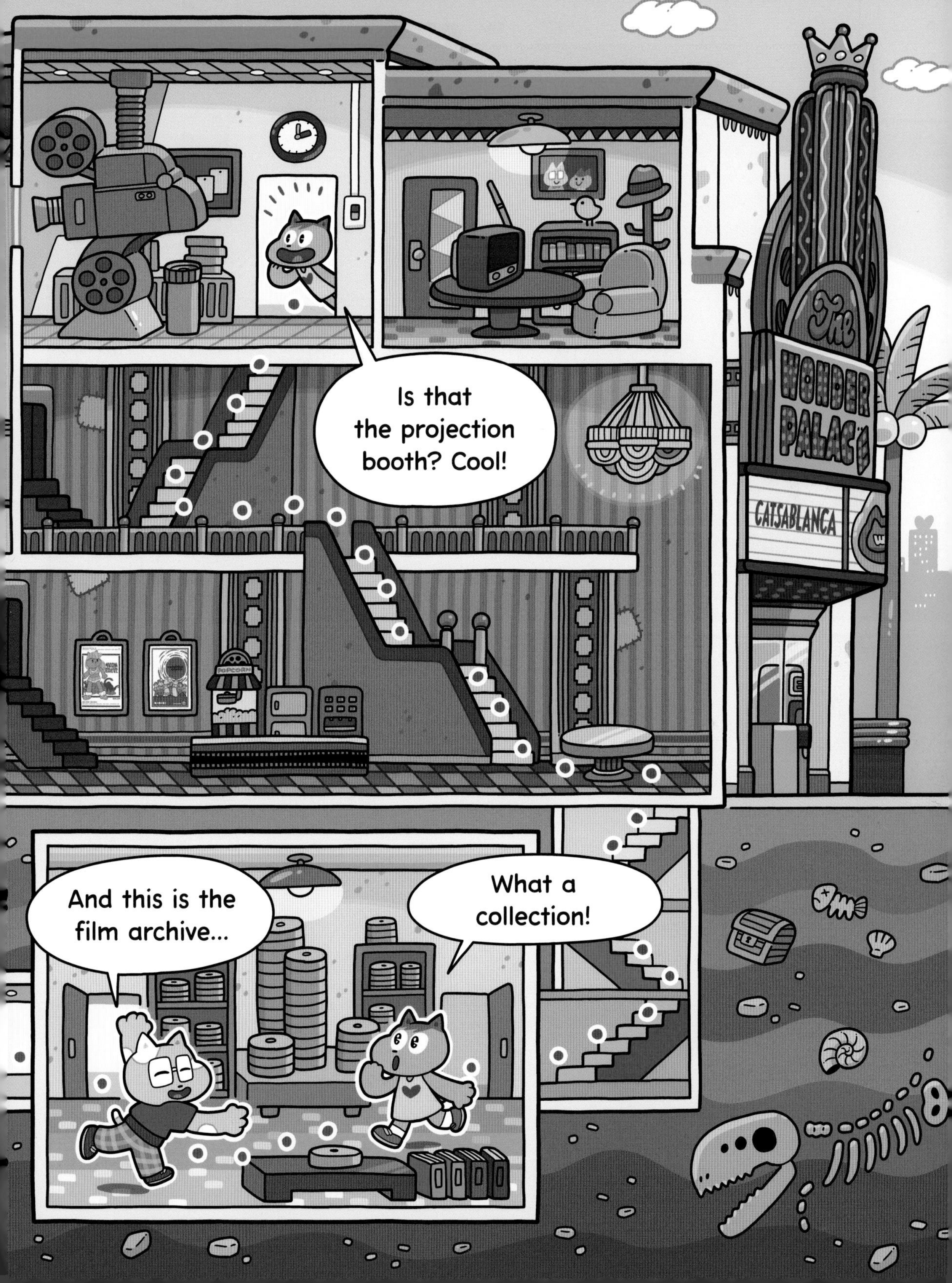

The WONDER PALACE
CATSABLANCA
POPCORN
Is that the projection booth? Cool!
And this is the film archive...
What a collection!

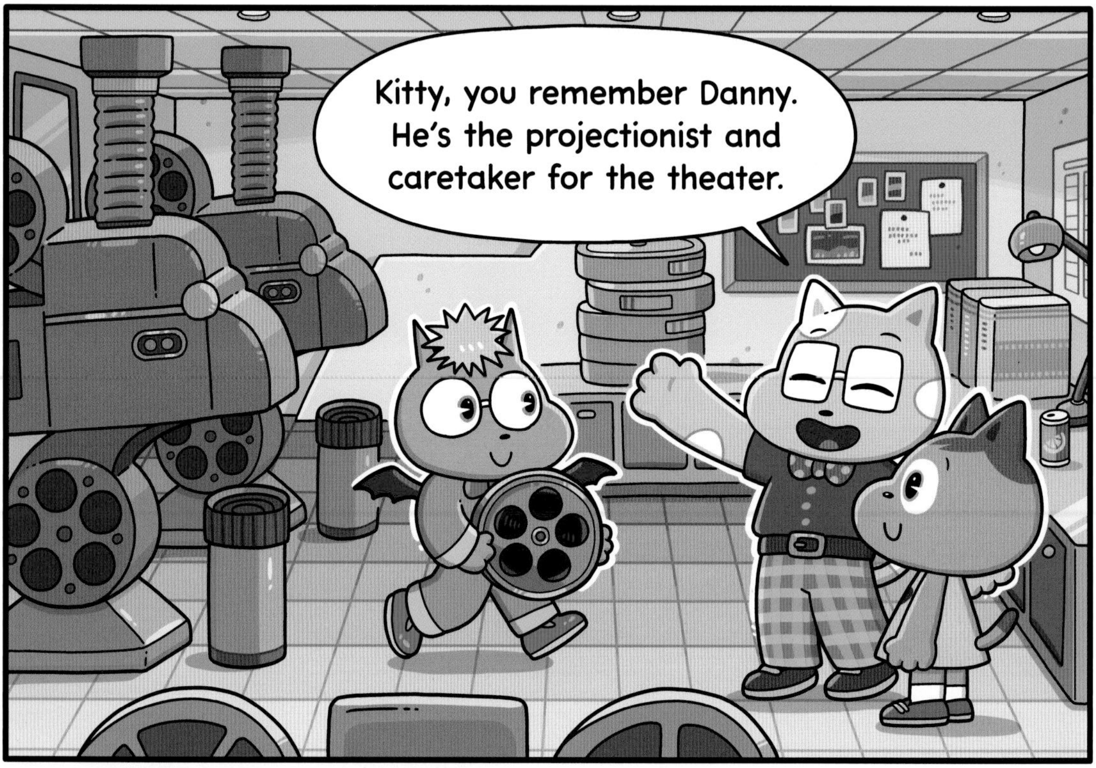
Kitty, you remember Danny. He's the projectionist and caretaker for the theater.

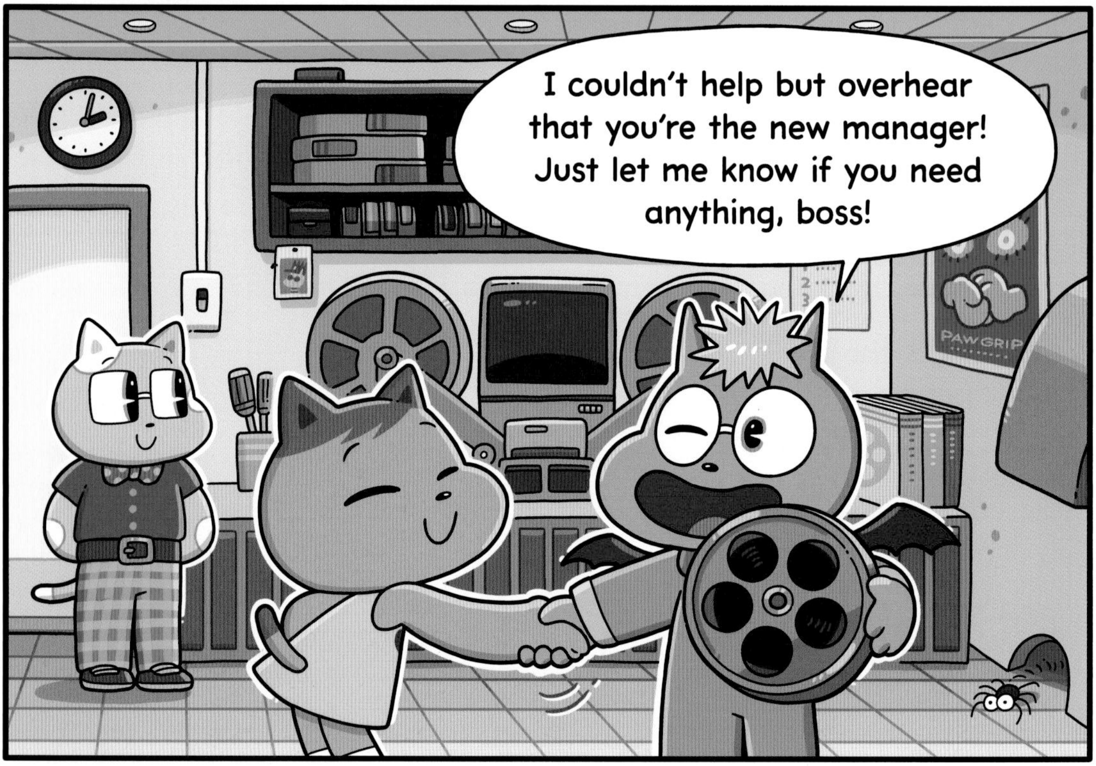
I couldn't help but overhear that you're the new manager! Just let me know if you need anything, boss!
PAWGRIP

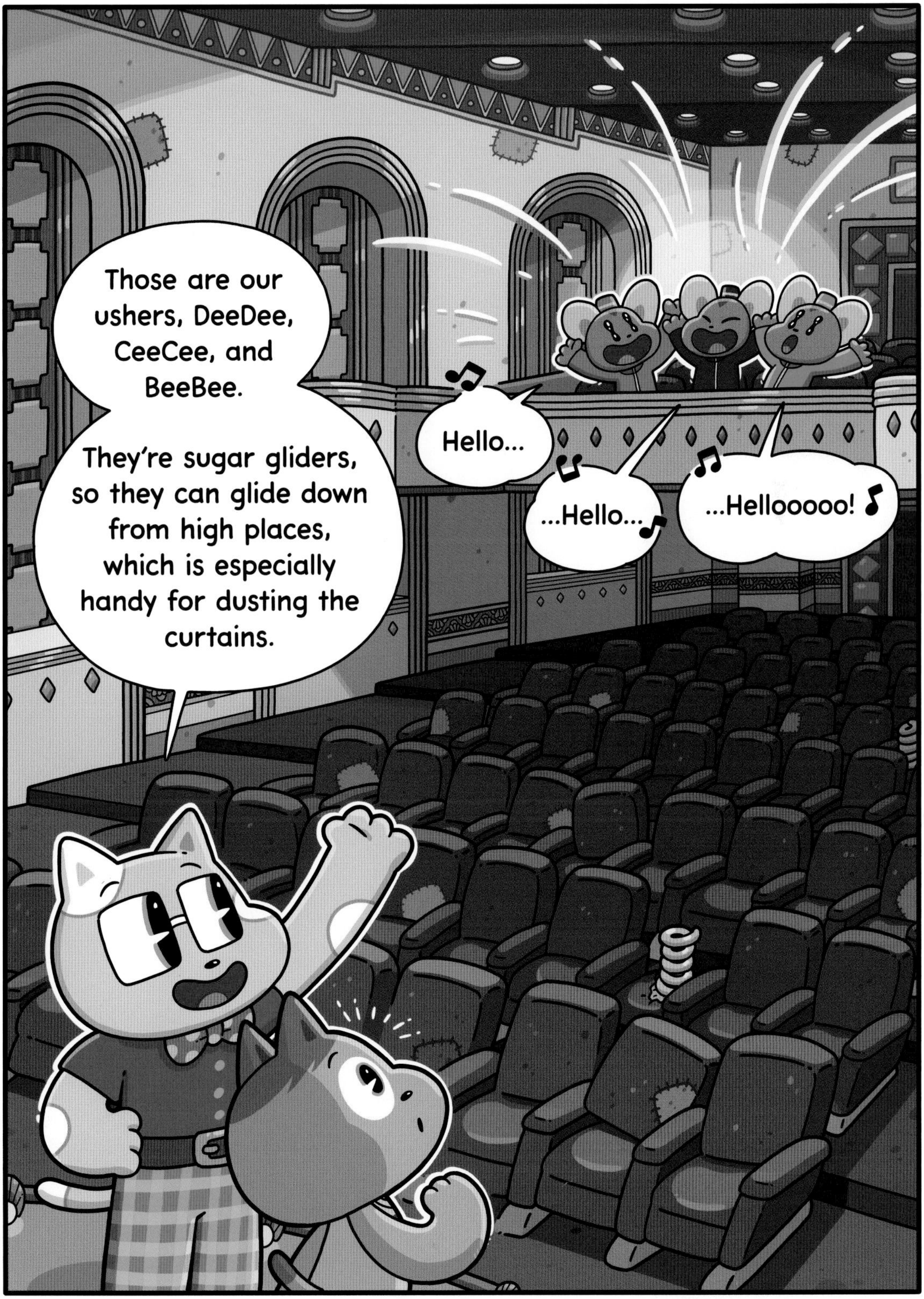

Those are our ushers, DeeDee, CeeCee, and BeeBee.
They're sugar gliders, so they can glide down from high places, which is especially handy for dusting the curtains.
Hello...
...Hello...
...Hellooooo!

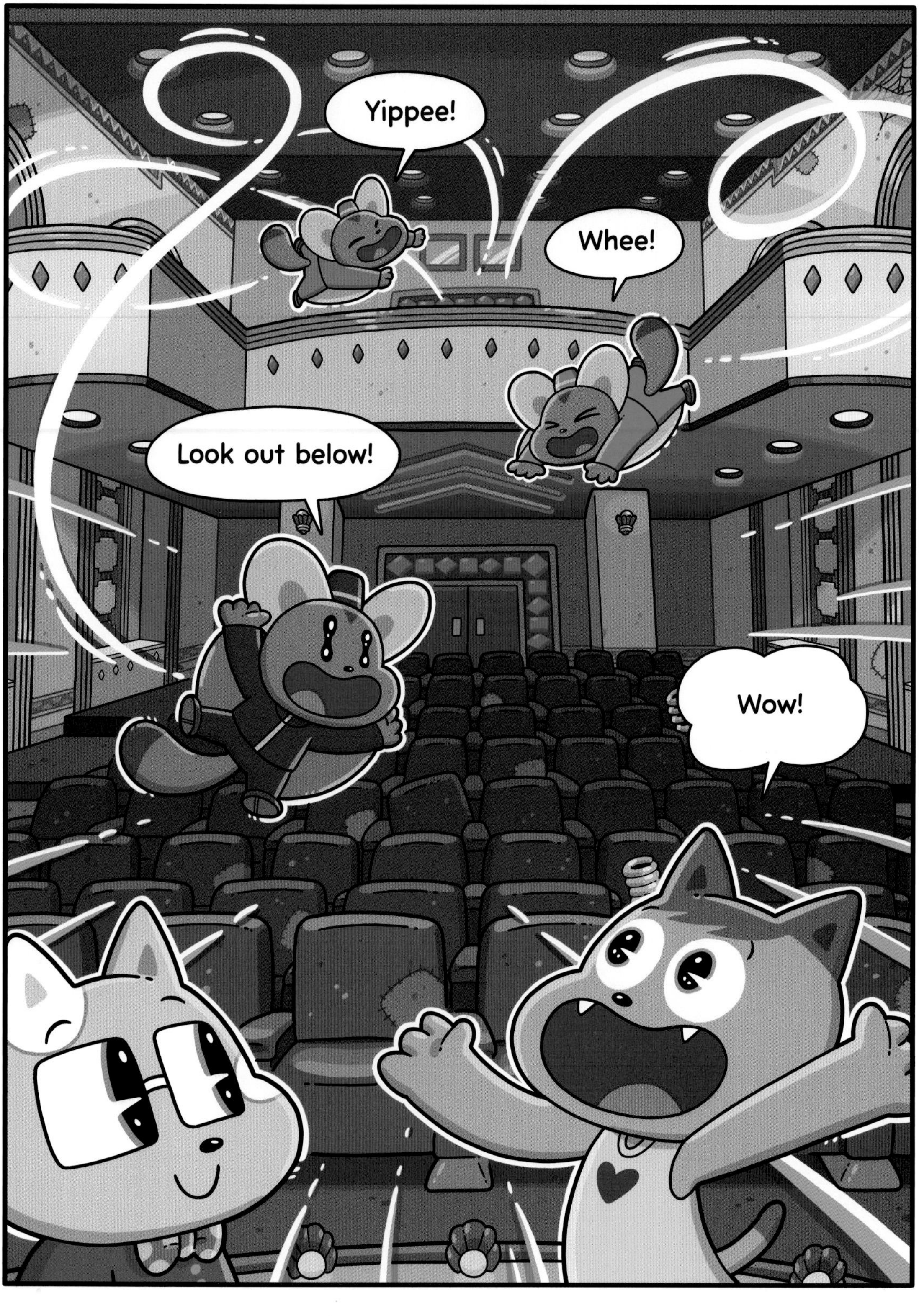
Yippee!
Whee!
Look out below!
Wow!

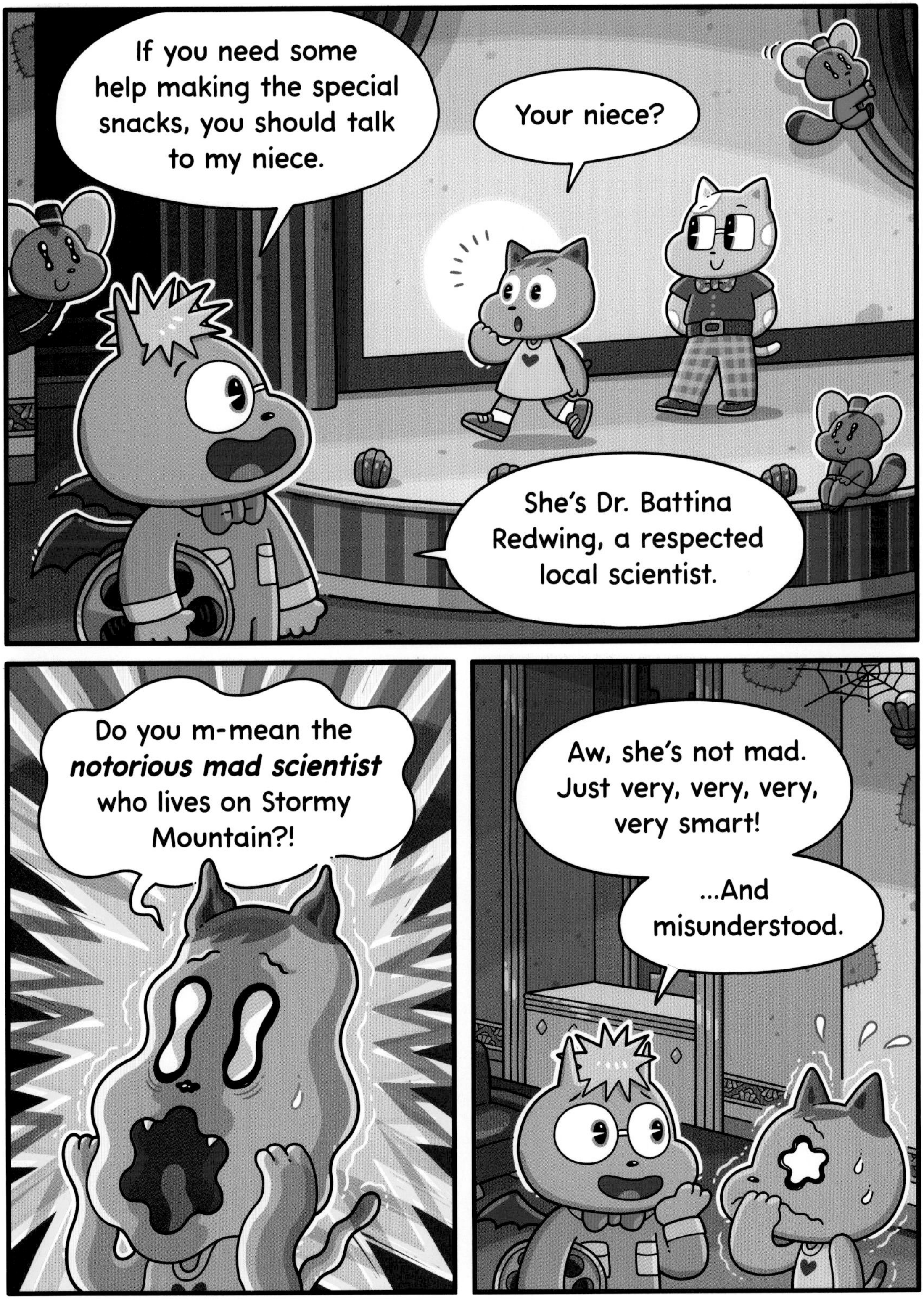
If you need some help making the special snacks, you should talk to my niece.
Your niece?
She's Dr. Battina Redwing, a respected local scientist.
Do you m-mean the ***notorious mad scientist*** who lives on Stormy Mountain?!
Aw, she's not mad. Just very, very, very, very smart!
...And misunderstood.

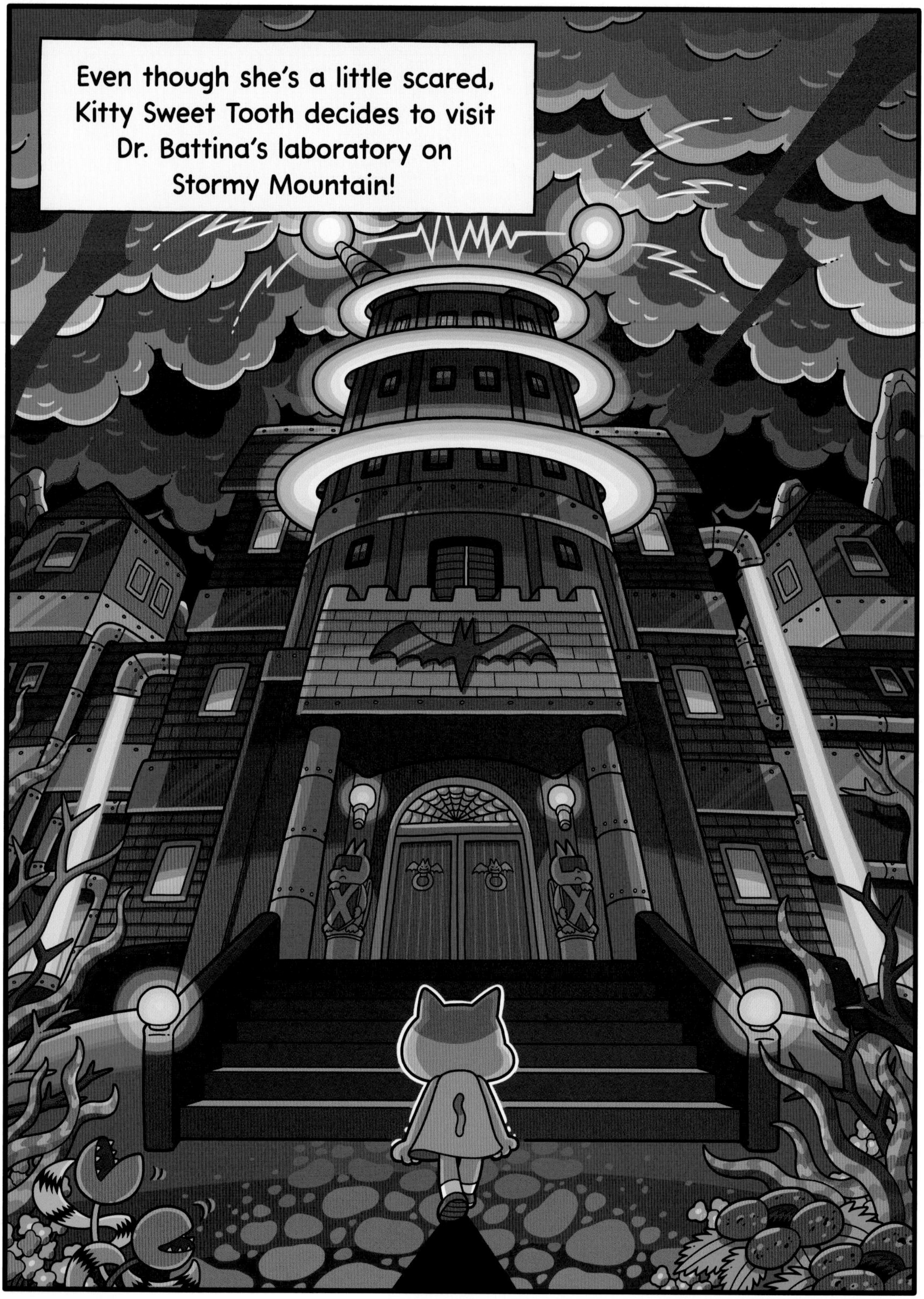
Even though she's a little scared, Kitty Sweet Tooth decides to visit Dr. Battina's laboratory on Stormy Mountain!

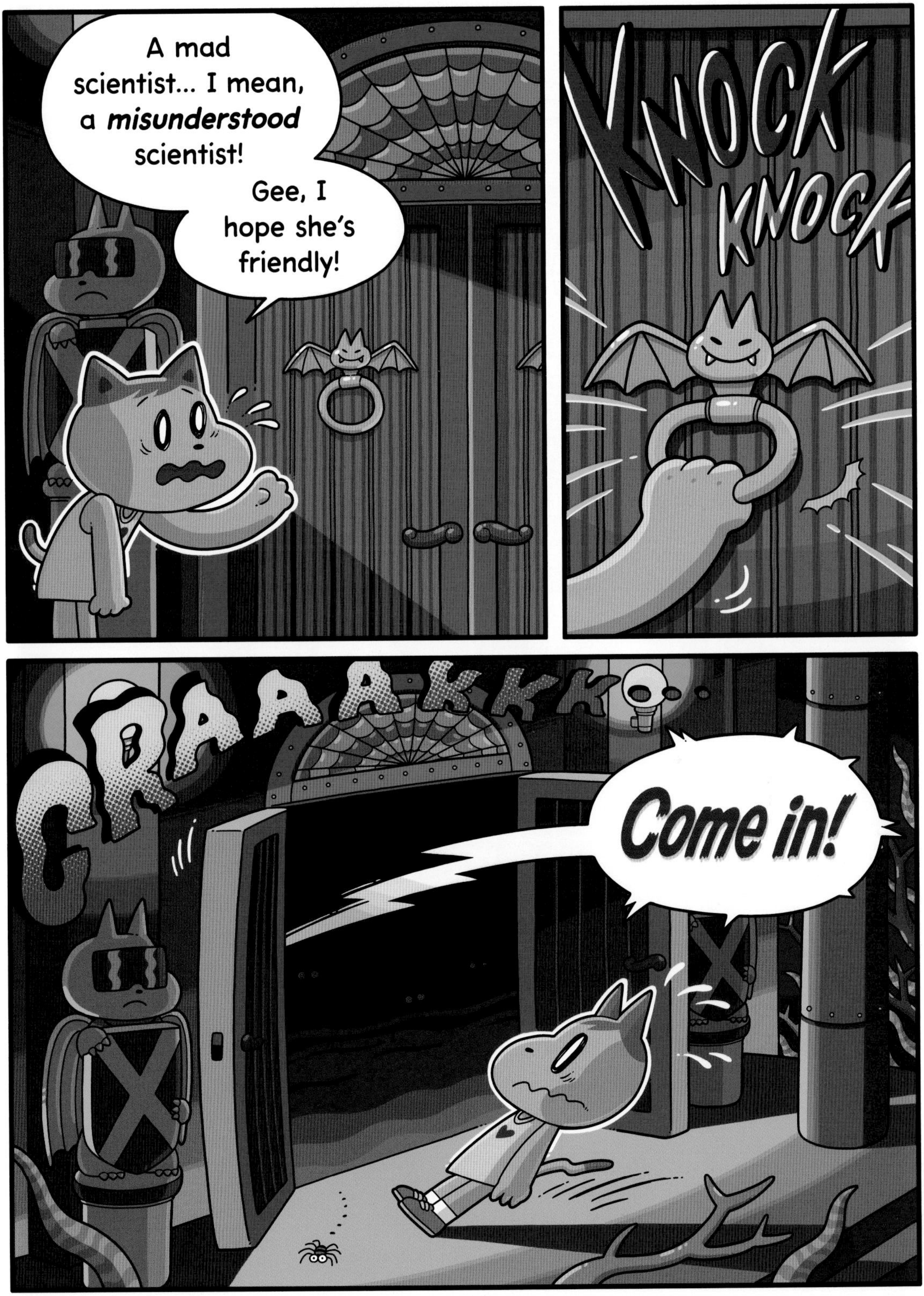
A mad scientist... I mean, a ***misunderstood*** scientist!
Gee, I hope she's friendly!
KNOCK
KNOCK
CRAAAKKK...
Come in!

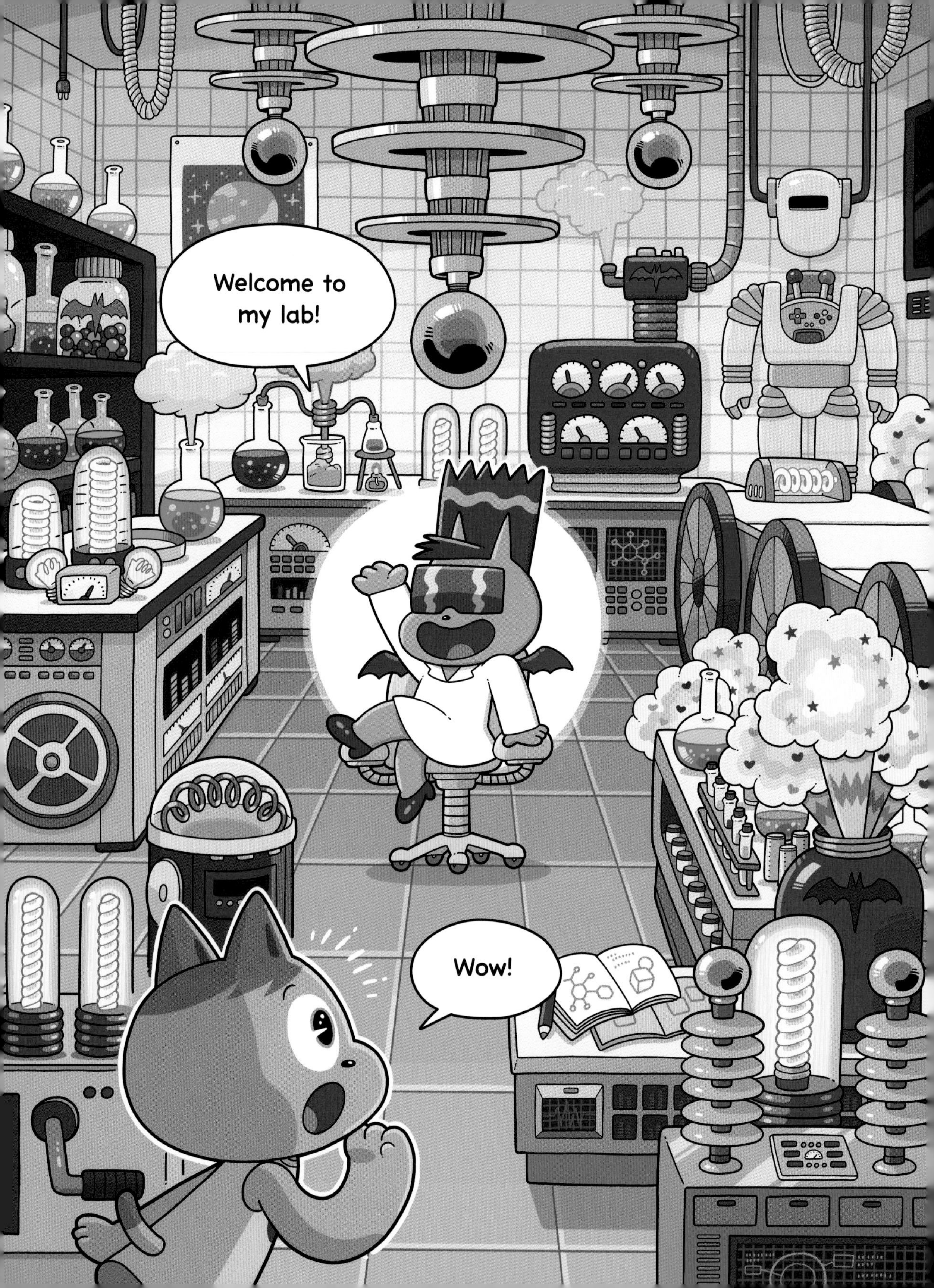
Welcome to my lab!
Wow!

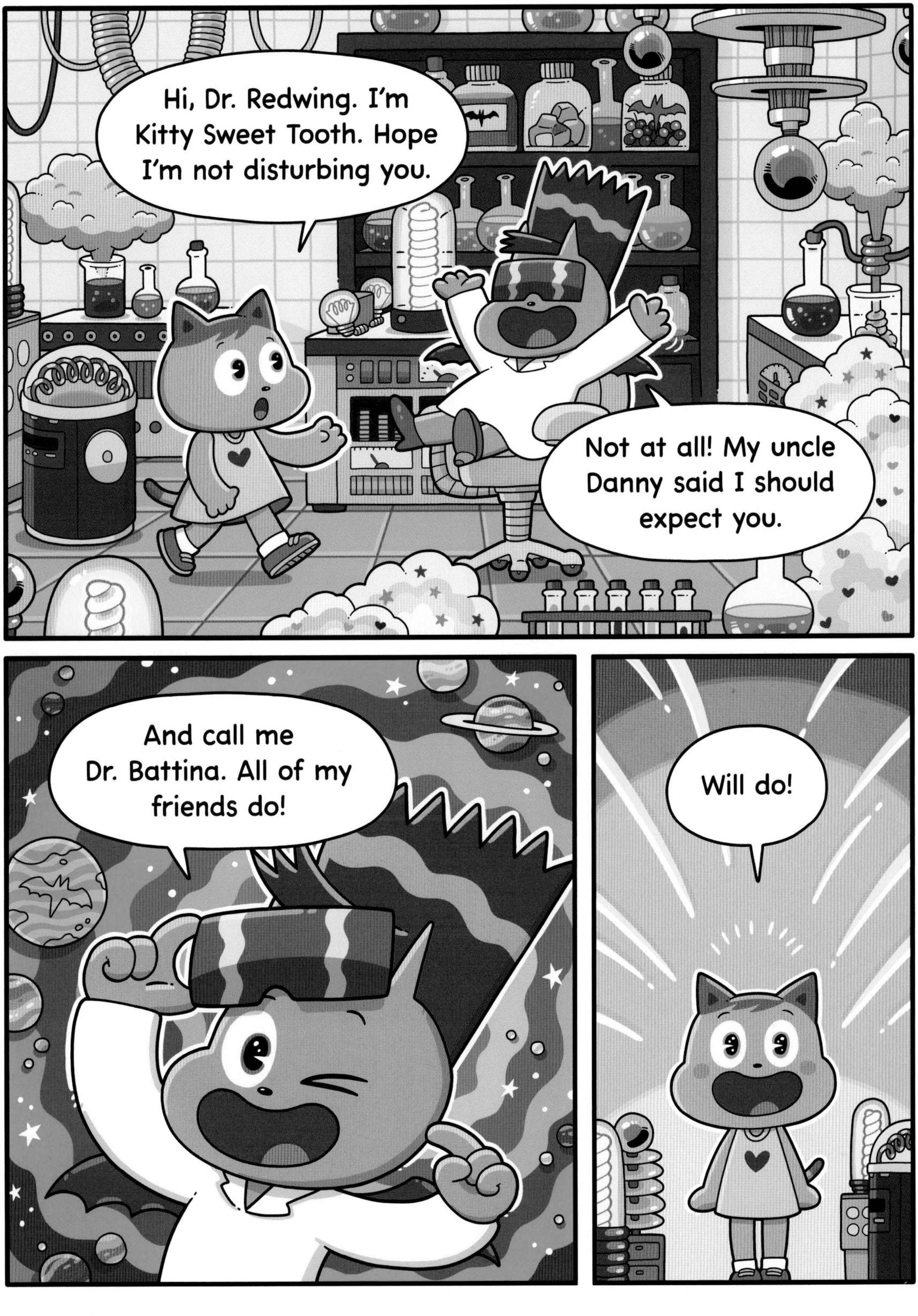
Hi, Dr. Redwing. I'm Kitty Sweet Tooth. Hope I'm not disturbing you.
Not at all! My uncle Danny said I should expect you.
And call me Dr. Battina. All of my friends do!
Will do!

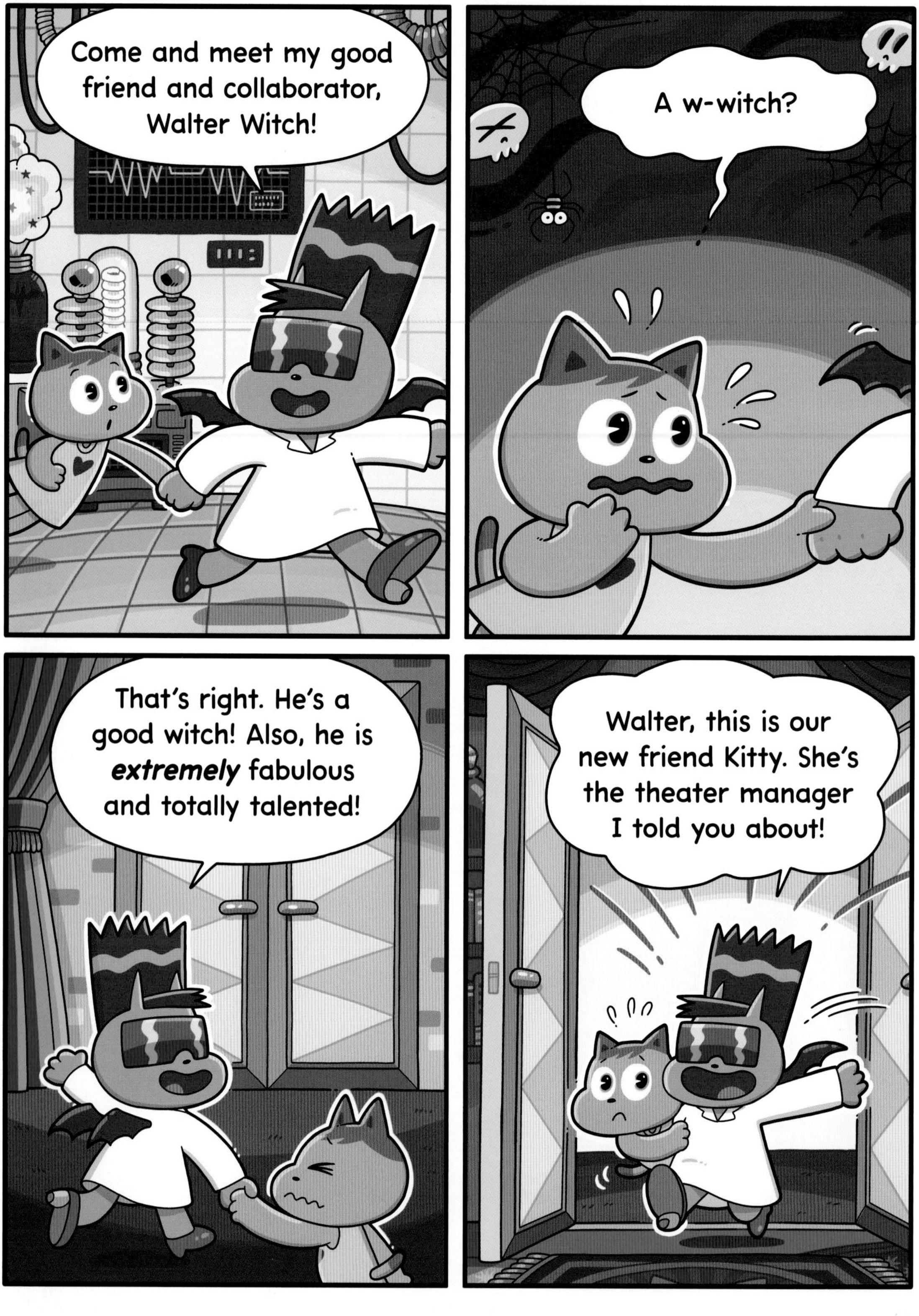
Come and meet my good friend and collaborator, Walter Witch!
A w-witch?
That's right. He's a good witch! Also, he is *extremely* fabulous and totally talented!
Walter, this is our new friend Kitty. She's the theater manager I told you about!

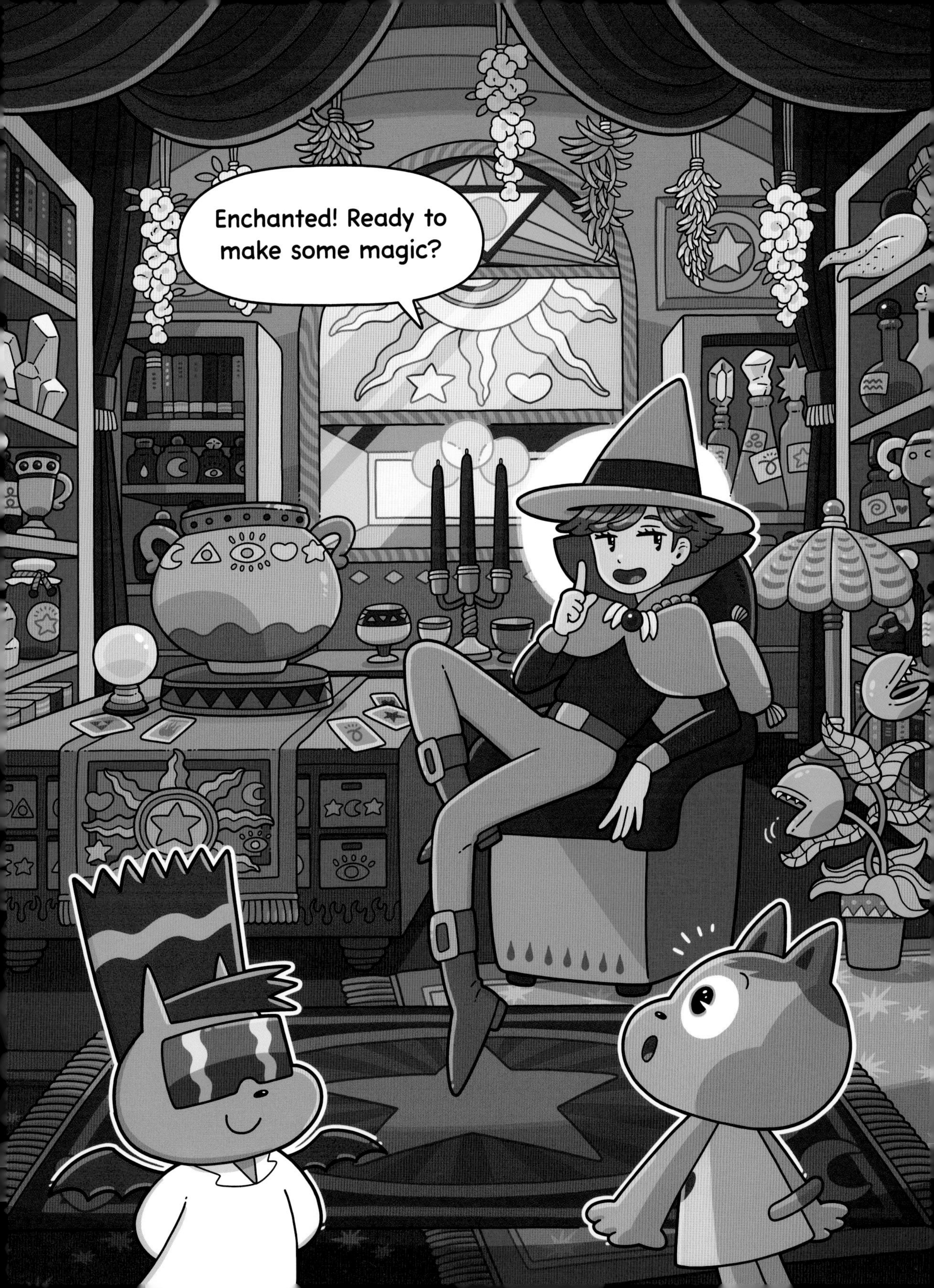
Enchanted! Ready to make some magic?

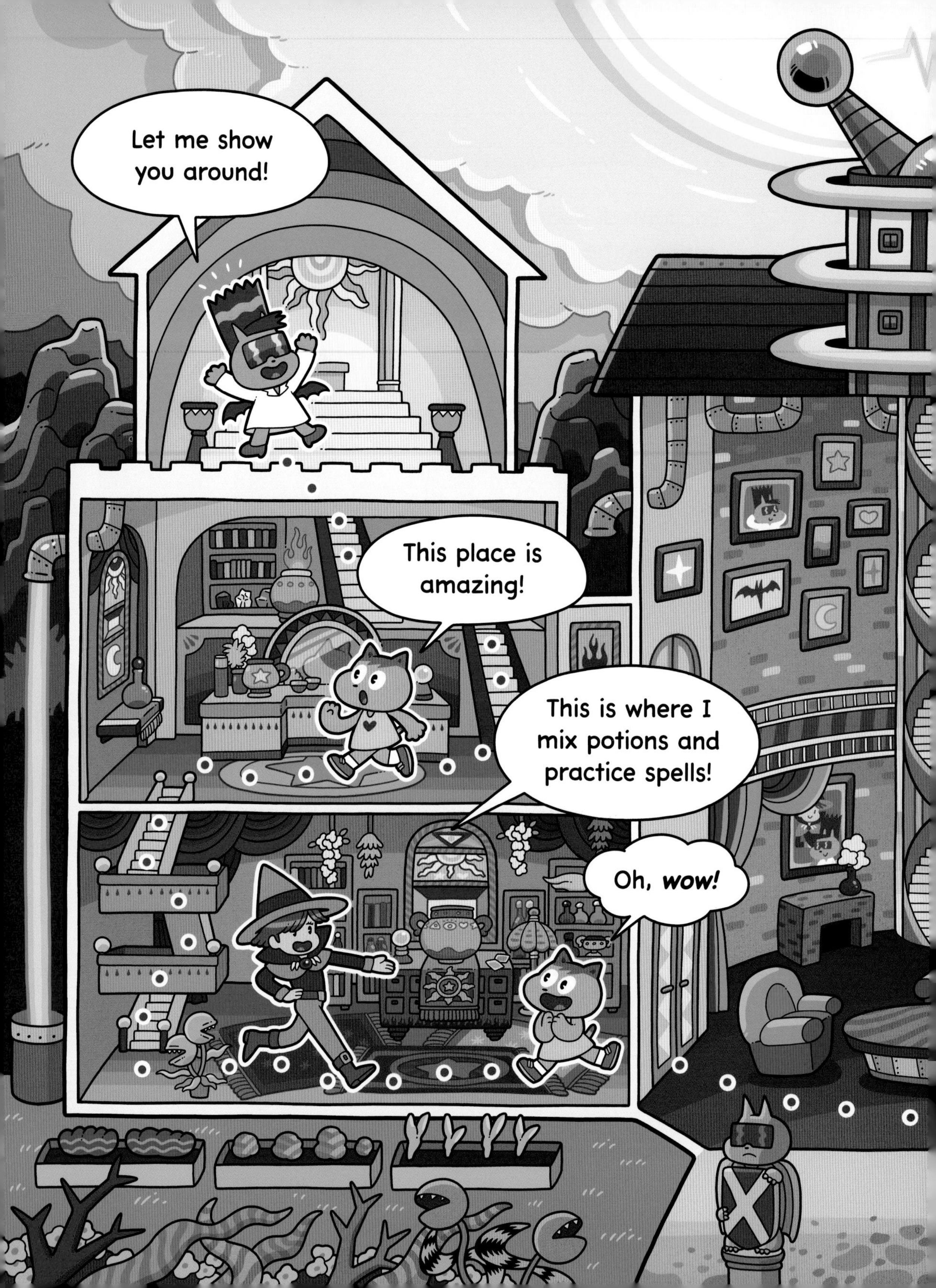
Let me show you around!
This place is amazing!
This is where I mix potions and practice spells!
Oh, *wow!*

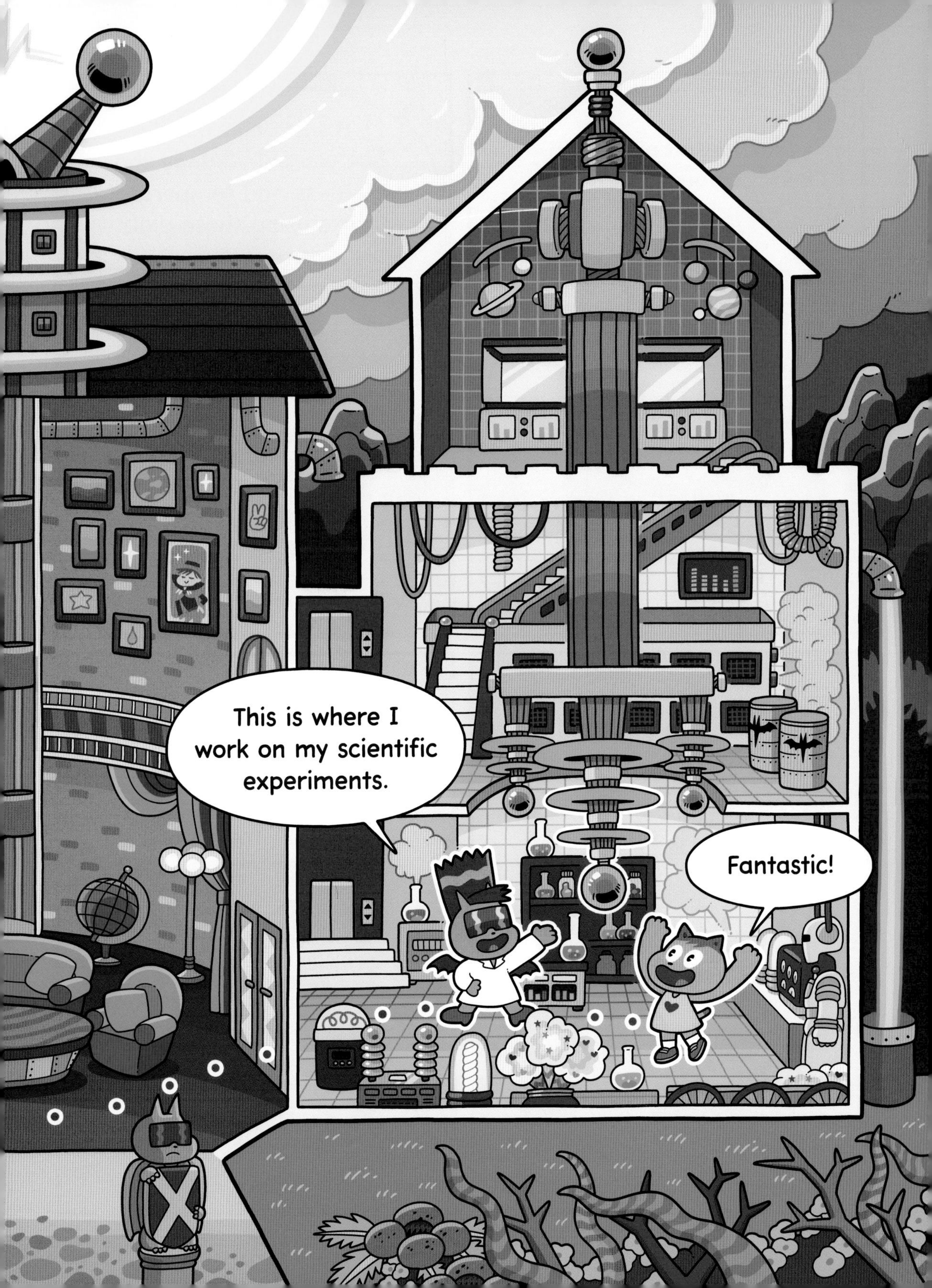
This is where I work on my scientific experiments.
Fantastic!

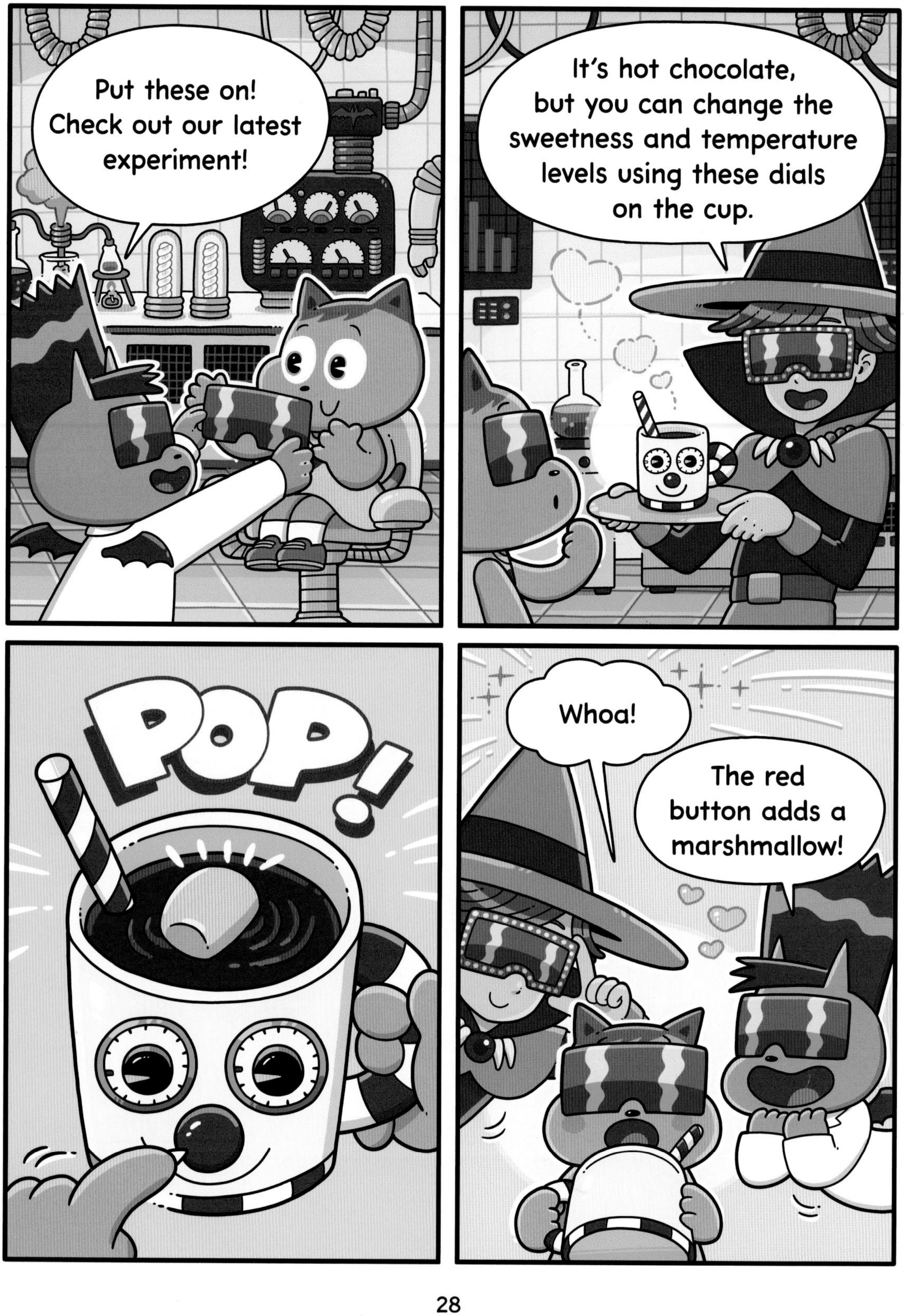
Put these on! Check out our latest experiment!
It's hot chocolate, but you can change the sweetness and temperature levels using these dials on the cup.
POP!
Whoa!
The red button adds a marshmallow!

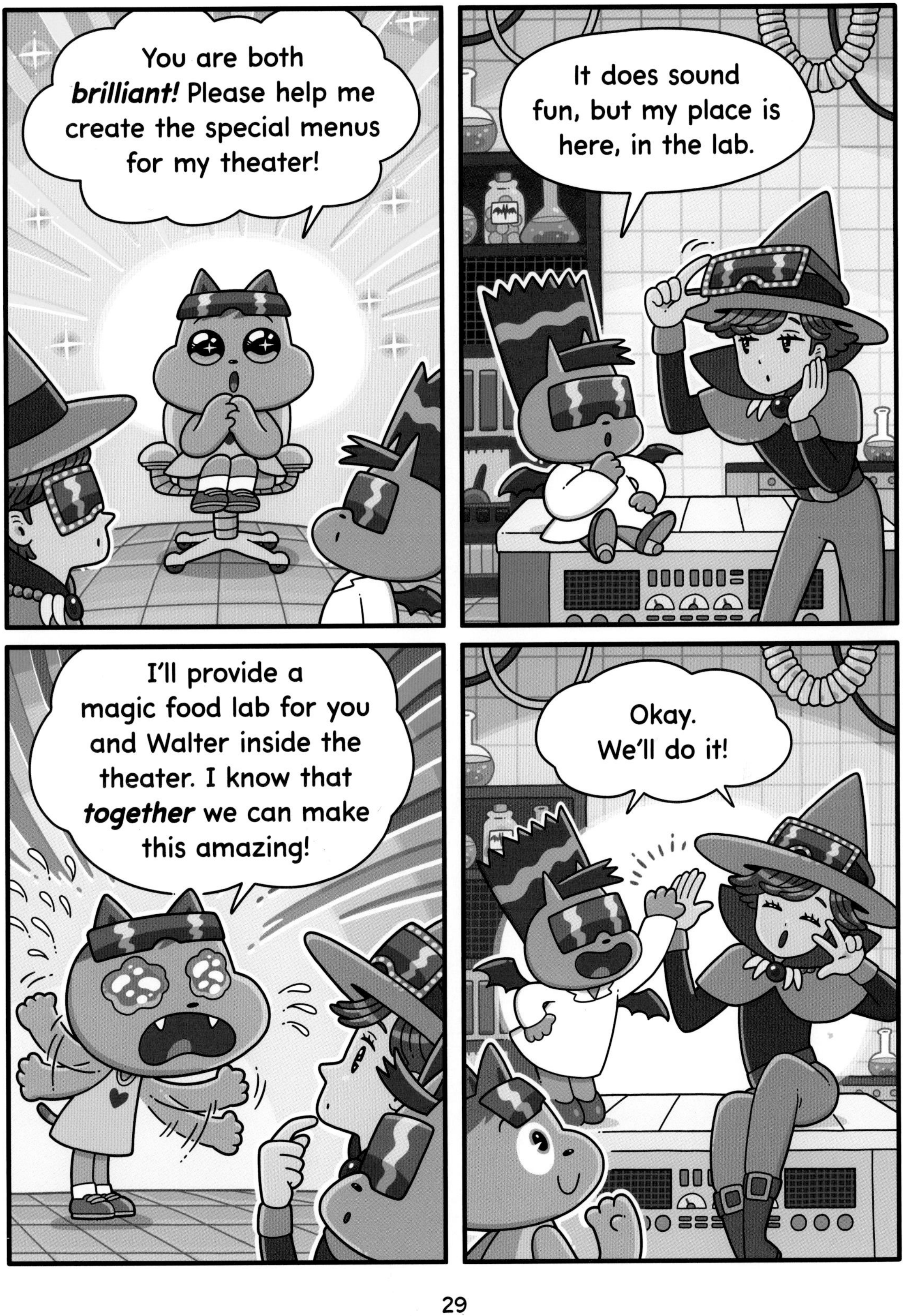
You are both *brilliant!* Please help me create the special menus for my theater!
It does sound fun, but my place is here, in the lab.
I'll provide a magic food lab for you and Walter inside the theater. I know that *together* we can make this amazing!
Okay. We'll do it!

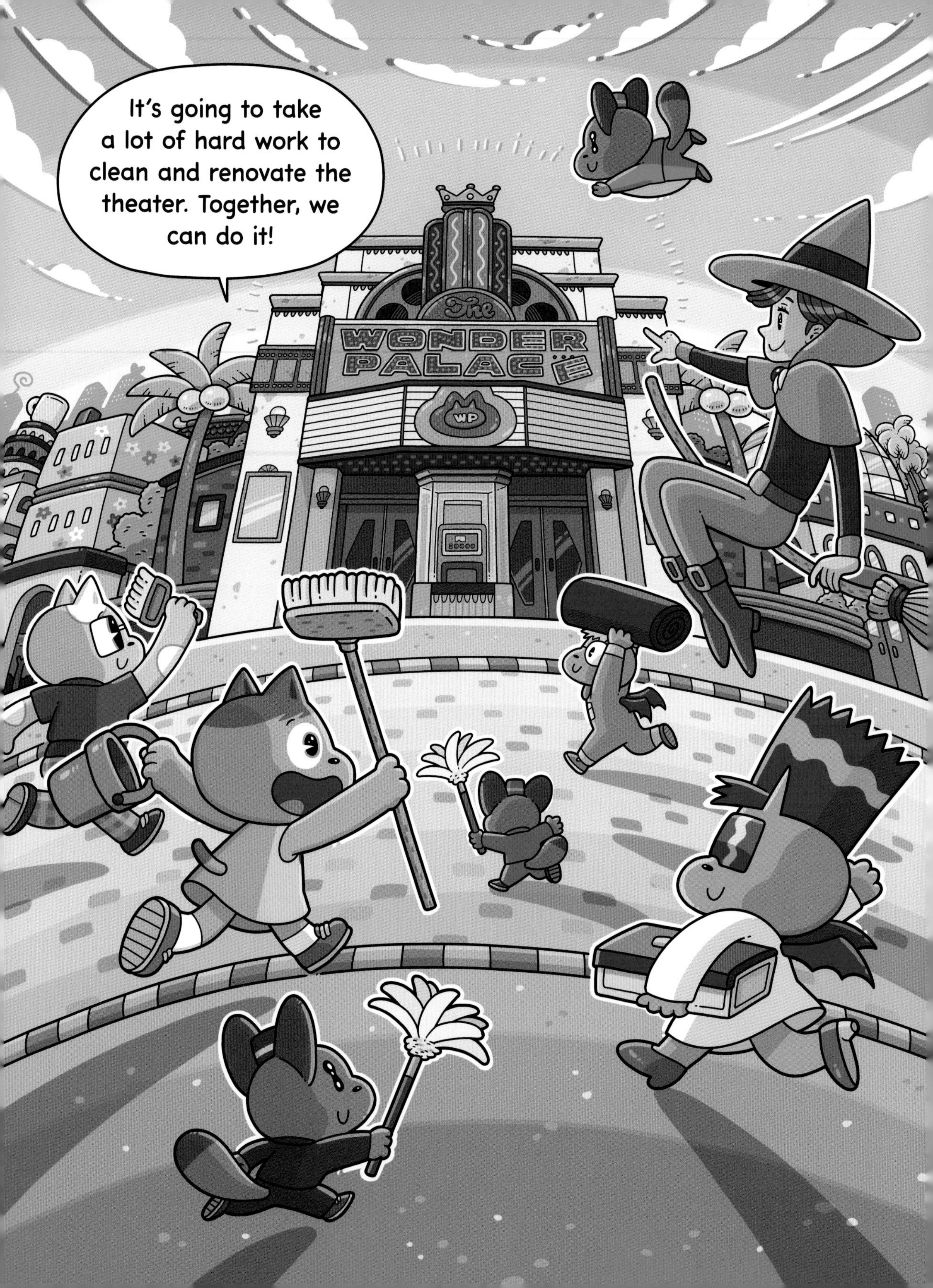
It's going to take a lot of hard work to clean and renovate the theater. Together, we can do it!
The
WONDER
PALACE
WP

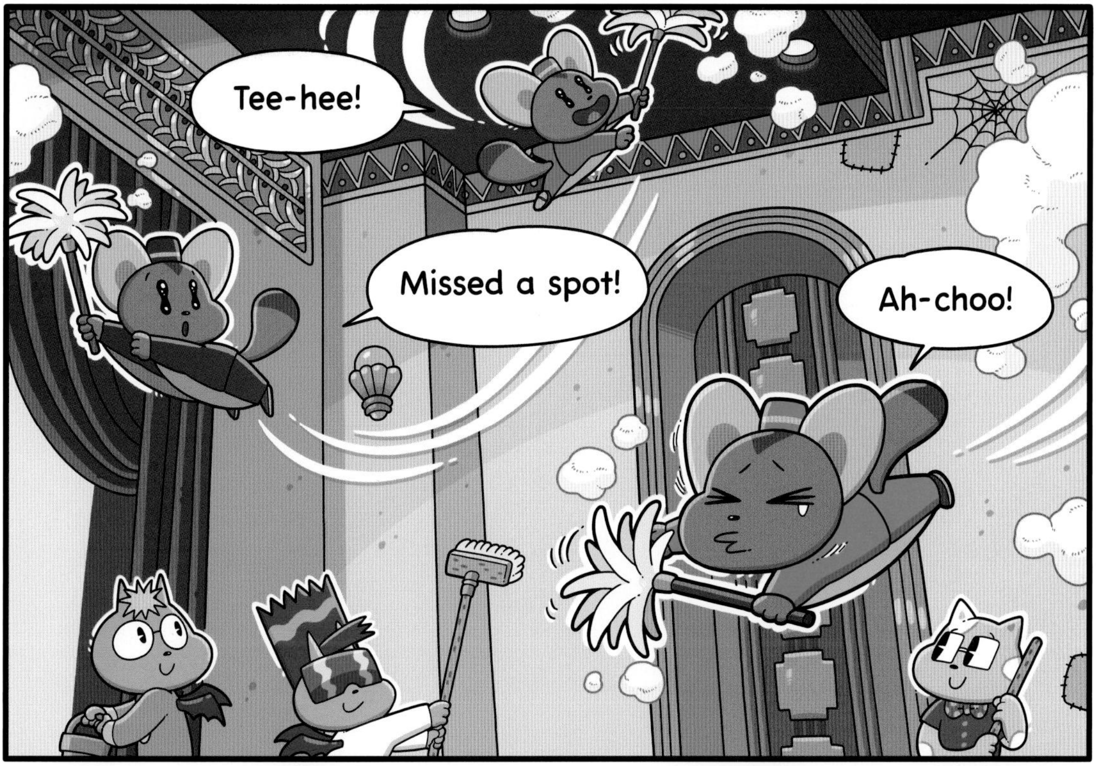
Tee-hee!
Missed a spot!
Ah-choo!

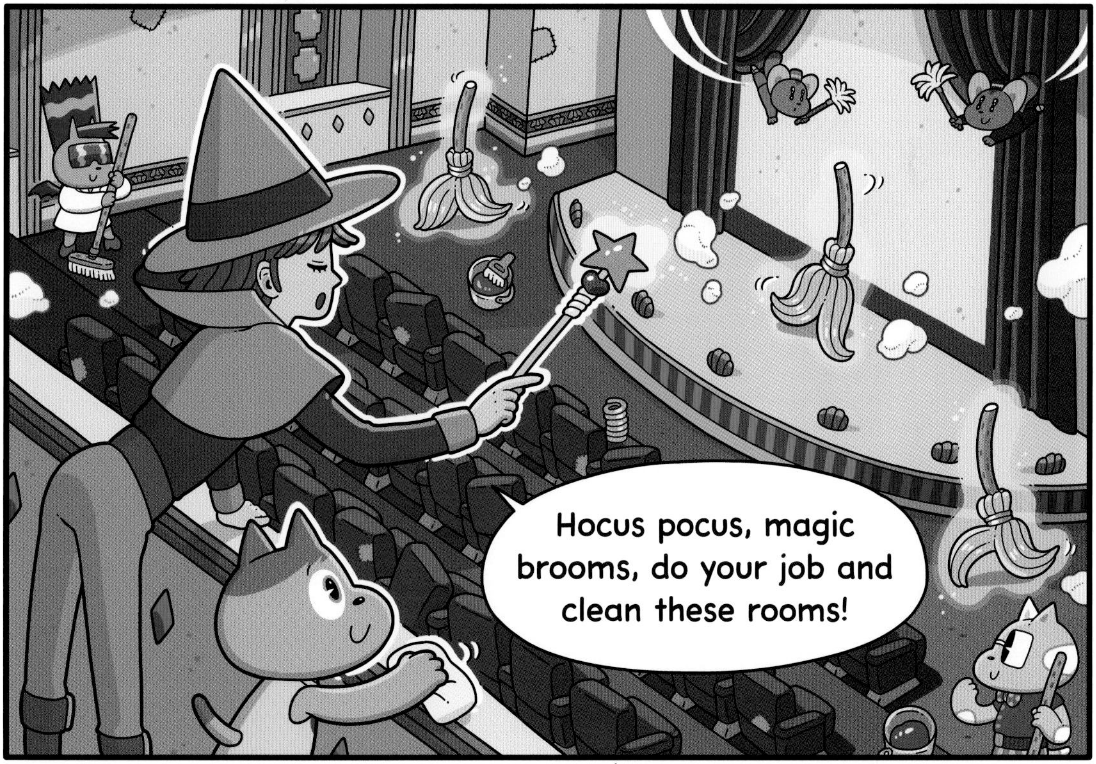
Hocus pocus, magic brooms, do your job and clean these rooms!

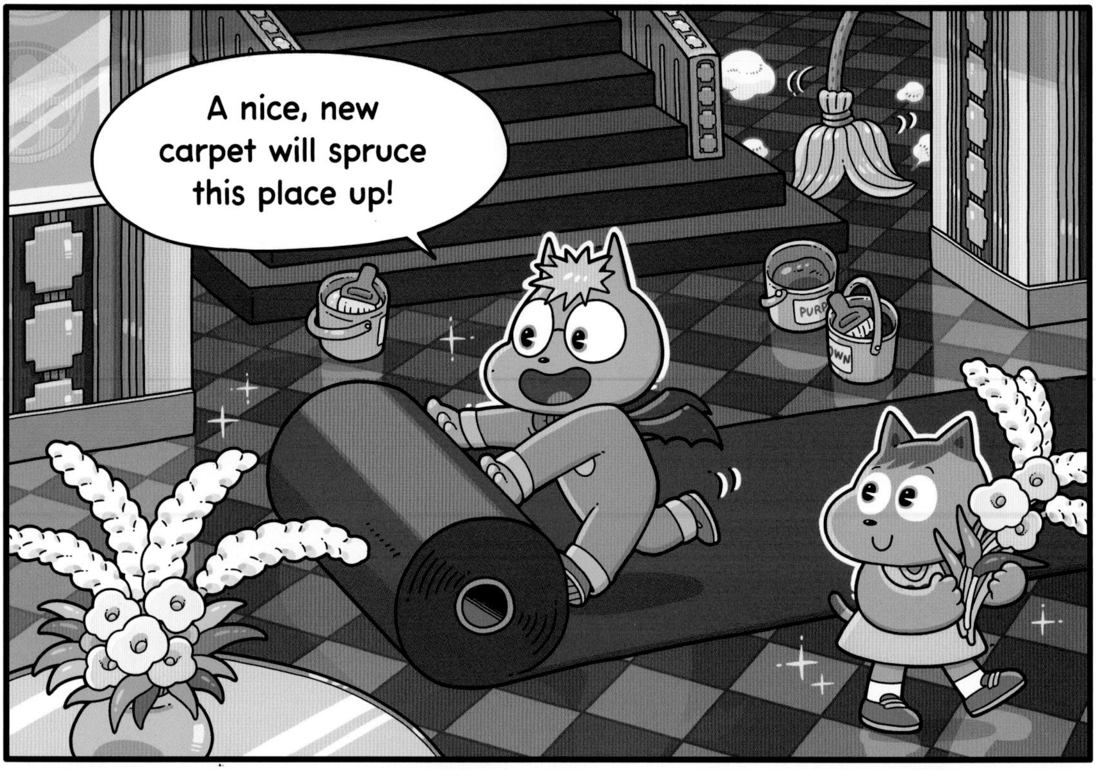
A nice, new carpet will spruce this place up!
PURP
OWN

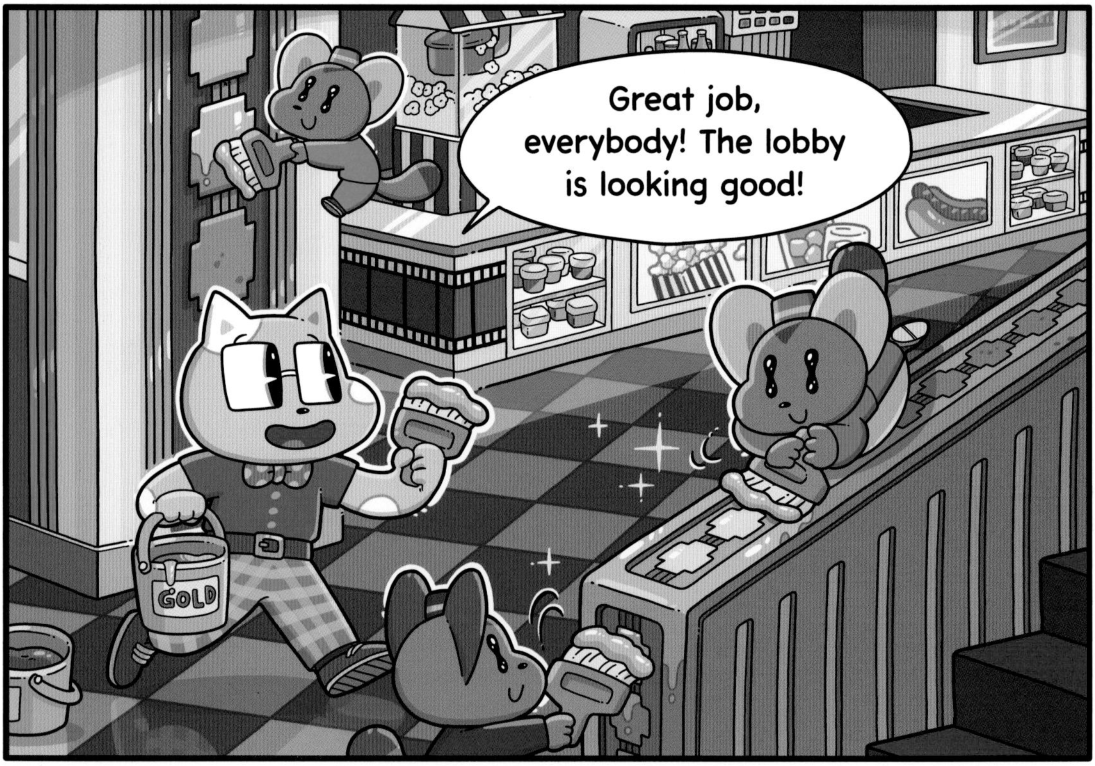
Great job, everybody! The lobby is looking good!
GOLD

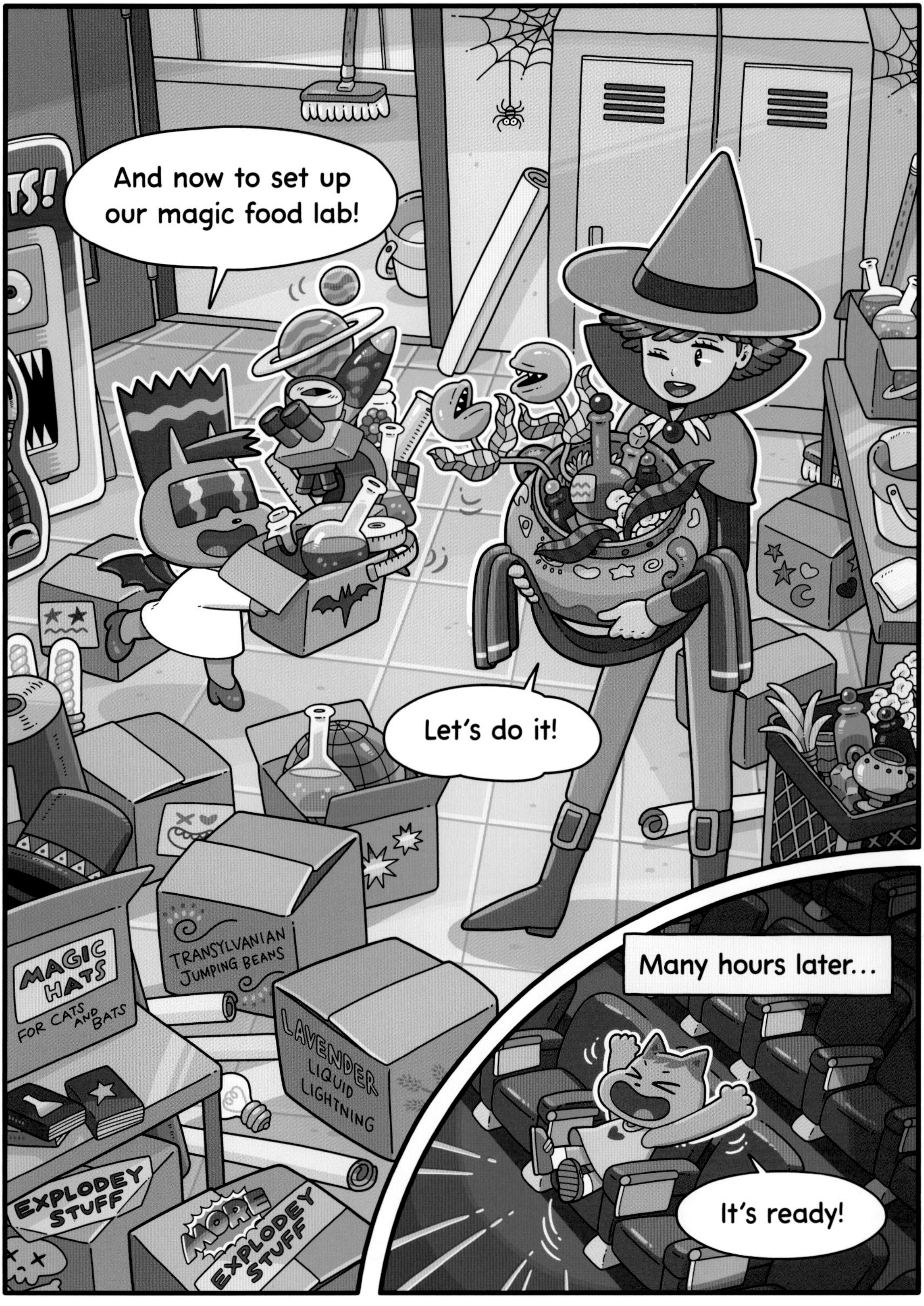
And now to set up our magic food lab!
Let's do it!
TRANSYLVANIAN JUMPING BEANS
MAGIC HATS FOR CATS AND BATS
LAVENDER LIQUID LIGHTNING
EXPLODEY STUFF
MORE EXPLODEY STUFF
Many hours later...
It's ready!

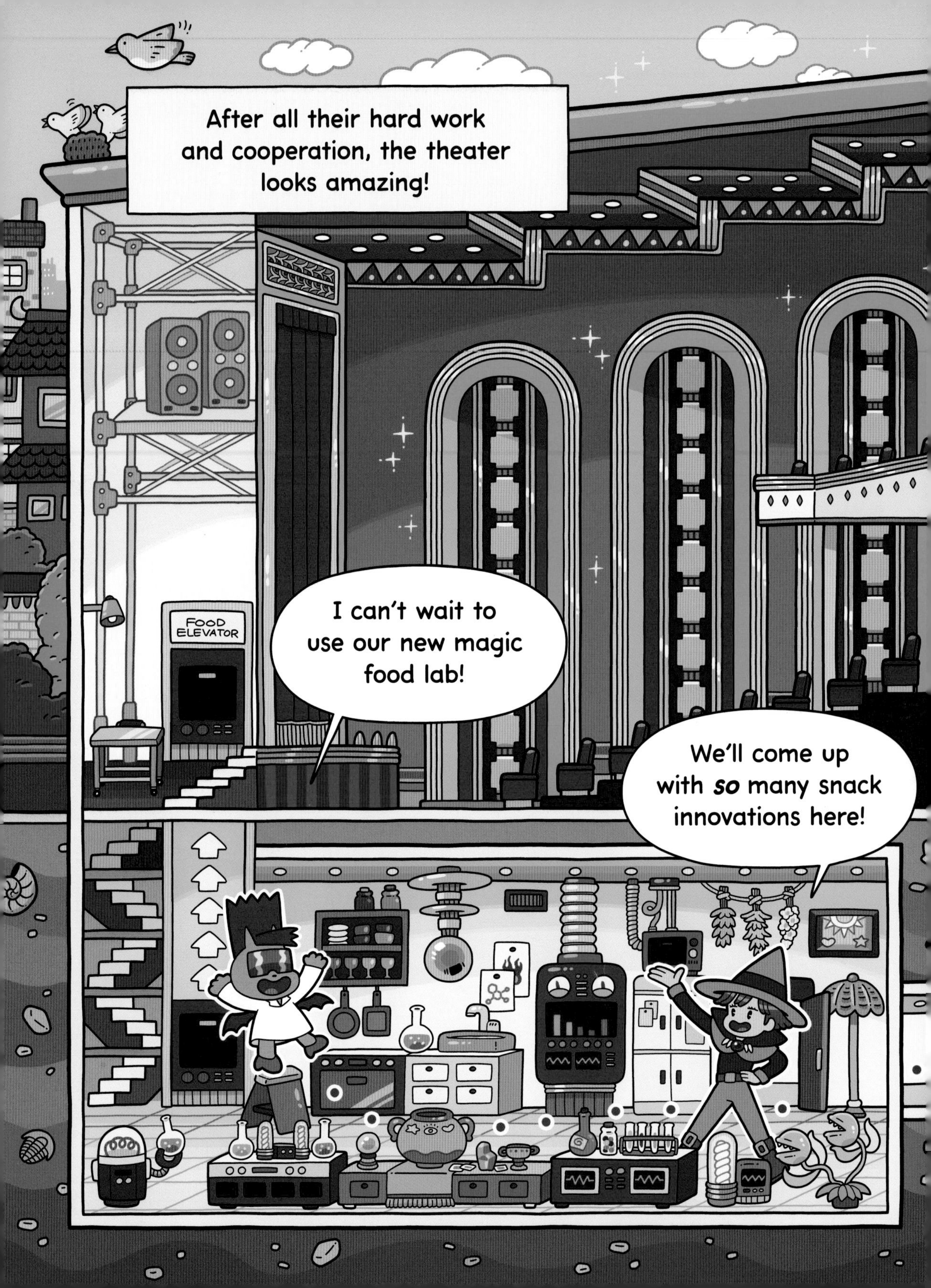

After all their hard work and cooperation, the theater looks amazing!
FOOD ELEVATOR
I can't wait to use our new magic food lab!
We'll come up with *so* many snack innovations here!

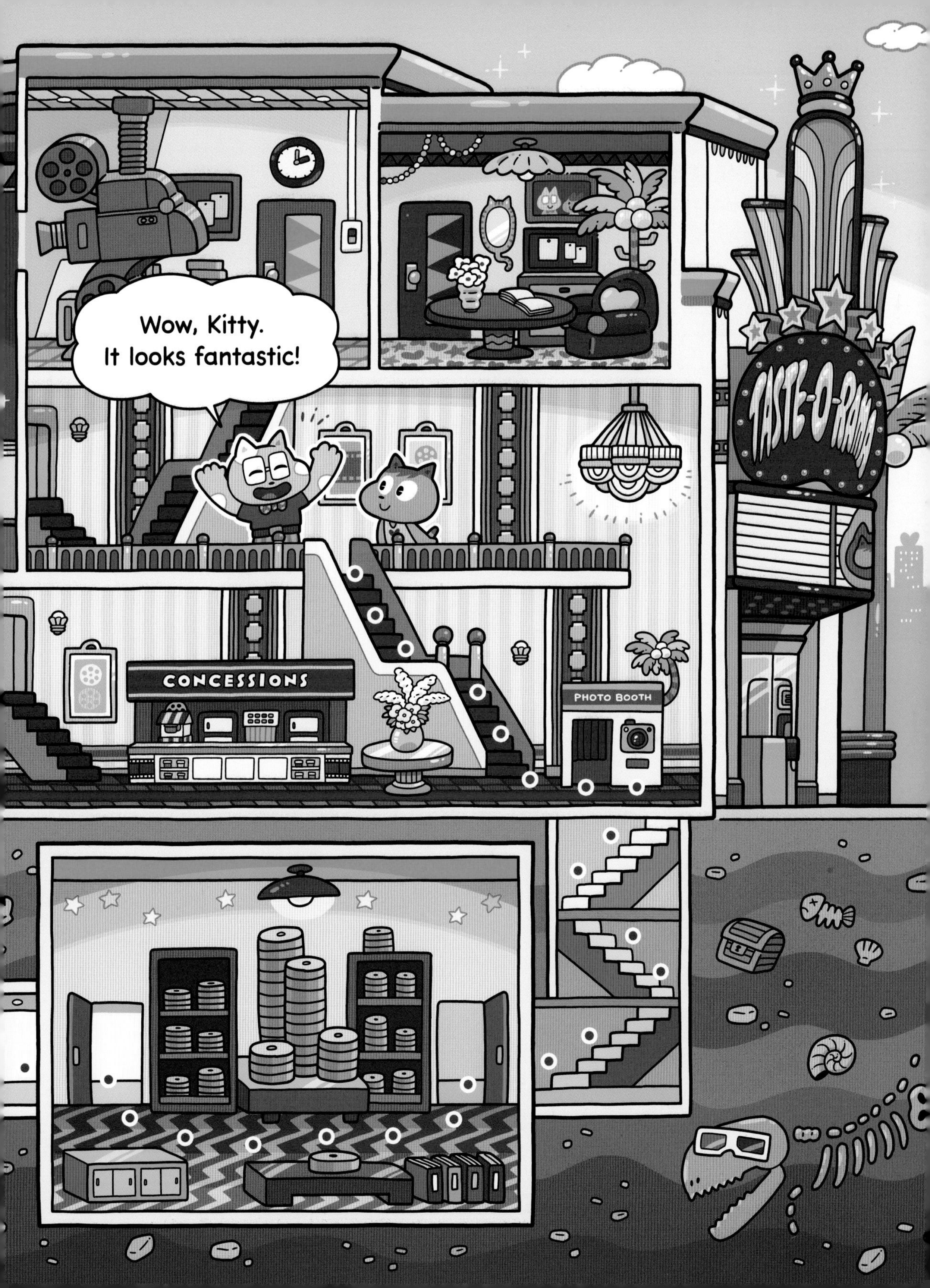

Wow, Kitty.
It looks fantastic!
TASTE-O-RAMA
CONCESSIONS
PHOTO BOOTH

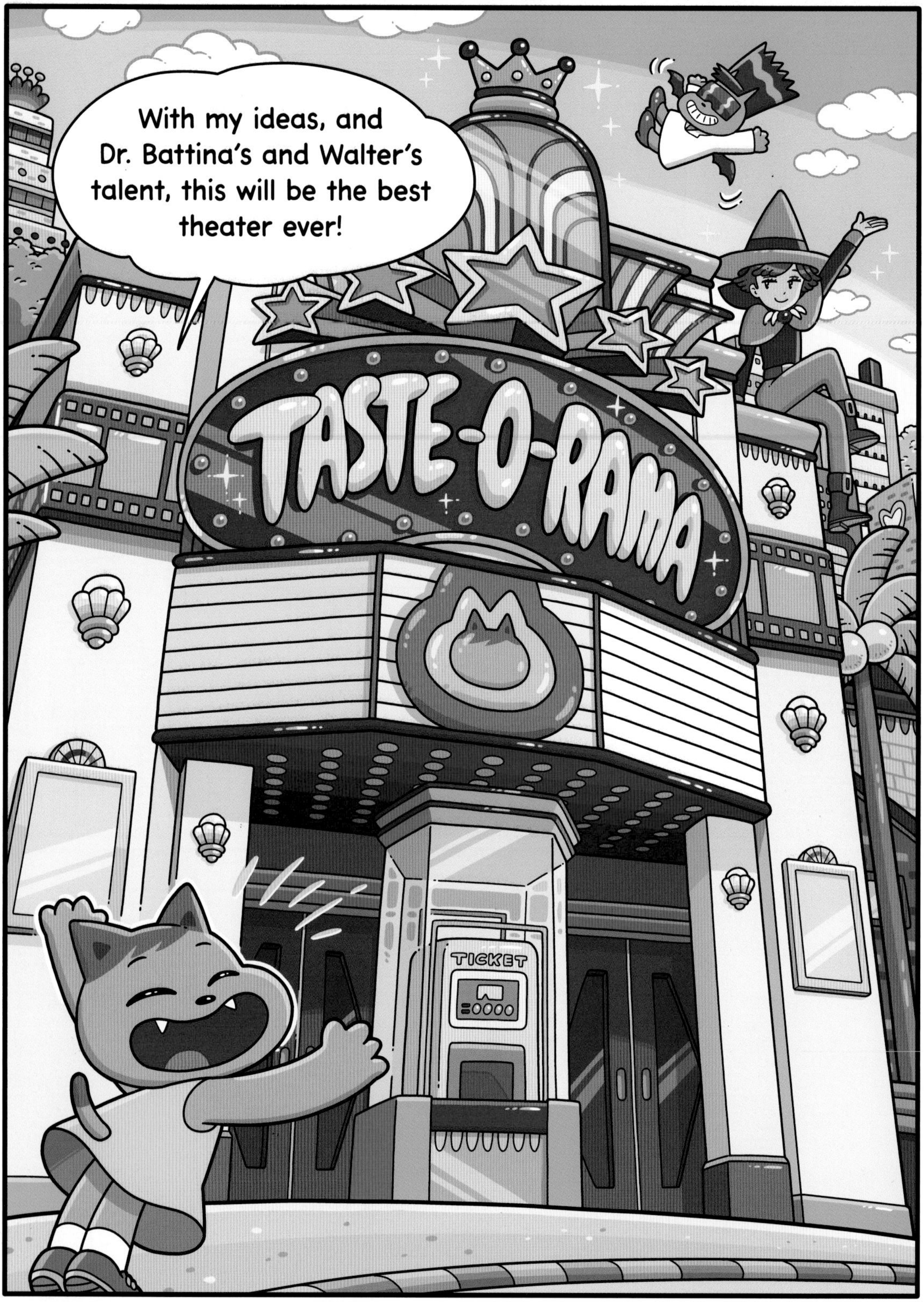
With my ideas, and Dr. Battina's and Walter's talent, this will be the best theater ever!
TASTE-O-RAMA
TICKET

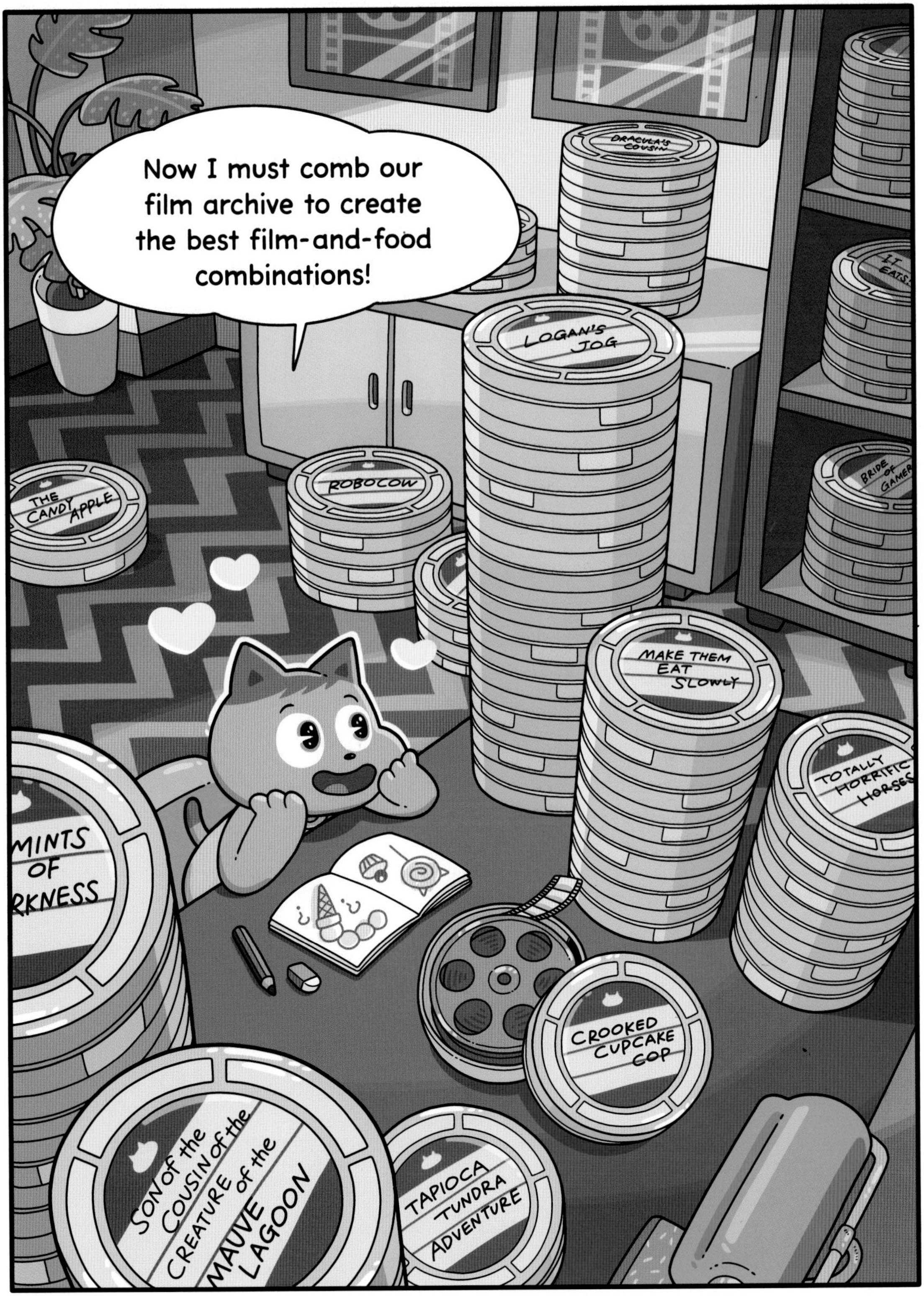
Now I must comb our film archive to create the best film-and-food combinations!
DRACULA'S COUSIN
IT EATS!
LOGAN'S JOG
ROBOCOW
THE CANDY APPLE
BRIDE OF GAMER
MAKE THEM EAT SLOWLY
TOTALLY HORRIFIC HORSES
MINTS OF RKNESS
CROOKED CUPCAKE COP
SON of the COUSIN of the CREATURE of the MAUVE LAGOON
TAPIOCA TUNDRA ADVENTURE

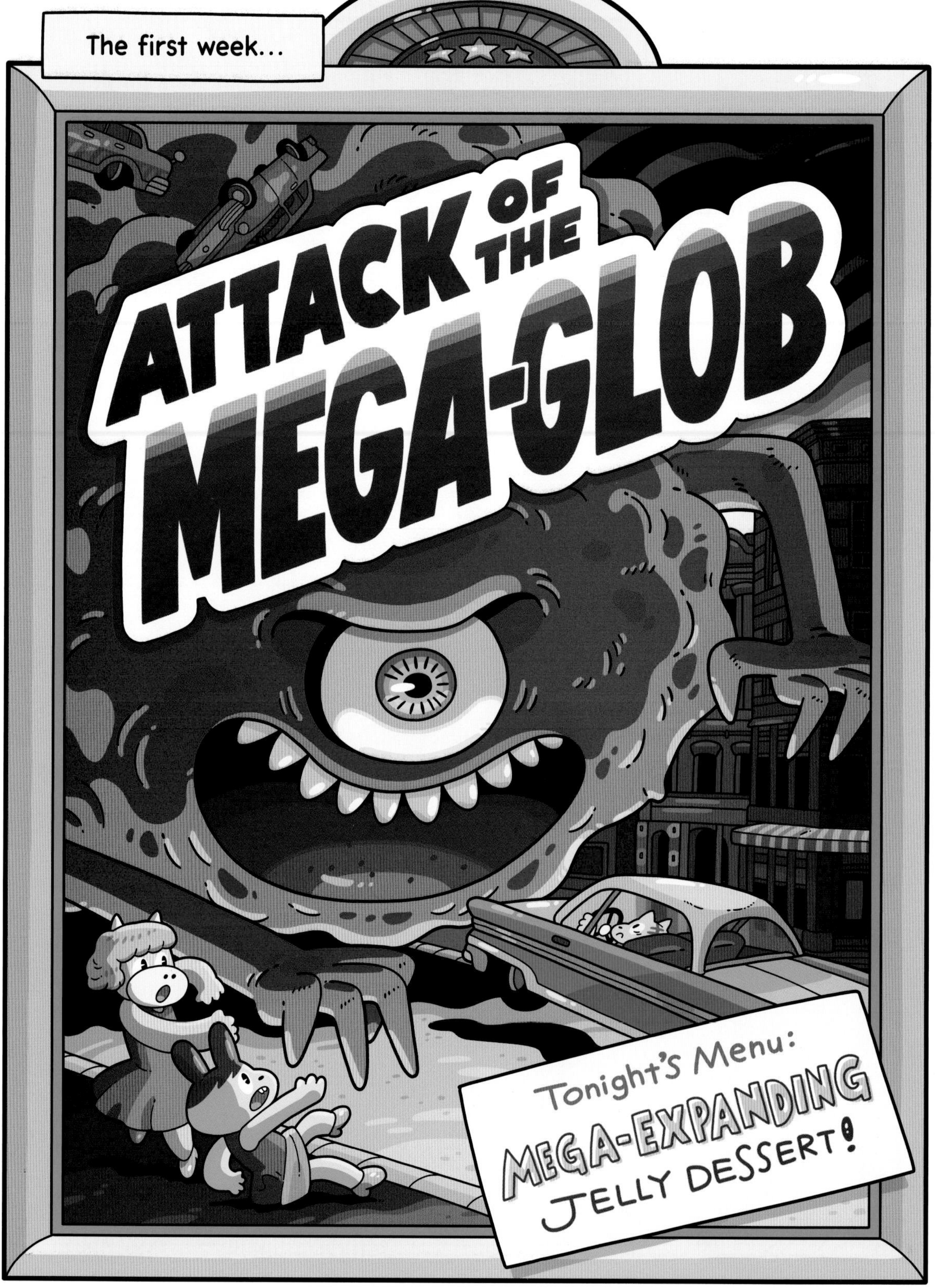
The first week...
ATTACK OF THE MEGA-GLOB
Tonight's Menu:
MEGA-EXPANDING
JELLY DESSERT!

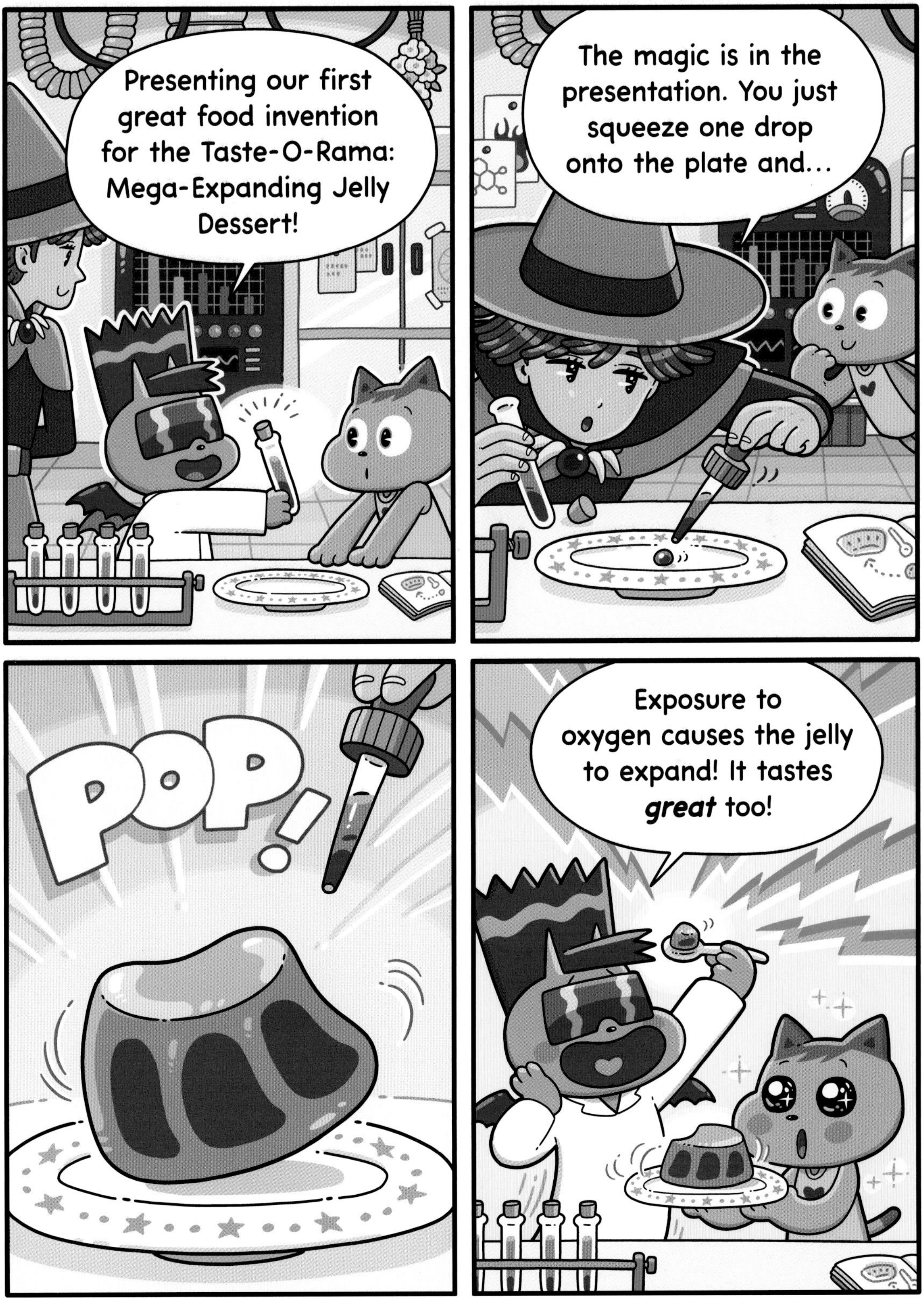
Presenting our first great food invention for the Taste-O-Rama: Mega-Expanding Jelly Dessert!
The magic is in the presentation. You just squeeze one drop onto the plate and...
POP!
Exposure to oxygen causes the jelly to expand! It tastes *great* too!

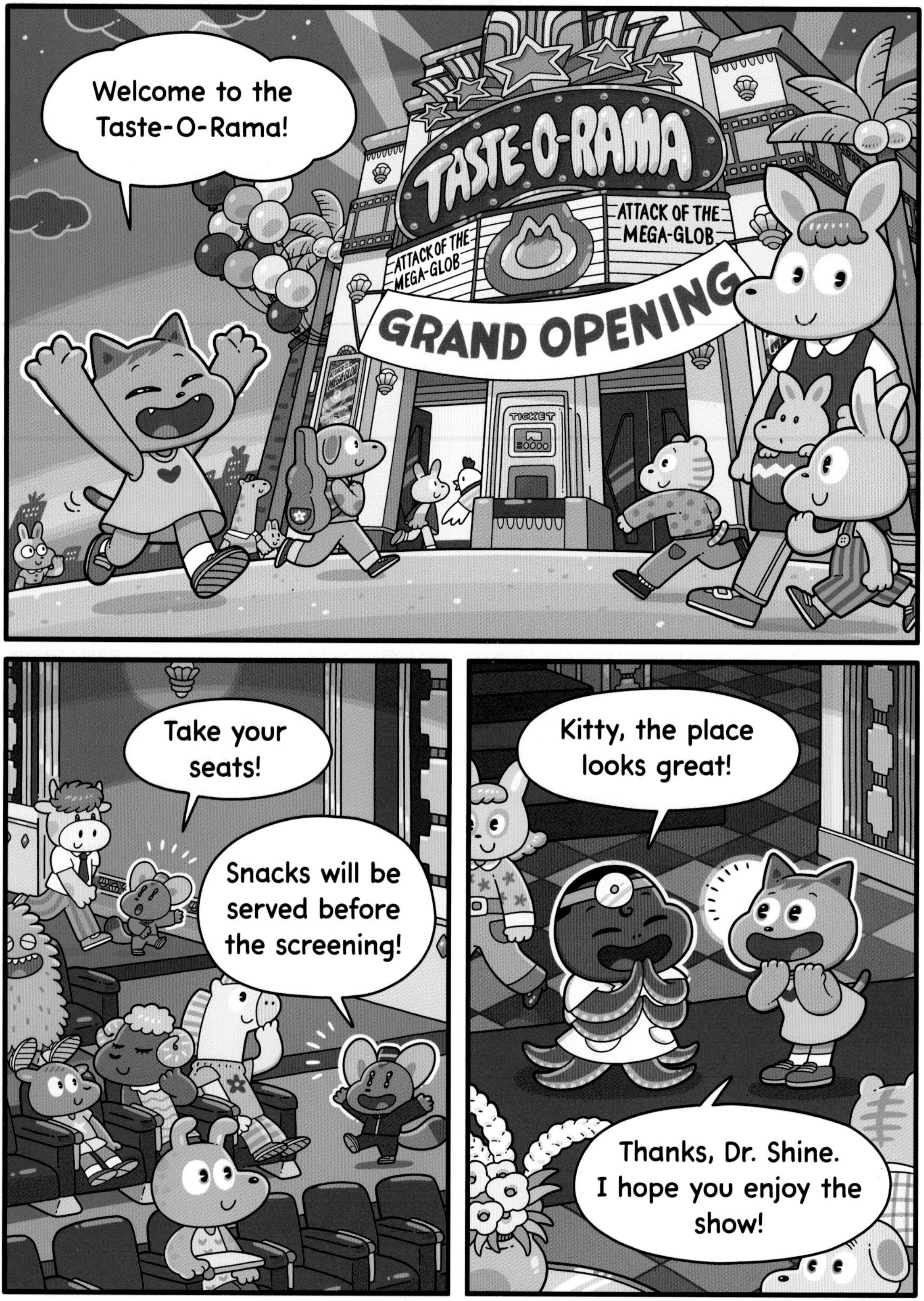
Welcome to the Taste-O-Rama!
TASTE-O-RAMA
ATTACK OF THE MEGA-GLOB
ATTACK OF THE MEGA-GLOB
GRAND OPENING
TICKET
Take your seats!
Snacks will be served before the screening!
Kitty, the place looks great!
Thanks, Dr. Shine. I hope you enjoy the show!

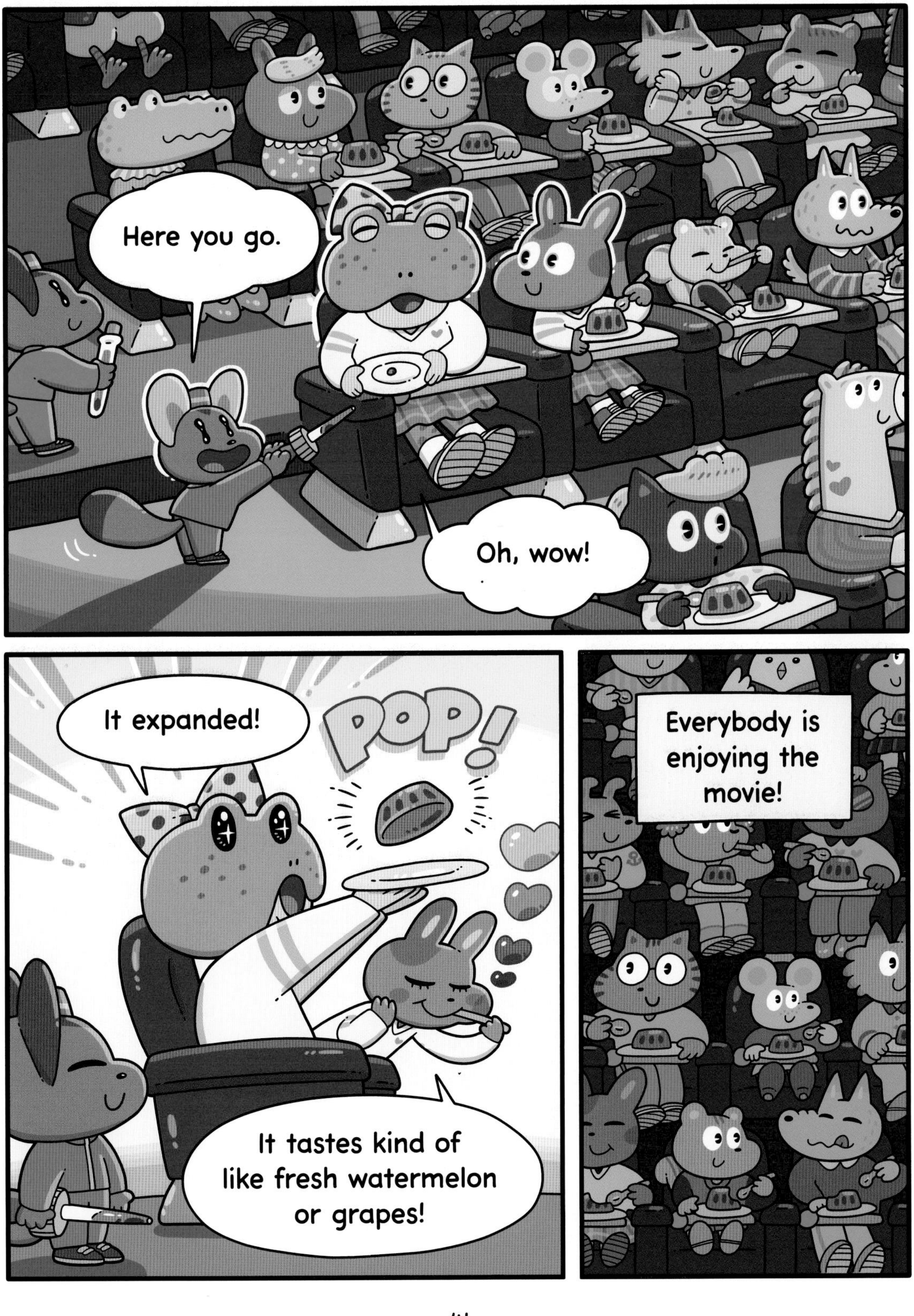

Here you go.
Oh, wow!
It expanded!
POP!
It tastes kind of like fresh watermelon or grapes!
Everybody is enjoying the movie!

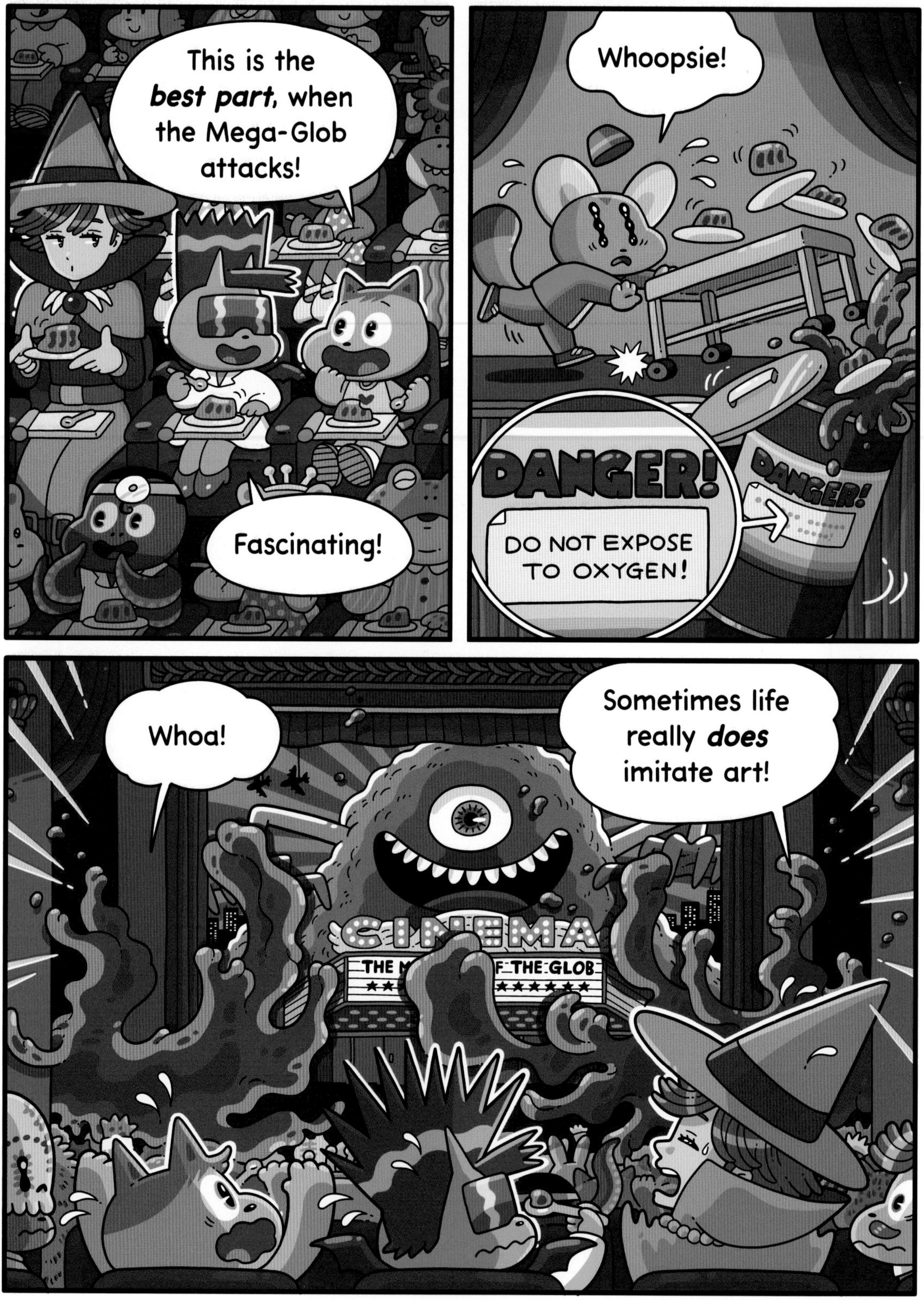
This is the *best part*, when the Mega-Glob attacks!
Fascinating!
Whoopsie!
DANGER!
DO NOT EXPOSE TO OXYGEN!
DANGER!
Whoa!
Sometimes life really *does* imitate art!
CINEMA
THE M F THE GLOB

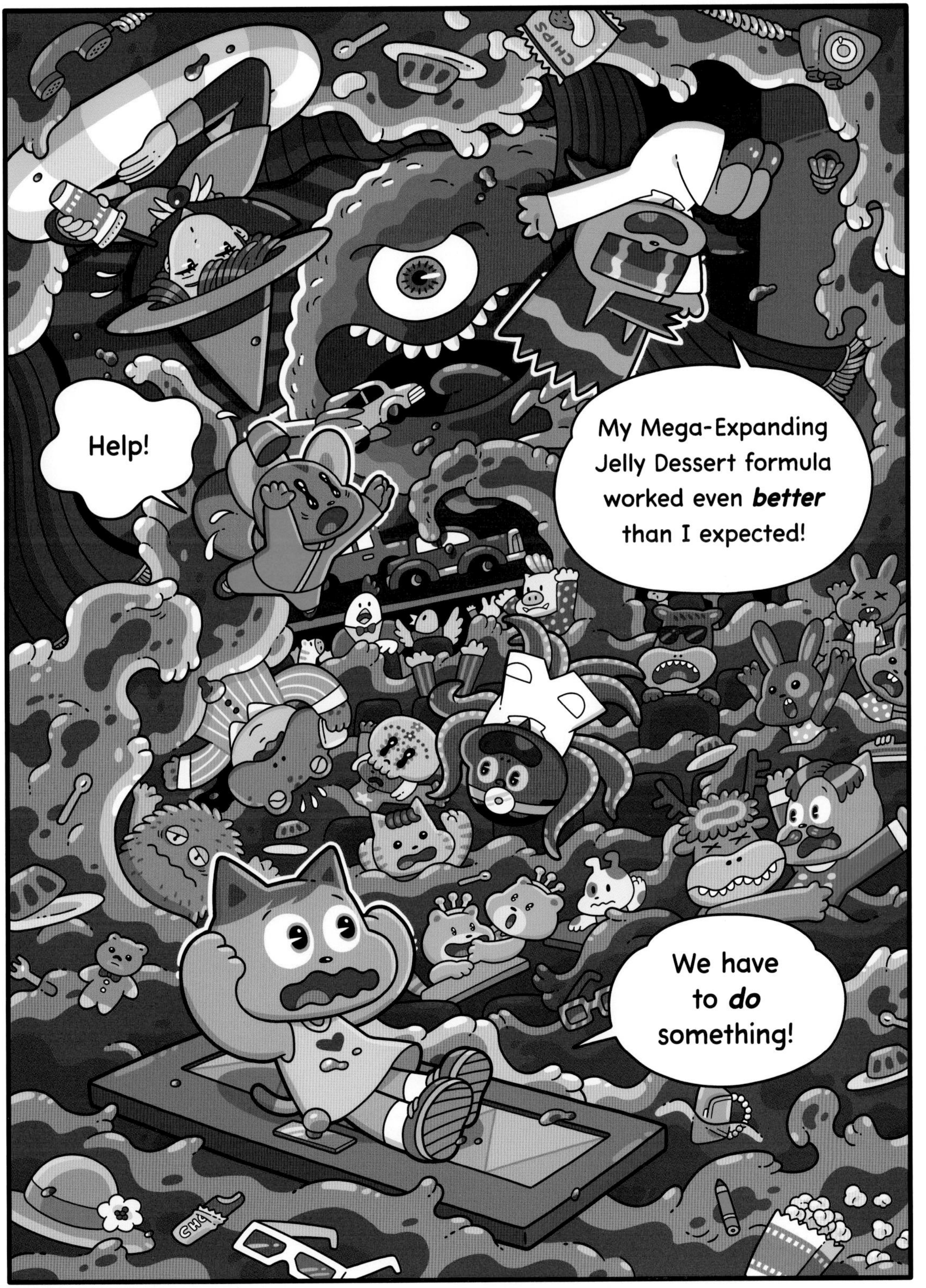
Help!
My Mega-Expanding Jelly Dessert formula worked even *better* than I expected!
We have to *do* something!
CHIPS

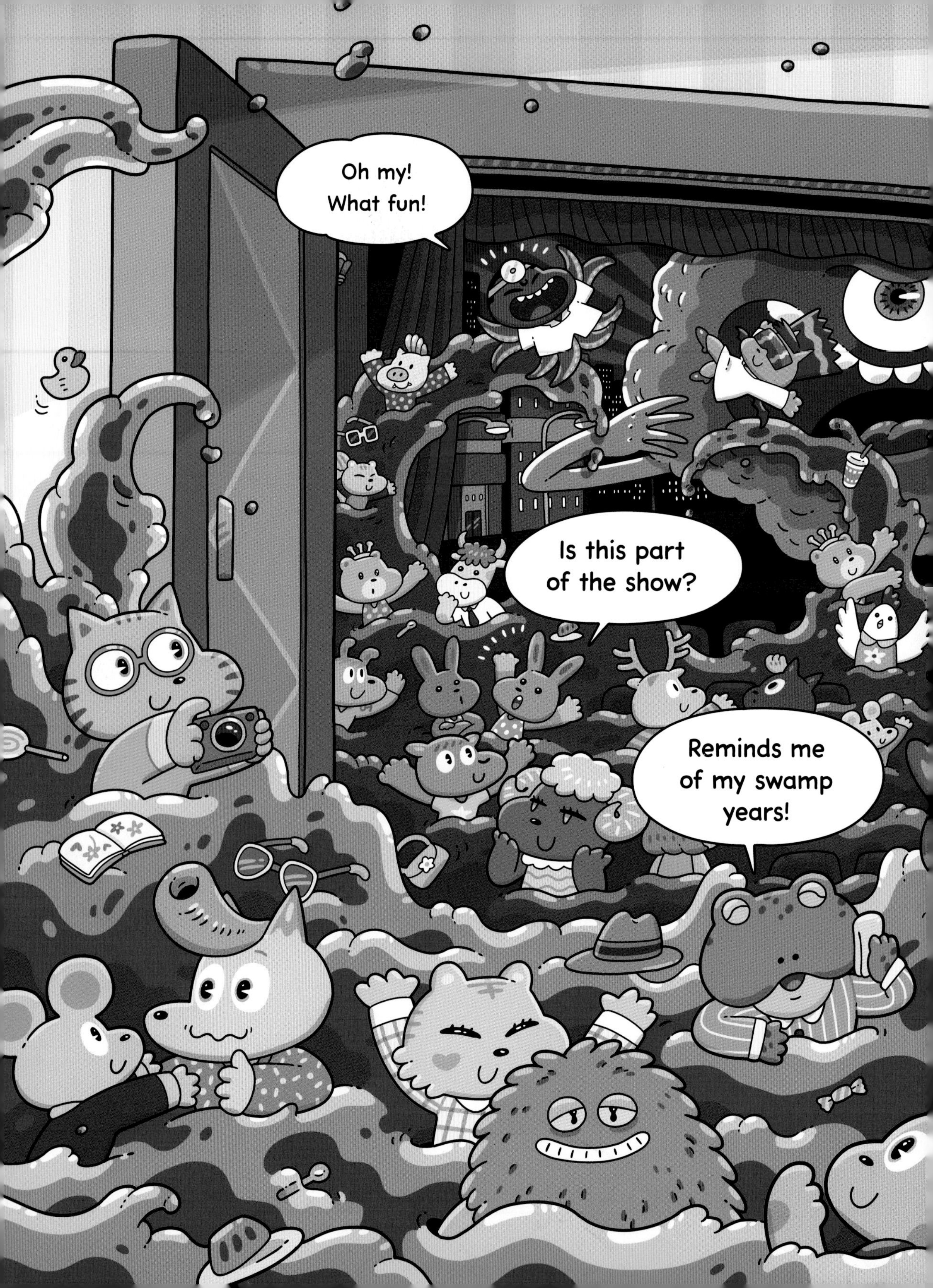
Oh my! What fun!
Is this part of the show?
Reminds me of my swamp years!

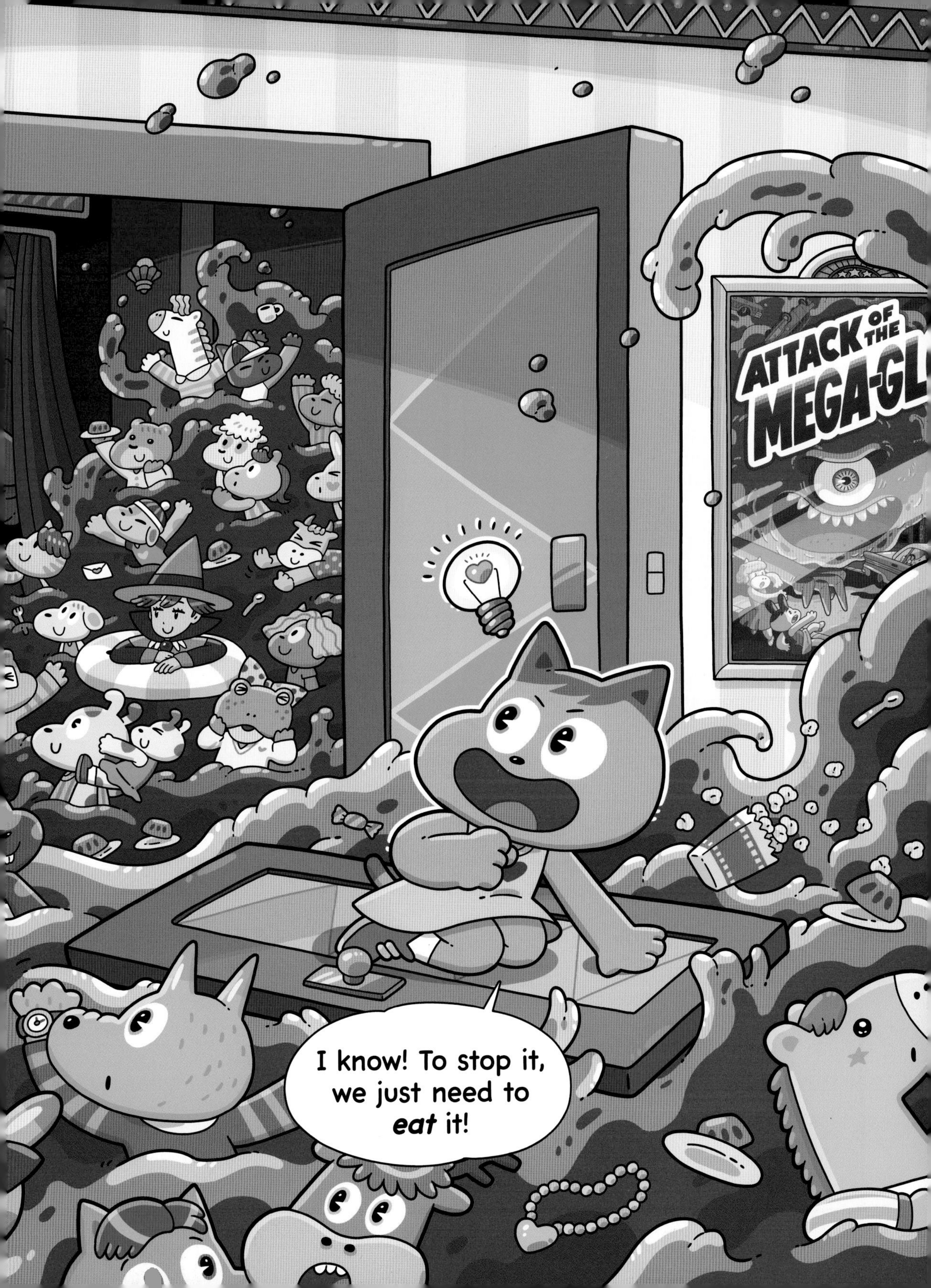
ATTACK OF THE MEGA-GL
I know! To stop it, we just need to *eat* it!

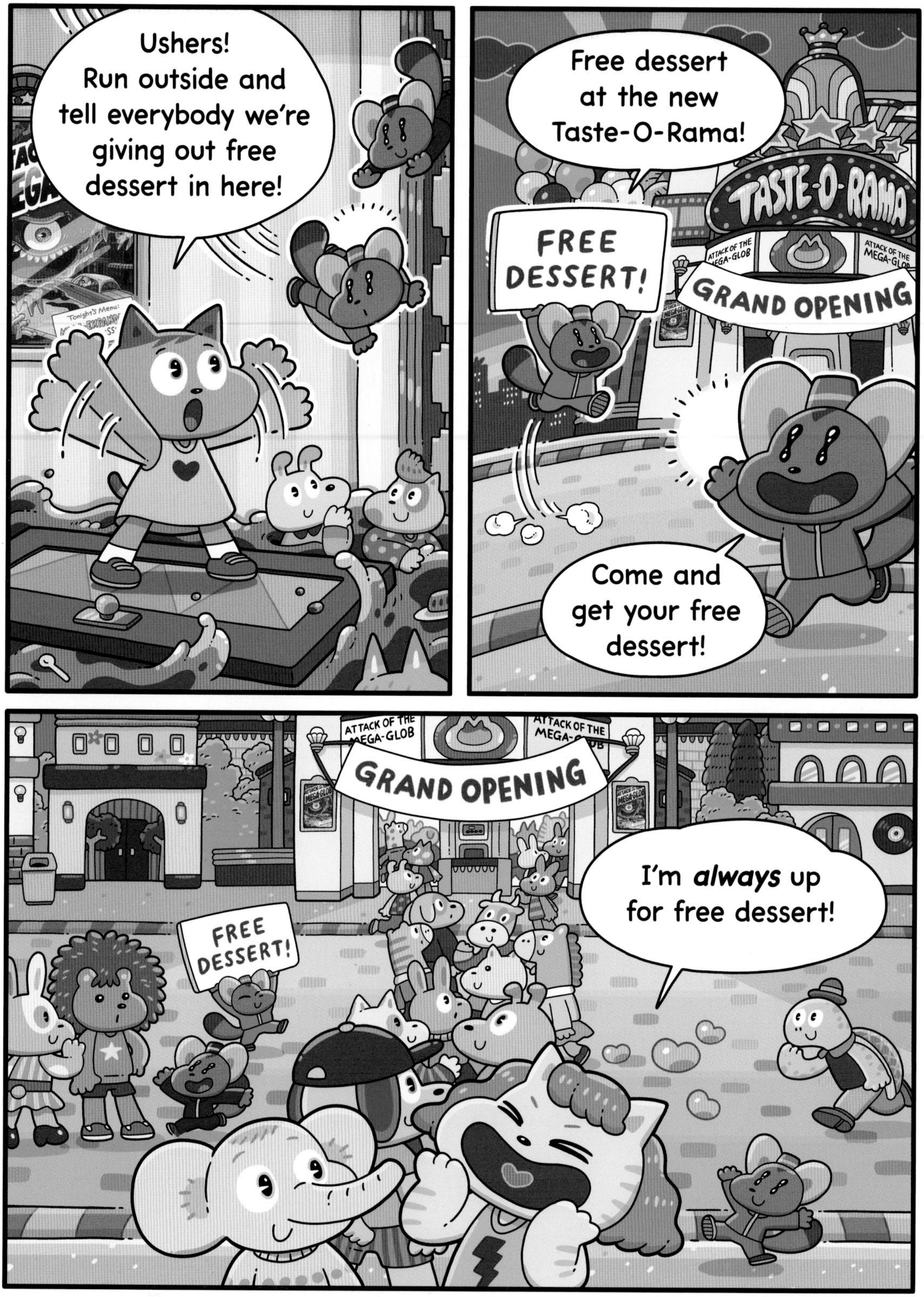
Ushers! Run outside and tell everybody we're giving out free dessert in here!
Free dessert at the new Taste-O-Rama!
FREE DESSERT!
TASTE-O-RAMA
ATTACK OF THE MEGA-GLOB
GRAND OPENING
Come and get your free dessert!
ATTACK OF THE MEGA-GLOB
GRAND OPENING
FREE DESSERT!
I'm *always* up for free dessert!

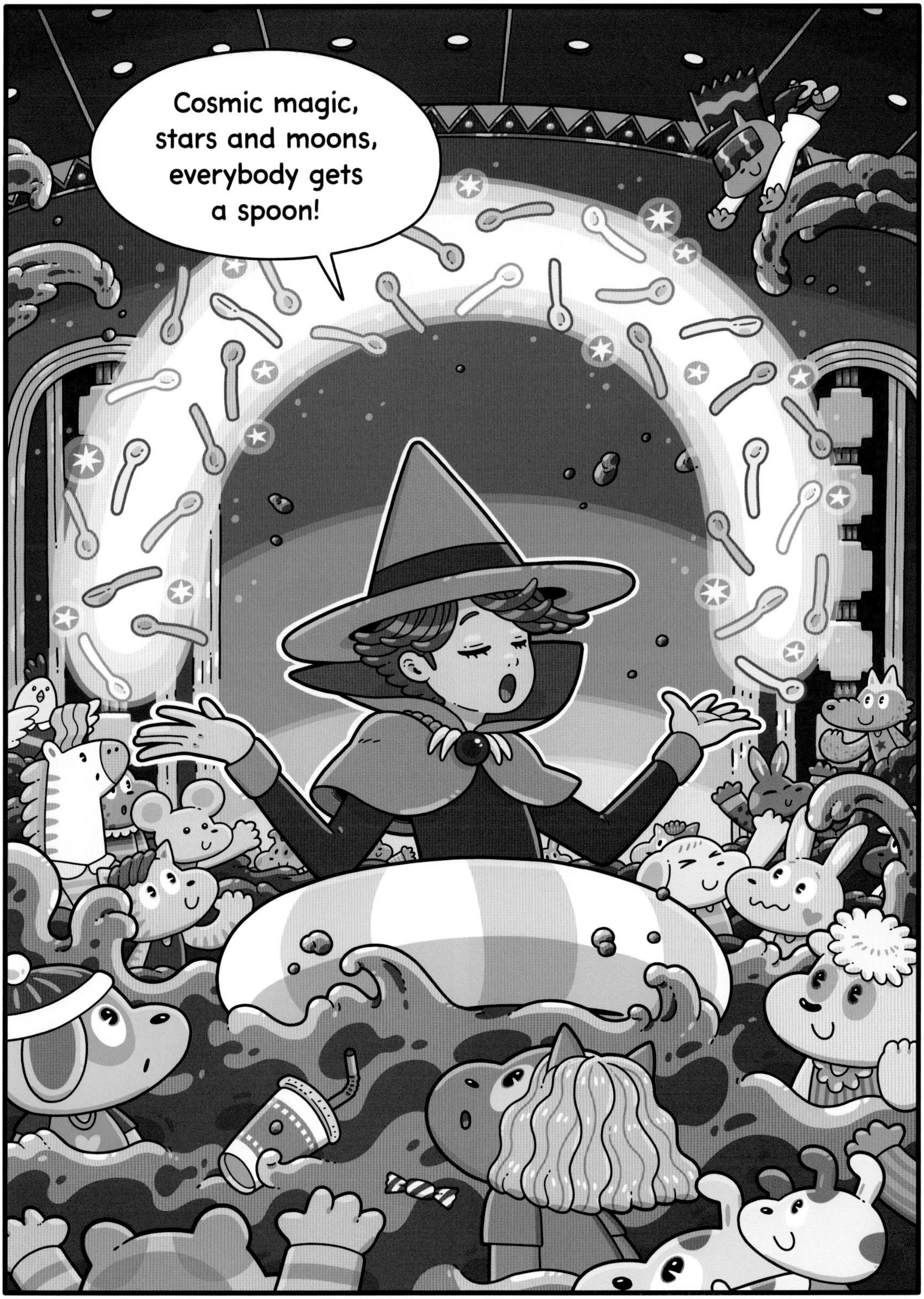
Cosmic magic, stars and moons, everybody gets a spoon!

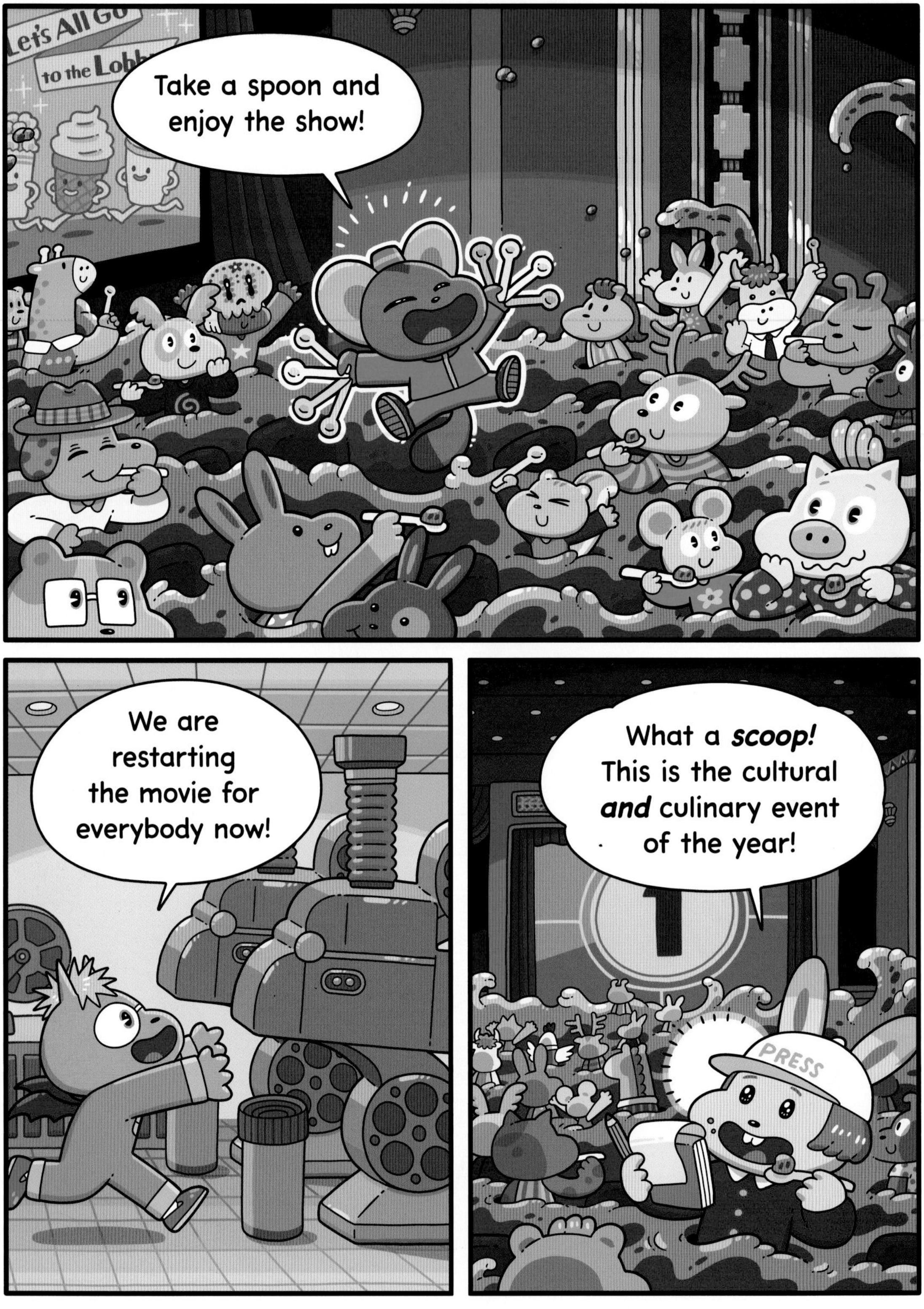
Take a spoon and enjoy the show!
We are restarting the movie for everybody now!
What a *scoop!* This is the cultural ***and*** culinary event of the year!
PRESS

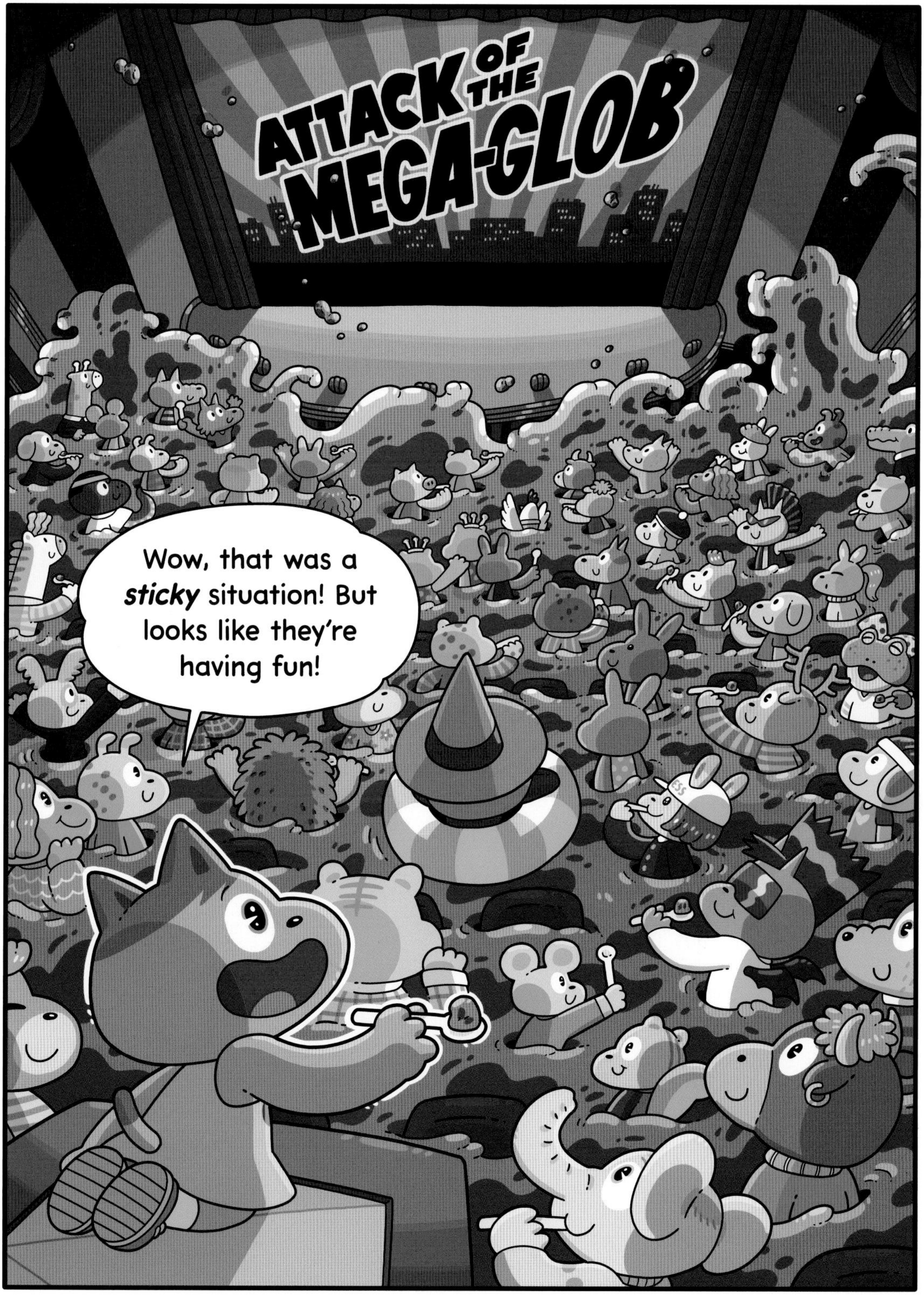
ATTACK OF THE MEGA-GLOB
Wow, that was a *sticky* situation! But looks like they're having fun!

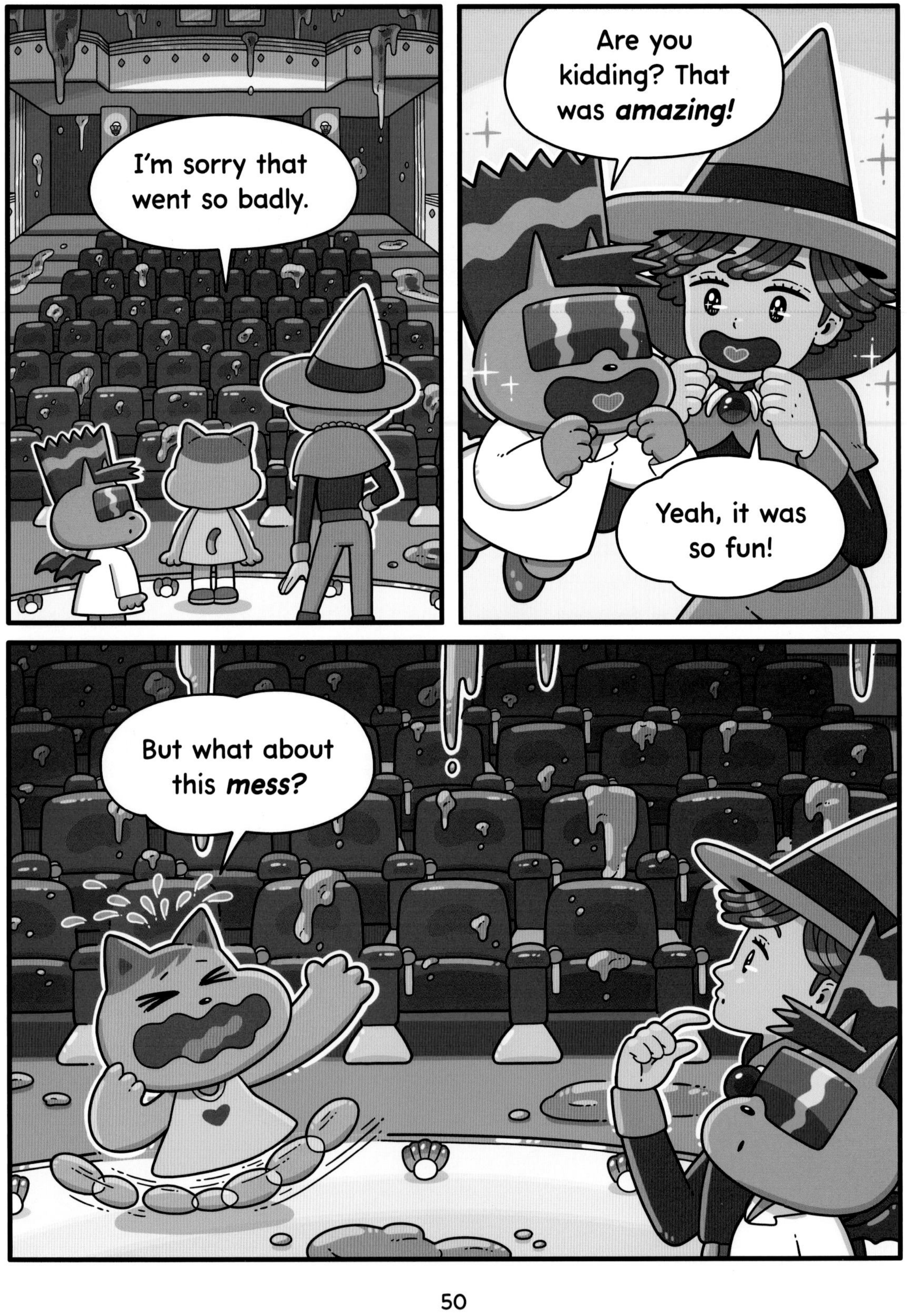
I'm sorry that went so badly.
Are you kidding? That was *amazing!*
Yeah, it was so fun!
But what about this *mess?*

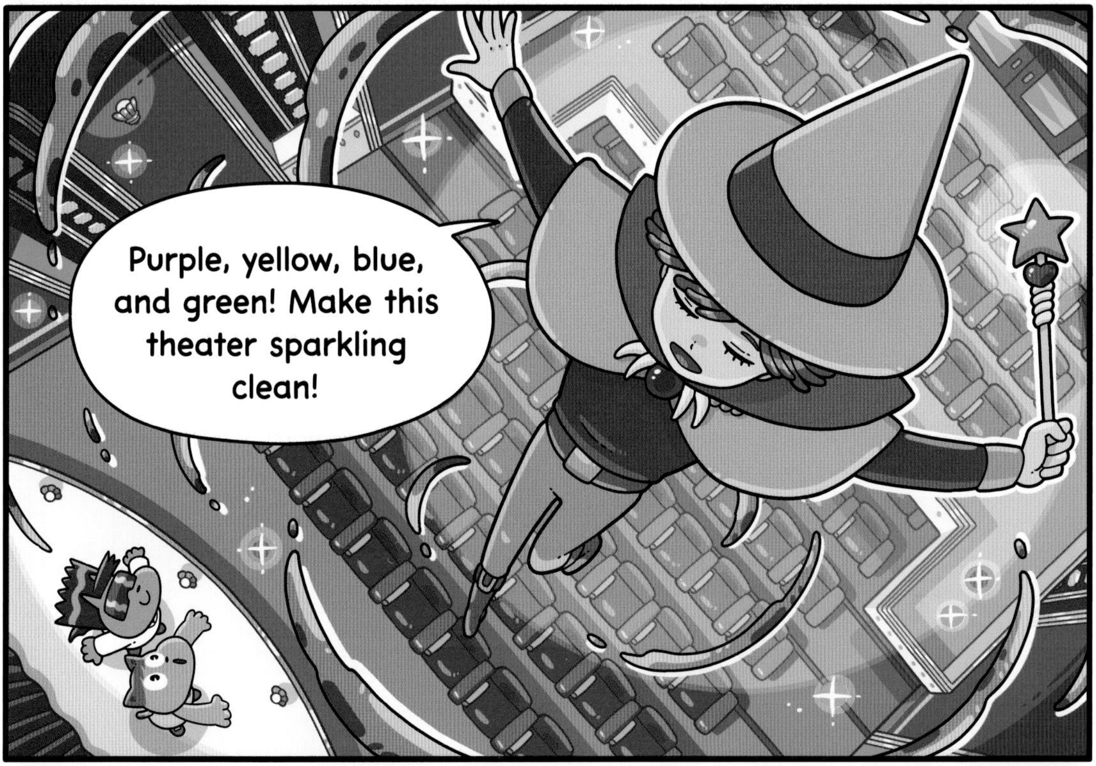
Purple, yellow, blue, and green! Make this theater sparkling clean!

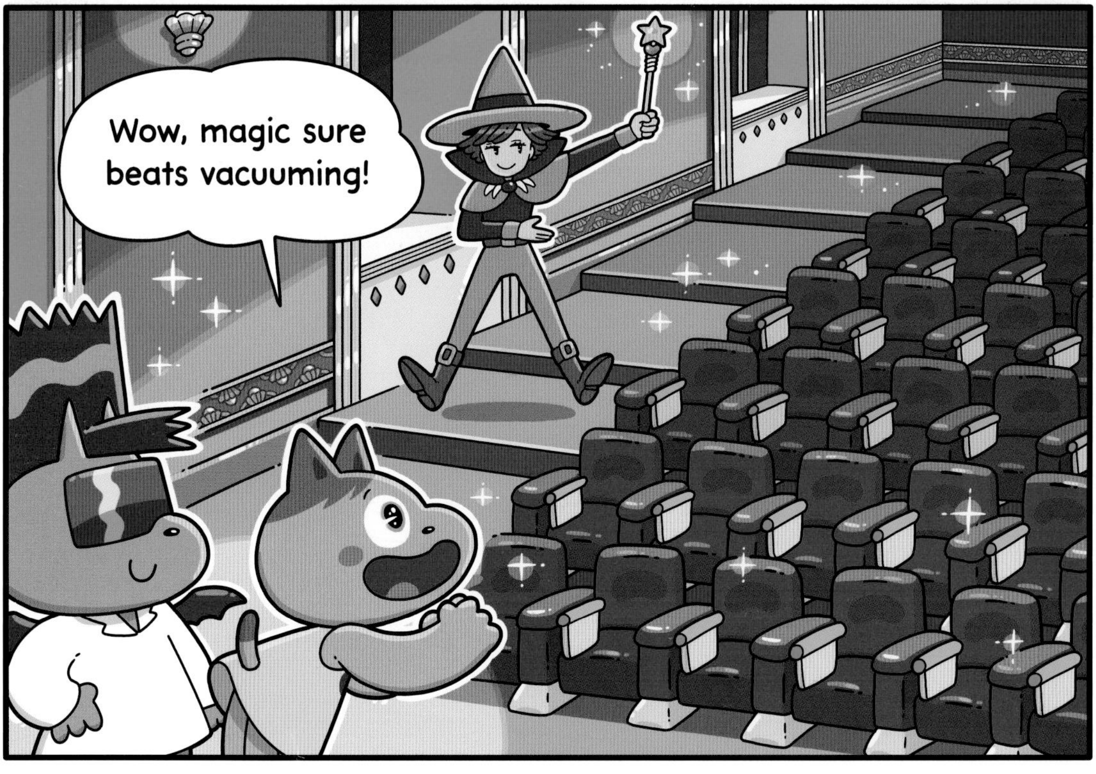
Wow, magic sure beats vacuuming!

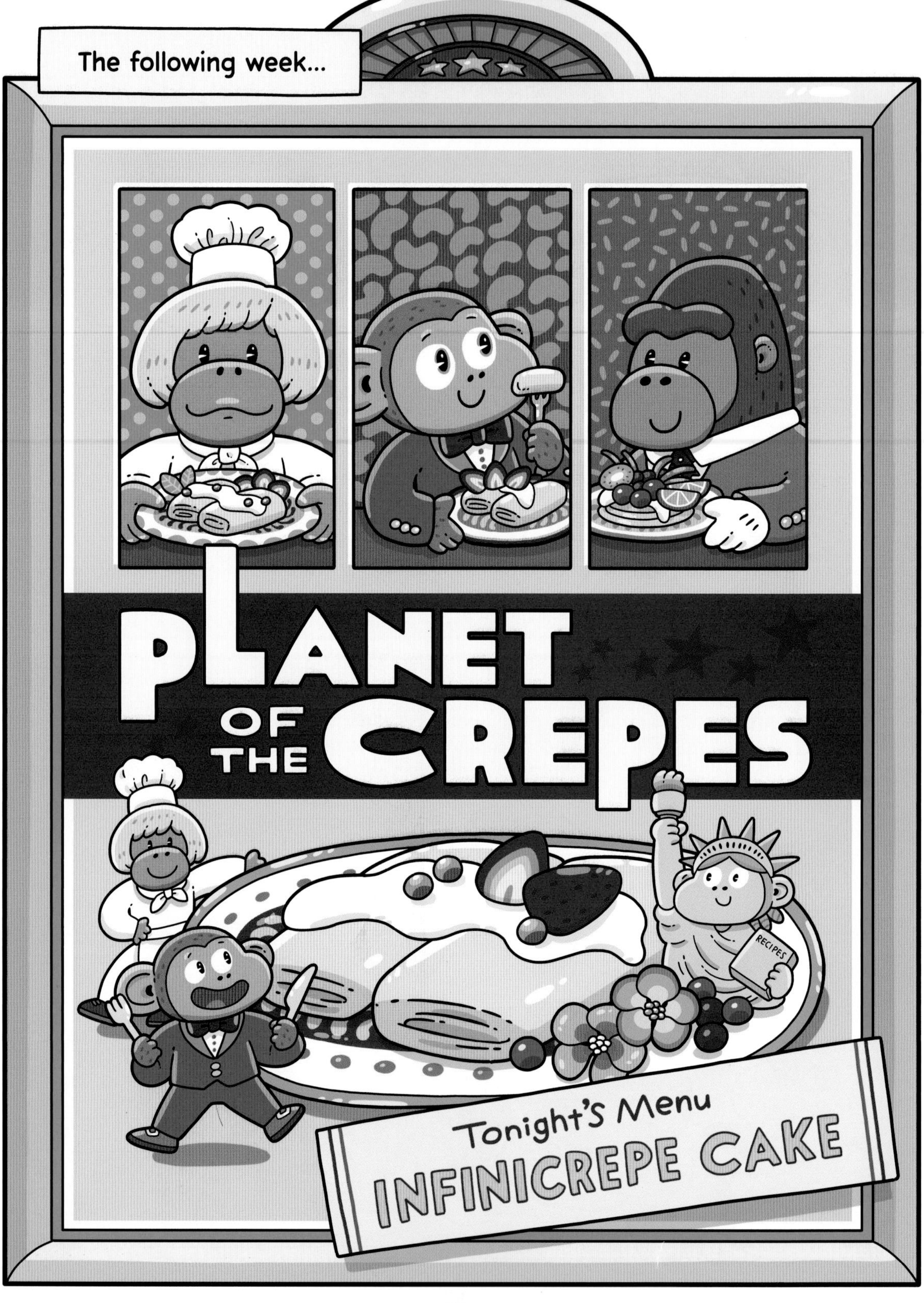
The following week...
PLANET OF THE CREPES
RECIPES
Tonight's Menu
INFINICREPE CAKE

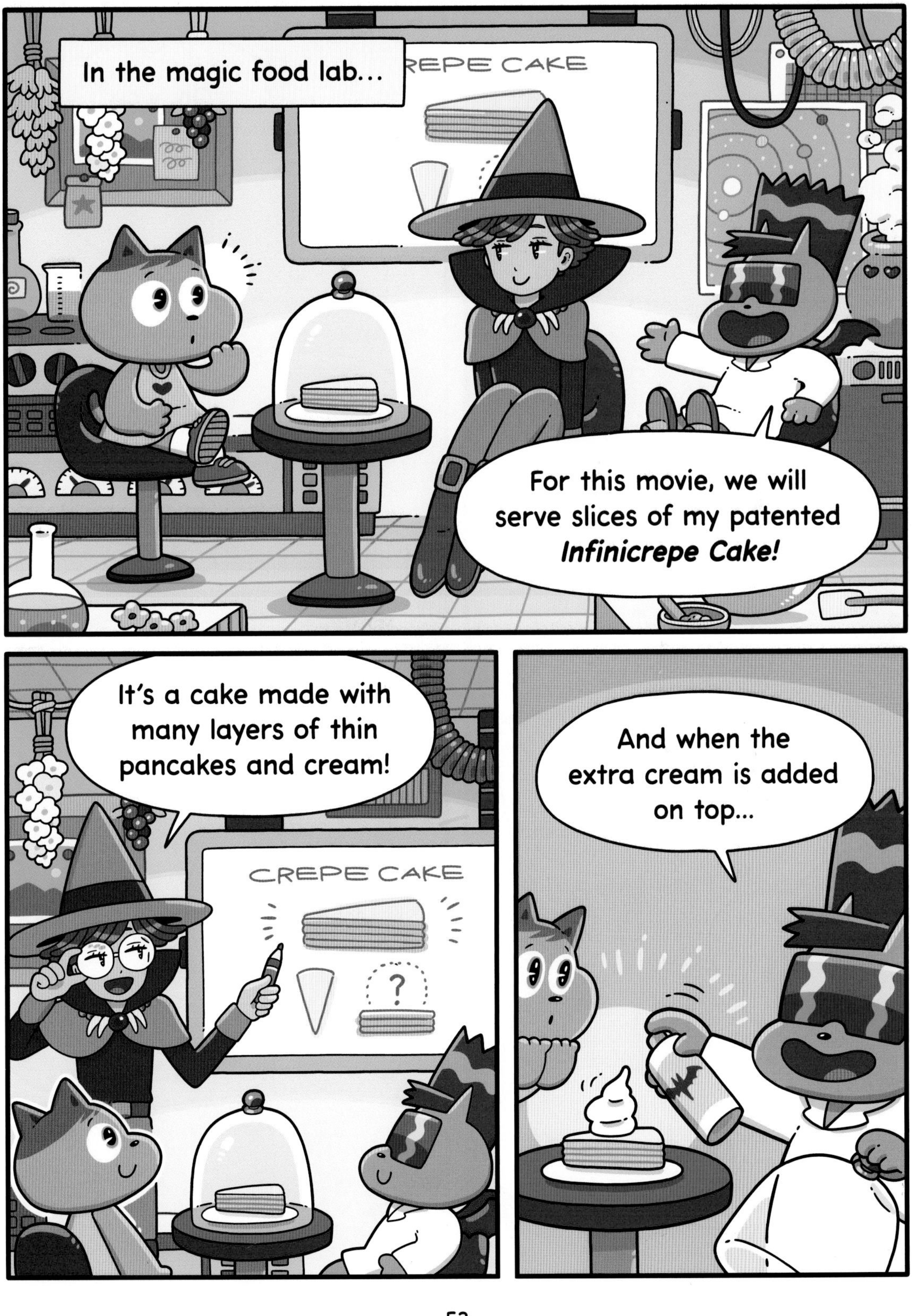
In the magic food lab...
CREPE CAKE
For this movie, we will serve slices of my patented *Infinicrepe Cake!*
It's a cake made with many layers of thin pancakes and cream!
CREPE CAKE
?
And when the extra cream is added on top...

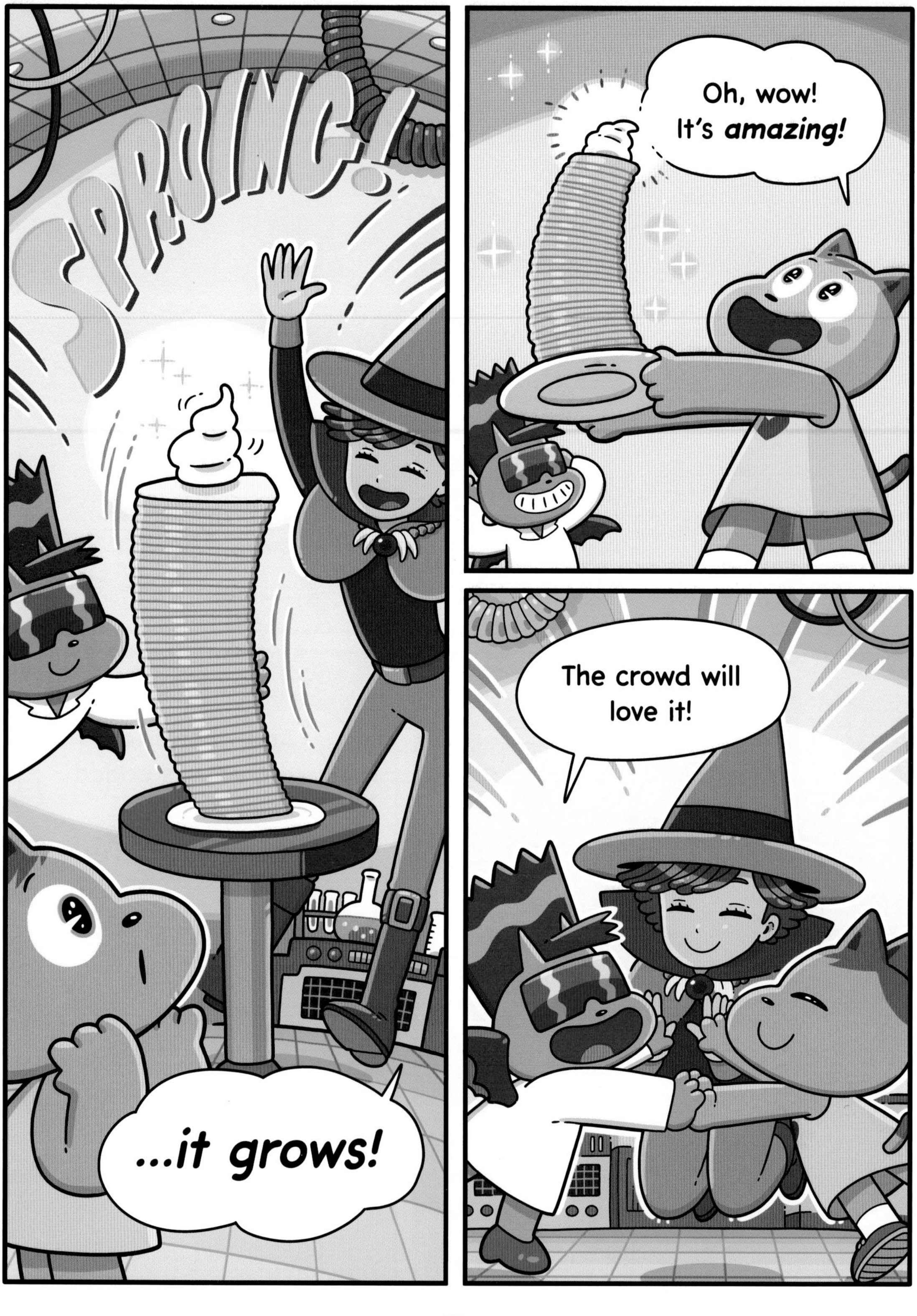
SPROING!
...it grows!
Oh, wow!
It's *amazing!*
The crowd will
love it!

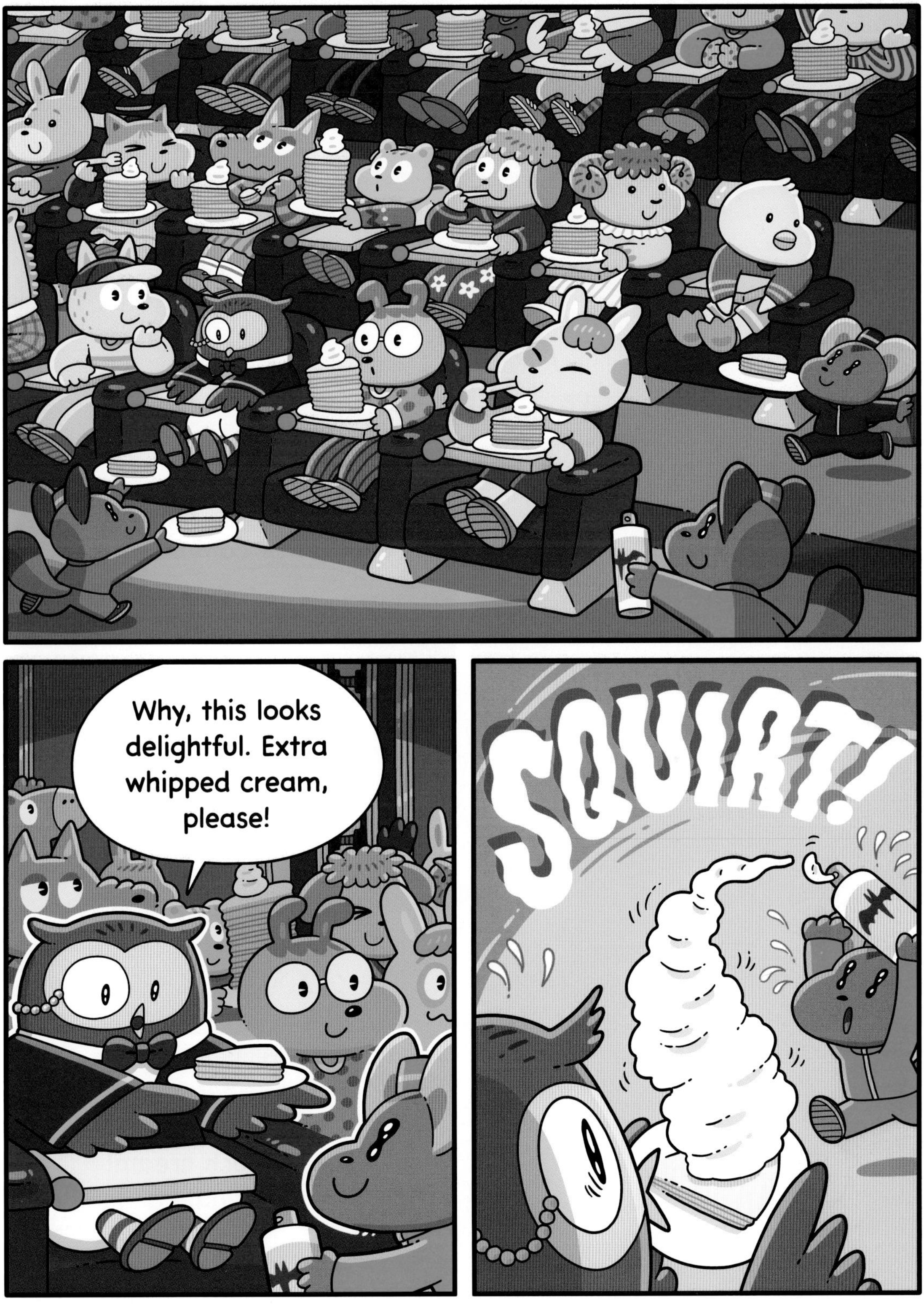
Why, this looks delightful. Extra whipped cream, please!
SQUIRT!

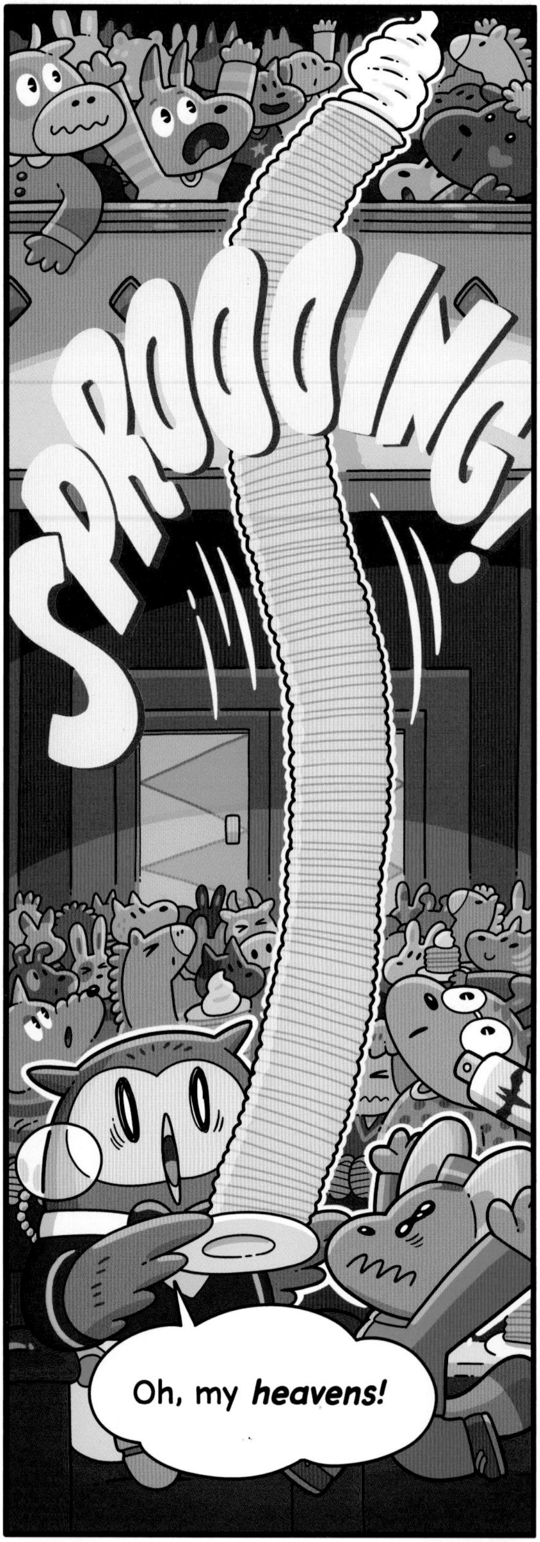
SPROOOING!
Oh, my *heavens!*

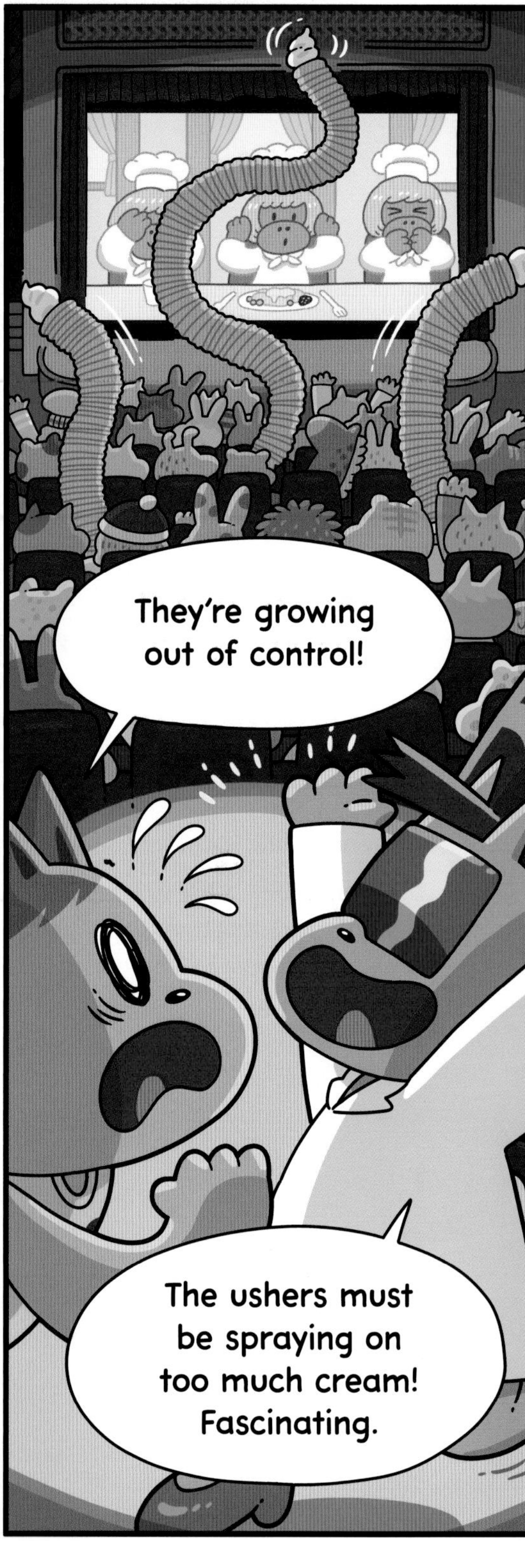
They're growing out of control!
The ushers must be spraying on too much cream! Fascinating.

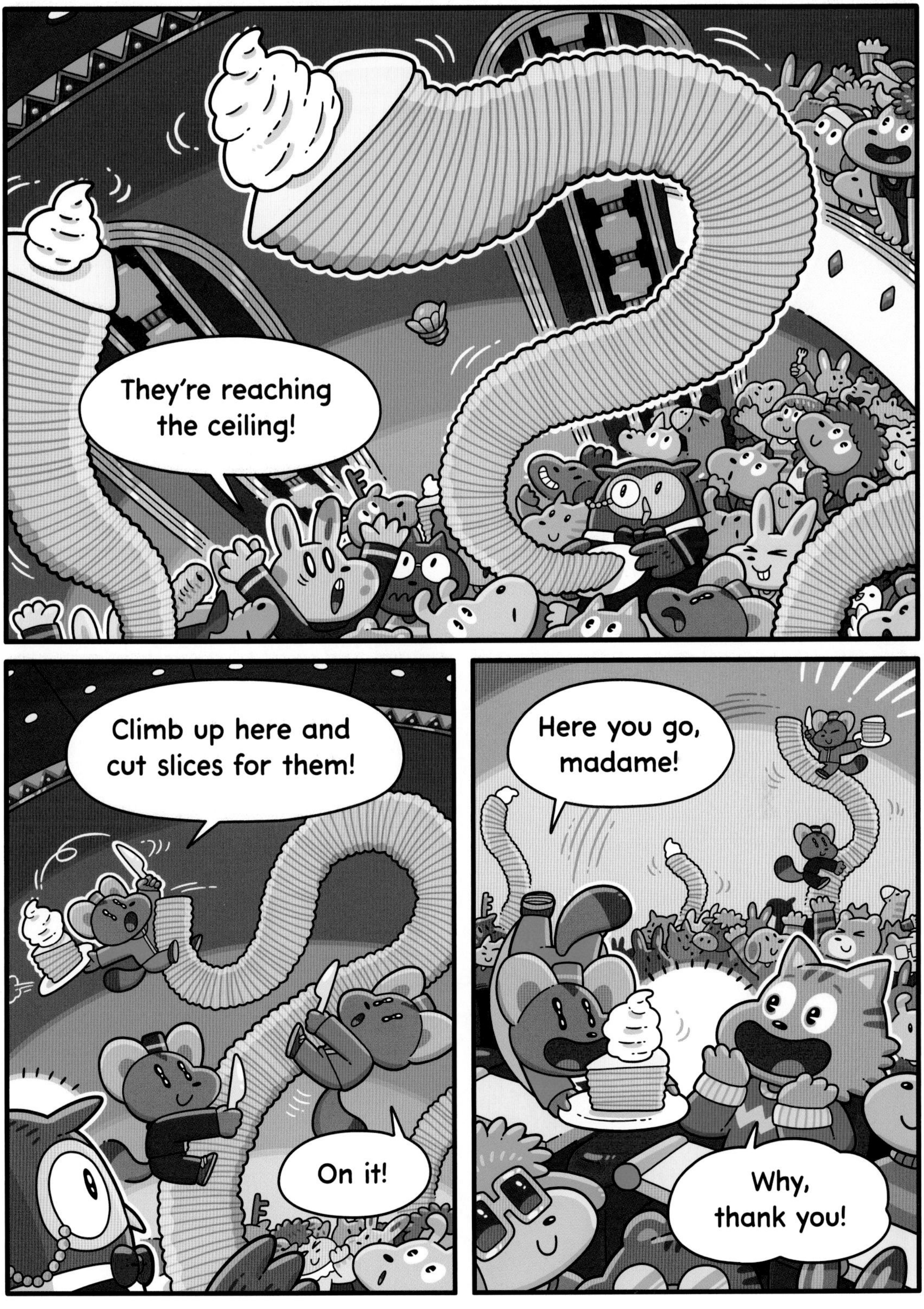
They're reaching the ceiling!
Climb up here and cut slices for them!
On it!
Here you go, madame!
Why, thank you!

We have to get more people in here to eat all this extra cake!

I'll cast a magic beacon to bring them in.

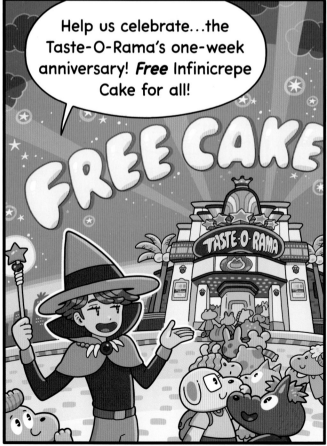

Help us celebrate...the Taste-O-Rama's one-week anniversary! *Free* Infinicrepe Cake for all!

FREE CAKE

TASTE-O-RAMA

Miss Kitty Sweet Tooth, I say, that was simply *delightful!*

Thank you for coming!

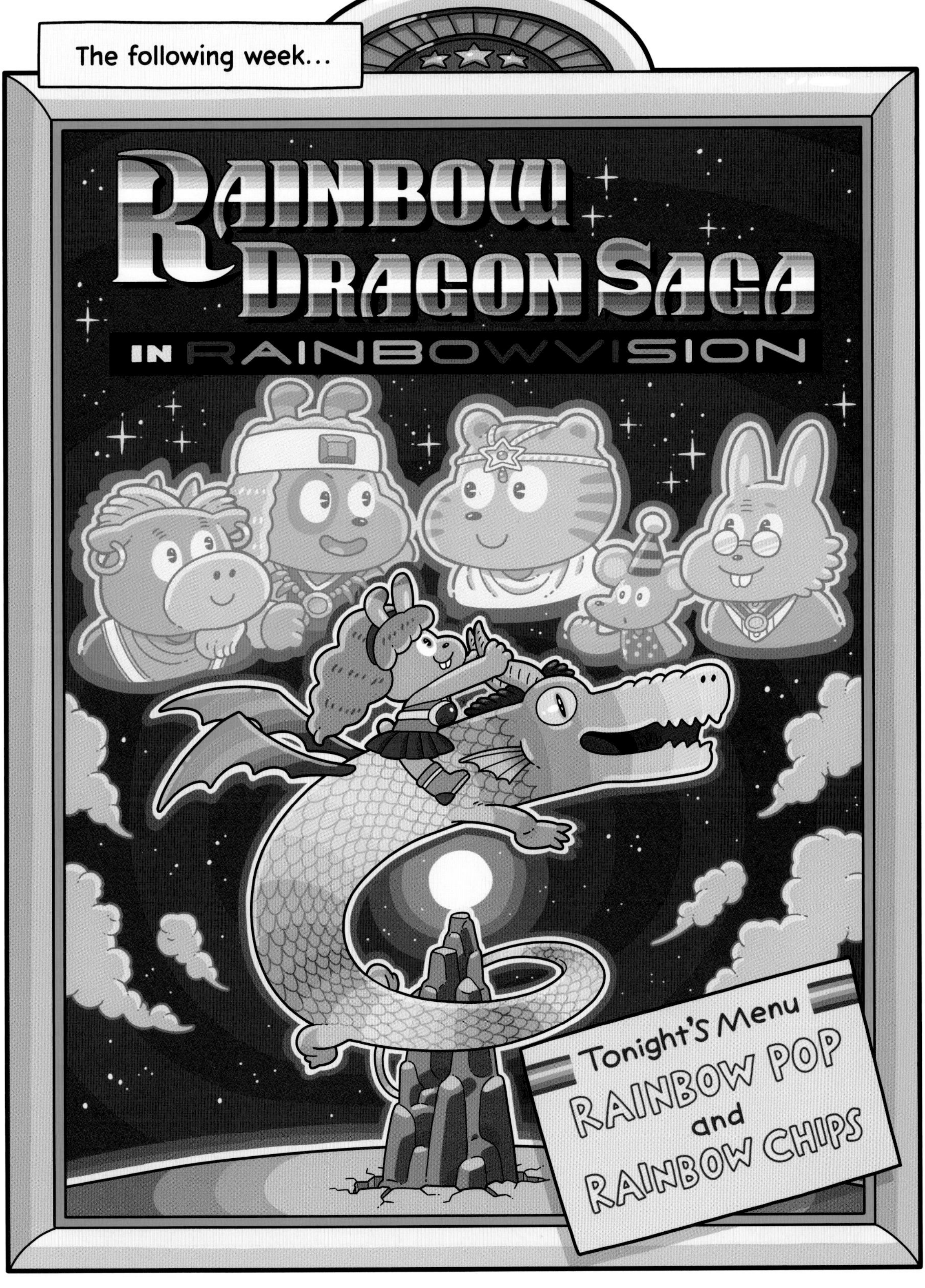

The following week...
RAINBOW DRAGON SAGA
IN RAINBOWVISION
Tonight's Menu
RAINBOW POP
and
RAINBOW CHIPS

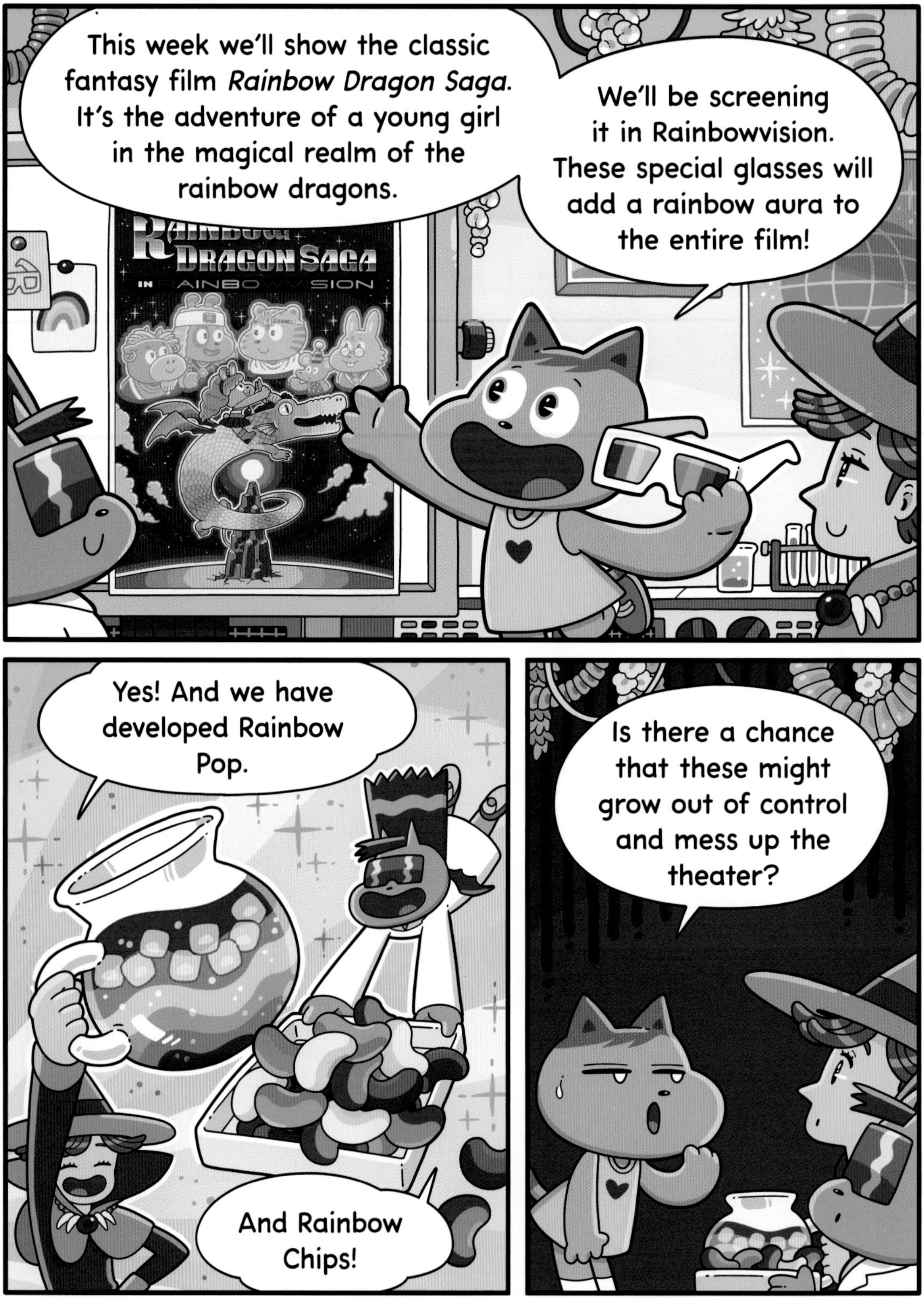
This week we'll show the classic fantasy film *Rainbow Dragon Saga.* It's the adventure of a young girl in the magical realm of the rainbow dragons.
DRAGON SAGA
We'll be screening it in Rainbowvision. These special glasses will add a rainbow aura to the entire film!
Yes! And we have developed Rainbow Pop.
And Rainbow Chips!
Is there a chance that these might grow out of control and mess up the theater?

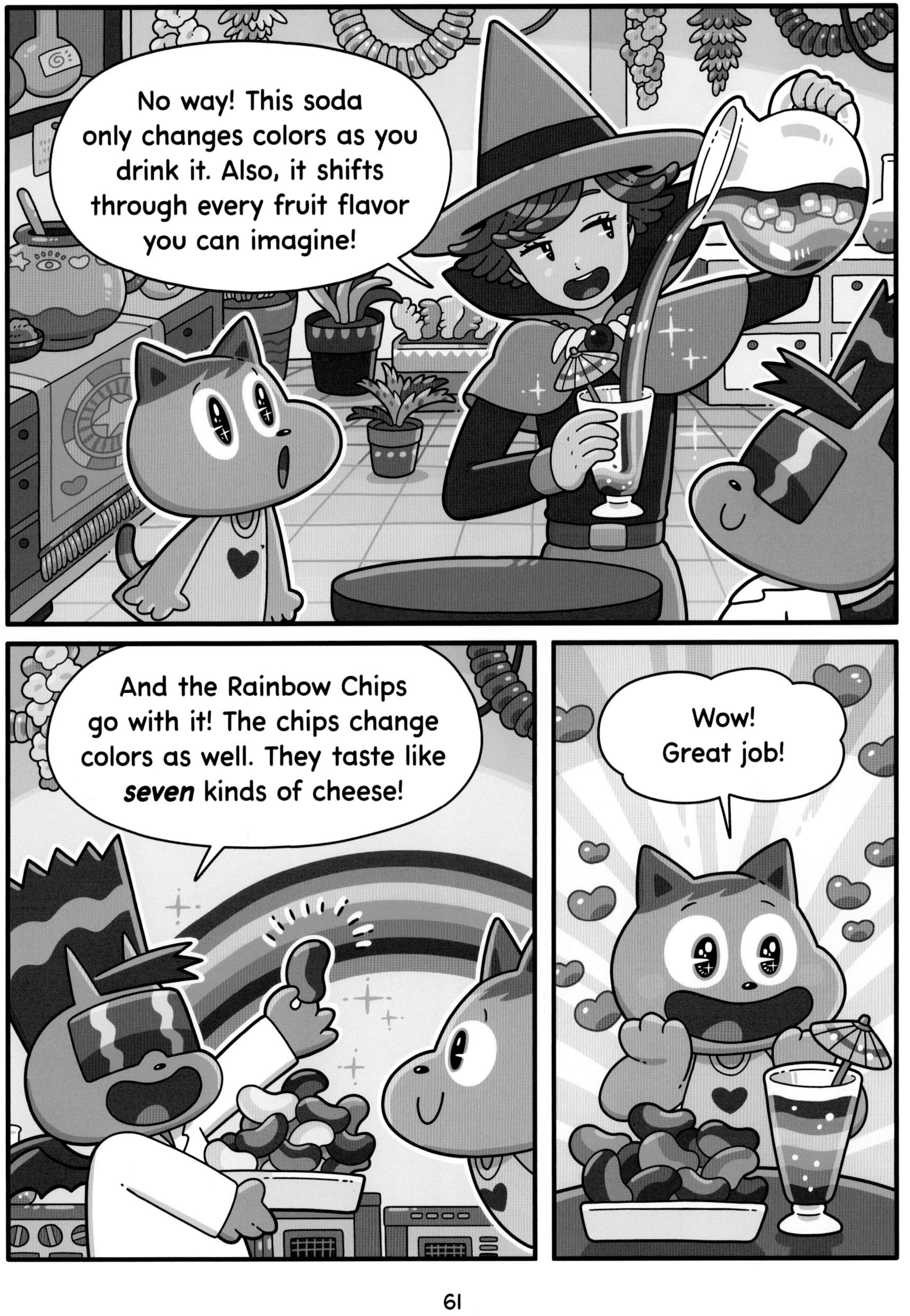
No way! This soda only changes colors as you drink it. Also, it shifts through every fruit flavor you can imagine!
And the Rainbow Chips go with it! The chips change colors as well. They taste like *seven* kinds of cheese!
Wow! Great job!

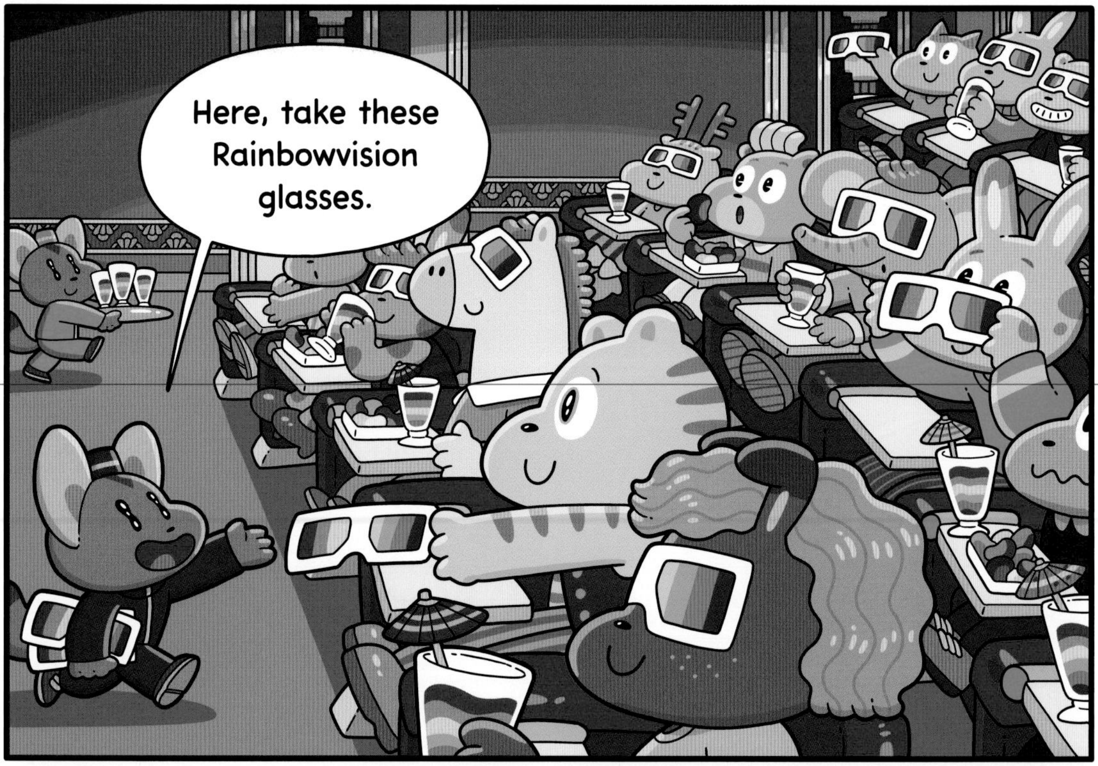
Here, take these Rainbowvision glasses.

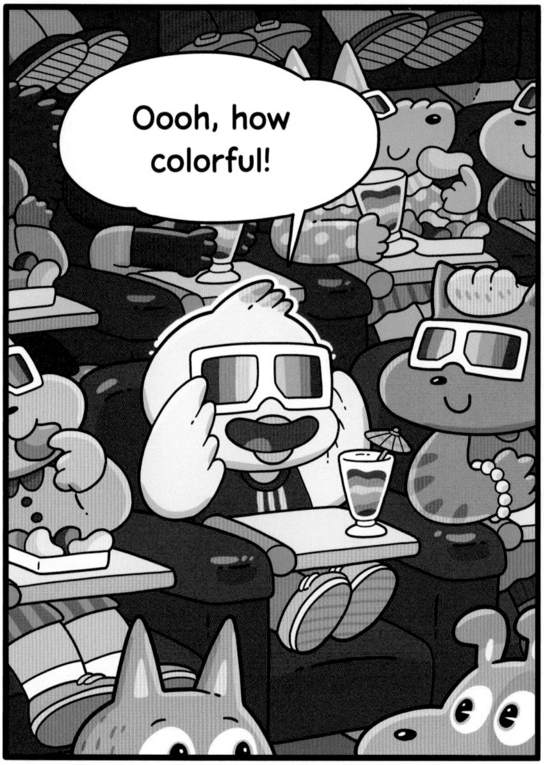
Oooh, how colorful!

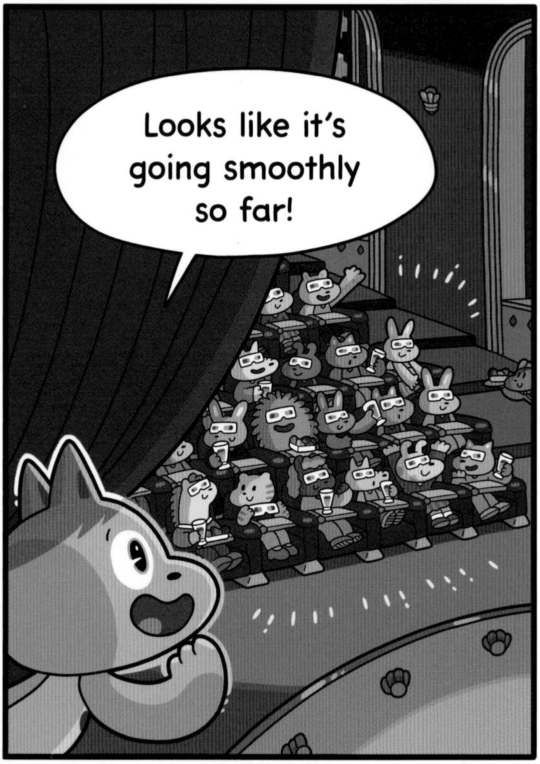
Looks like it's going smoothly so far!

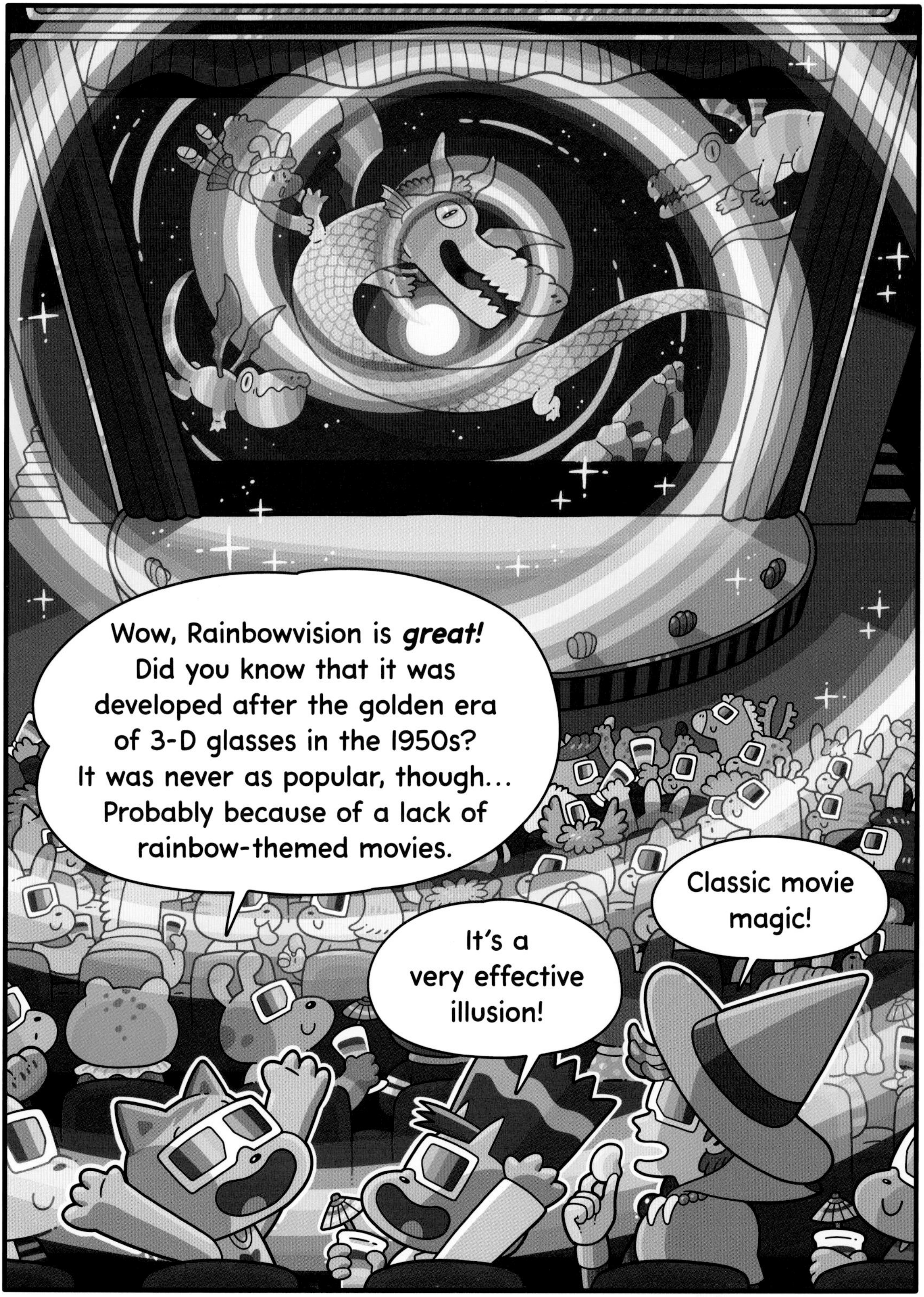
Wow, Rainbowvision is *great!* Did you know that it was developed after the golden era of 3-D glasses in the 1950s? It was never as popular, though... Probably because of a lack of rainbow-themed movies.
It's a very effective illusion!
Classic movie magic!

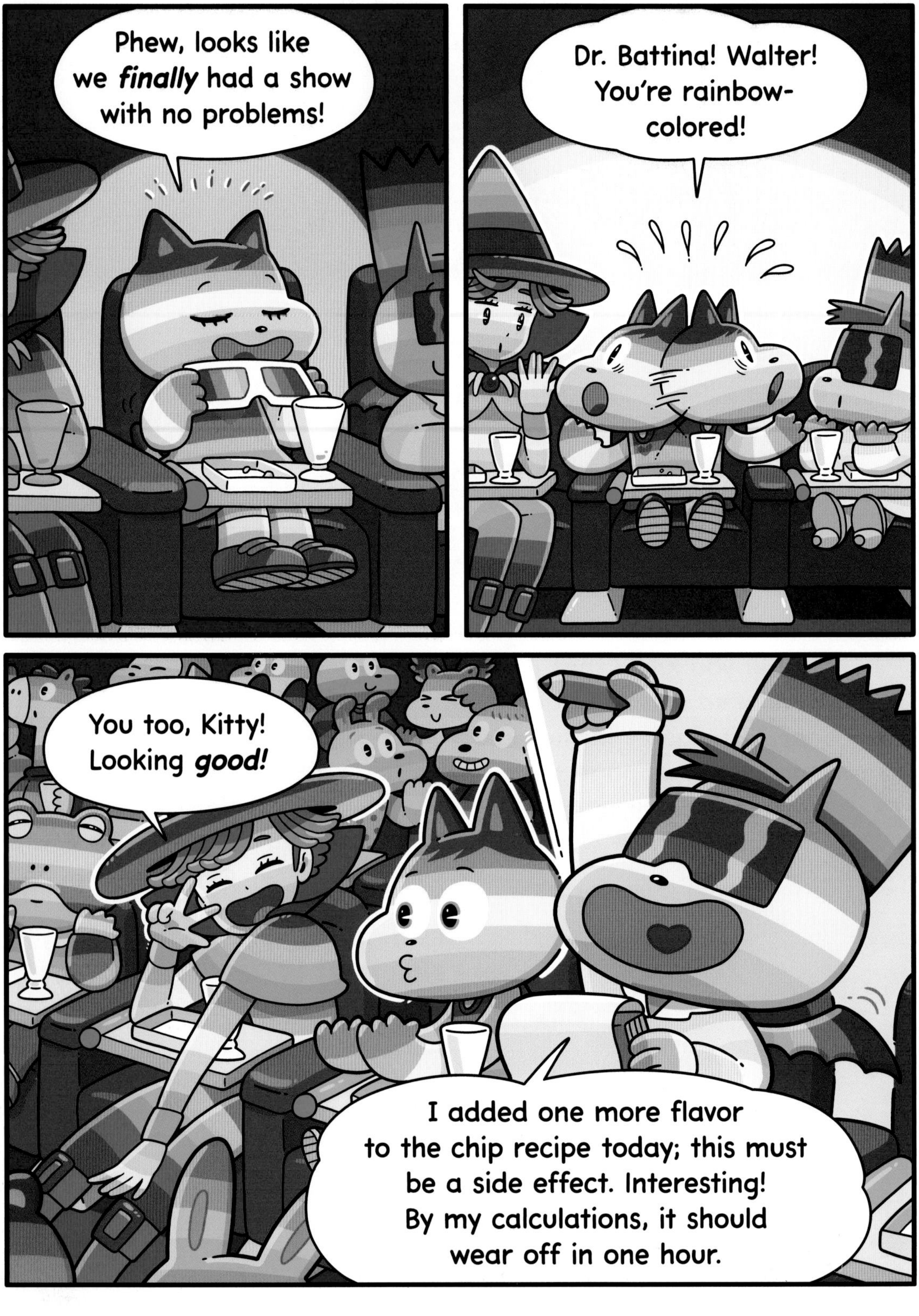
Phew, looks like we *finally* had a show with no problems!
Dr. Battina! Walter! You're rainbow-colored!
You too, Kitty! Looking *good!*
I added one more flavor to the chip recipe today; this must be a side effect. Interesting! By my calculations, it should wear off in one hour.

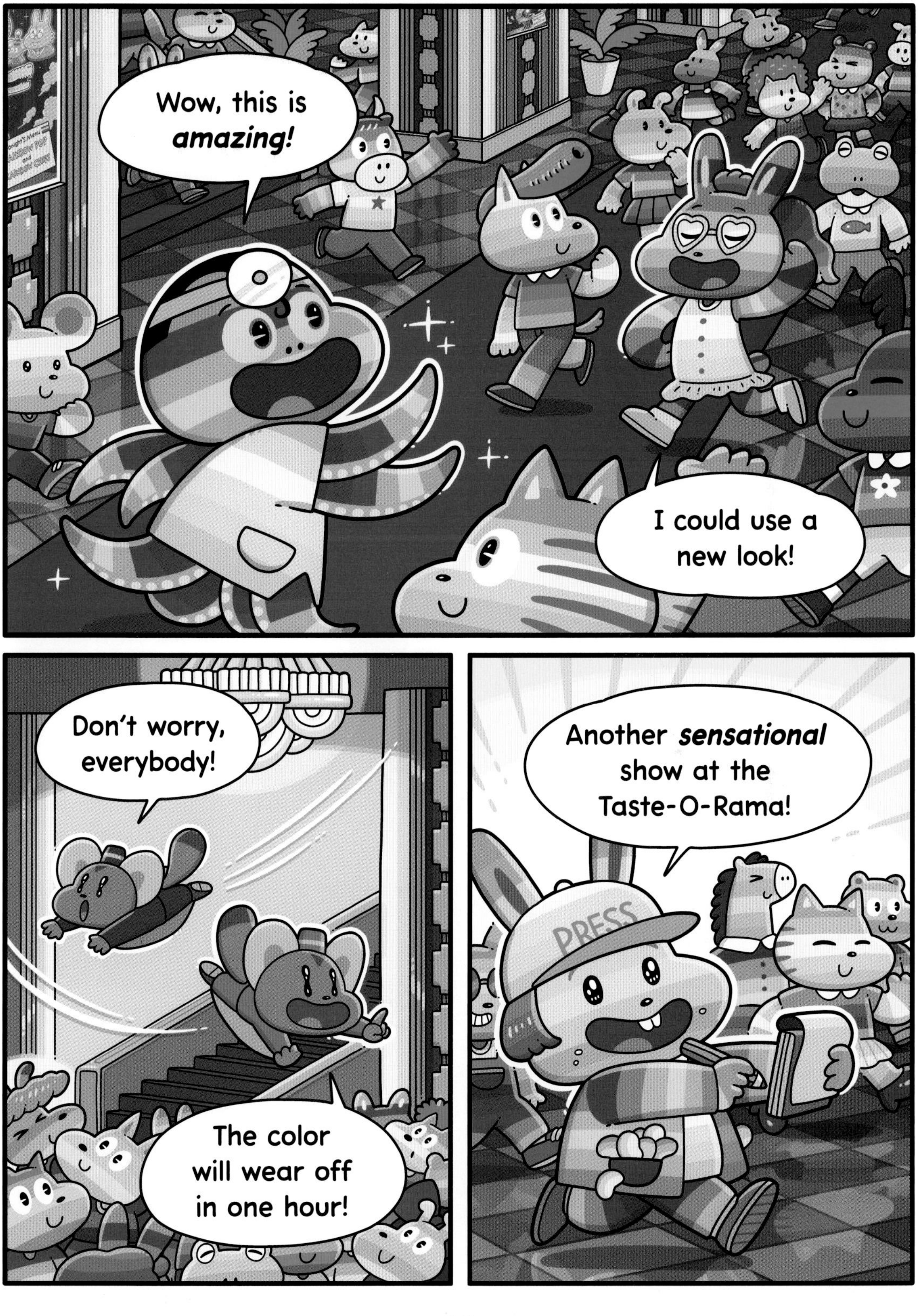
Wow, this is *amazing!*
I could use a new look!
Don't worry, everybody!
The color will wear off in one hour!
Another *sensational* show at the Taste-O-Rama!
PRESS

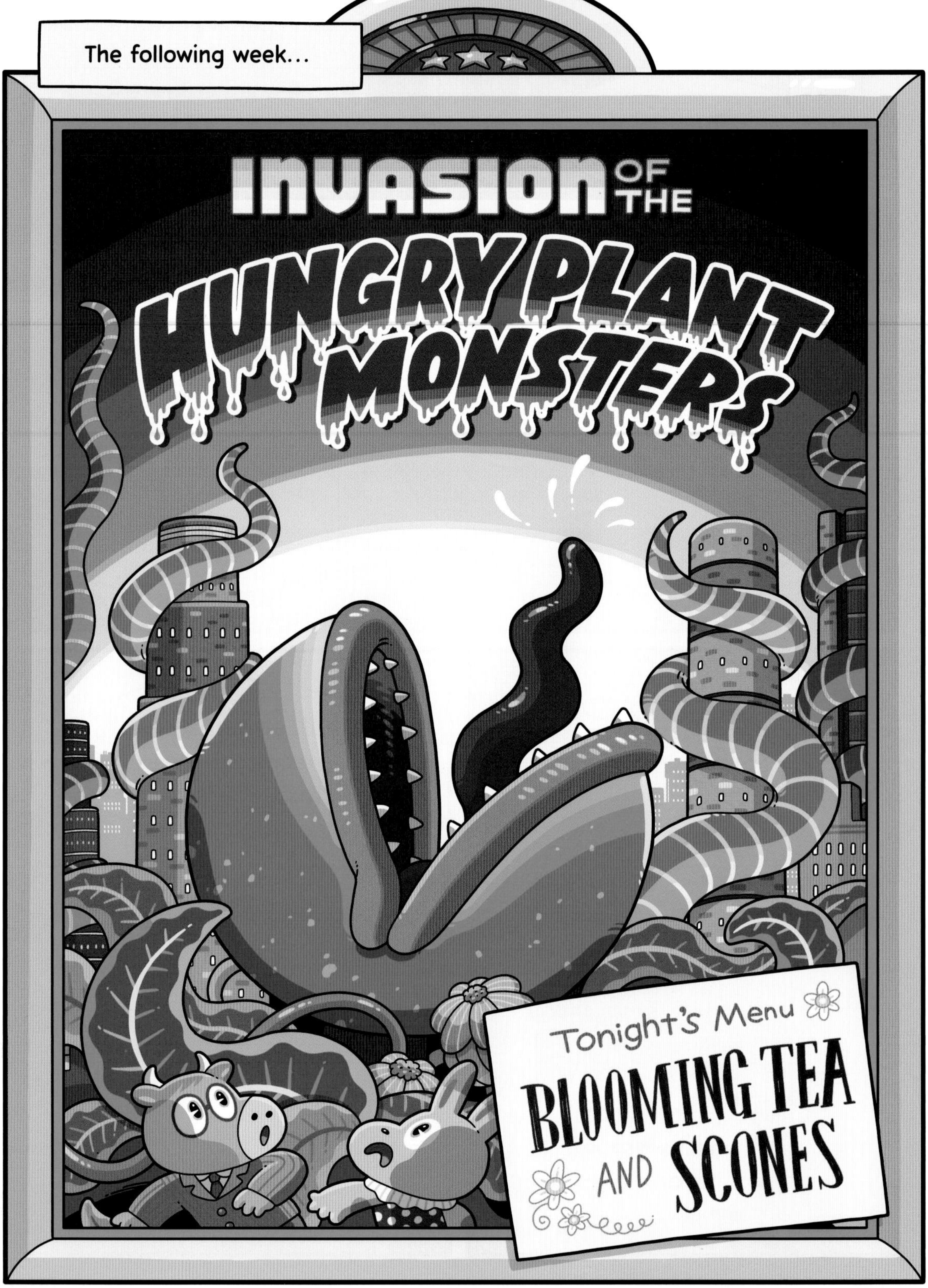
The following week...
INVASION OF THE
HUNGRY PLANT MONSTERS
Tonight's Menu
BLOOMING TEA AND SCONES

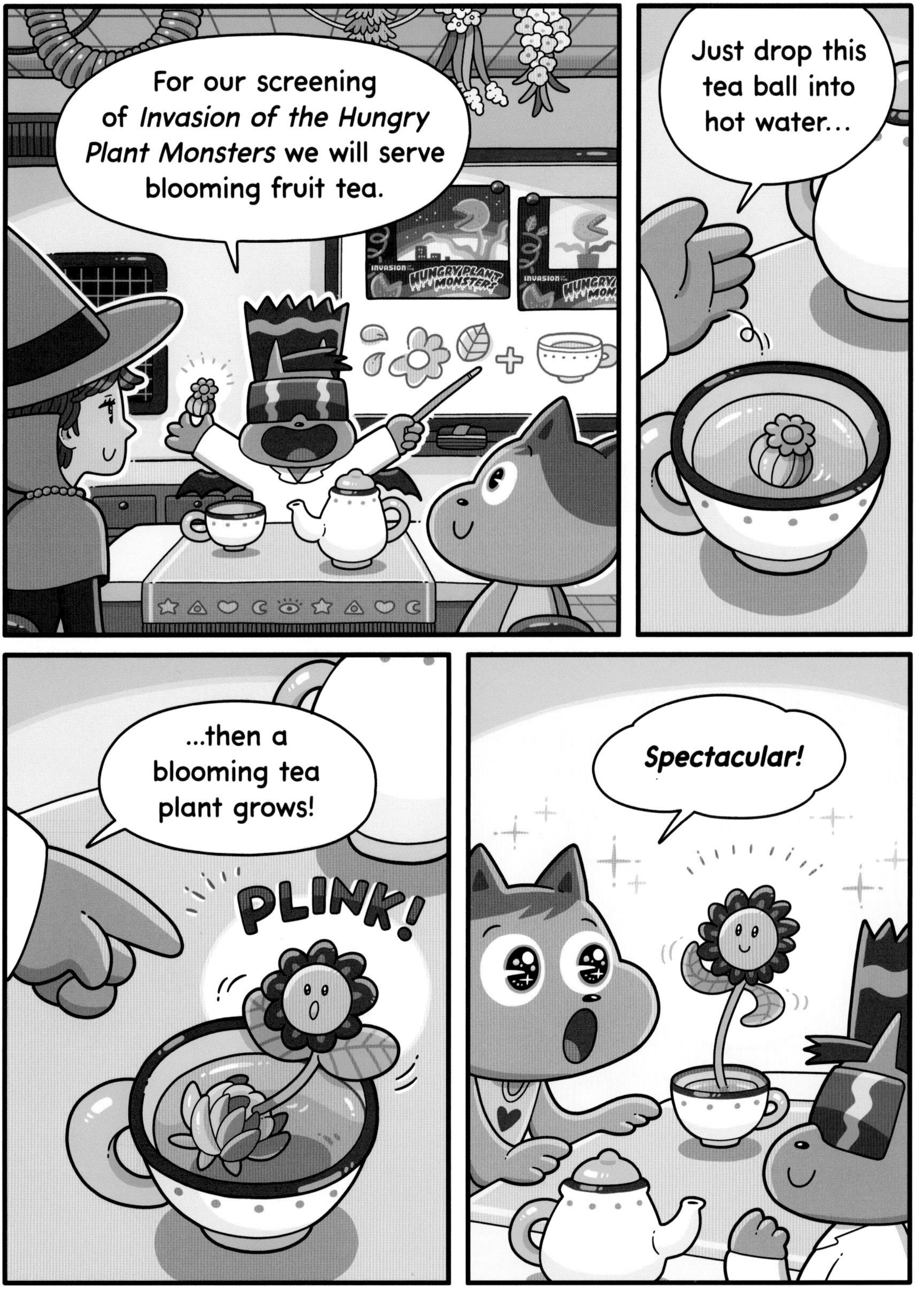
For our screening of *Invasion of the Hungry Plant Monsters* we will serve blooming fruit tea.
INVASION OF THE HUNGRY PLANT MONSTERS
Just drop this tea ball into hot water...
...then a blooming tea plant grows!
PLINK!
Spectacular!

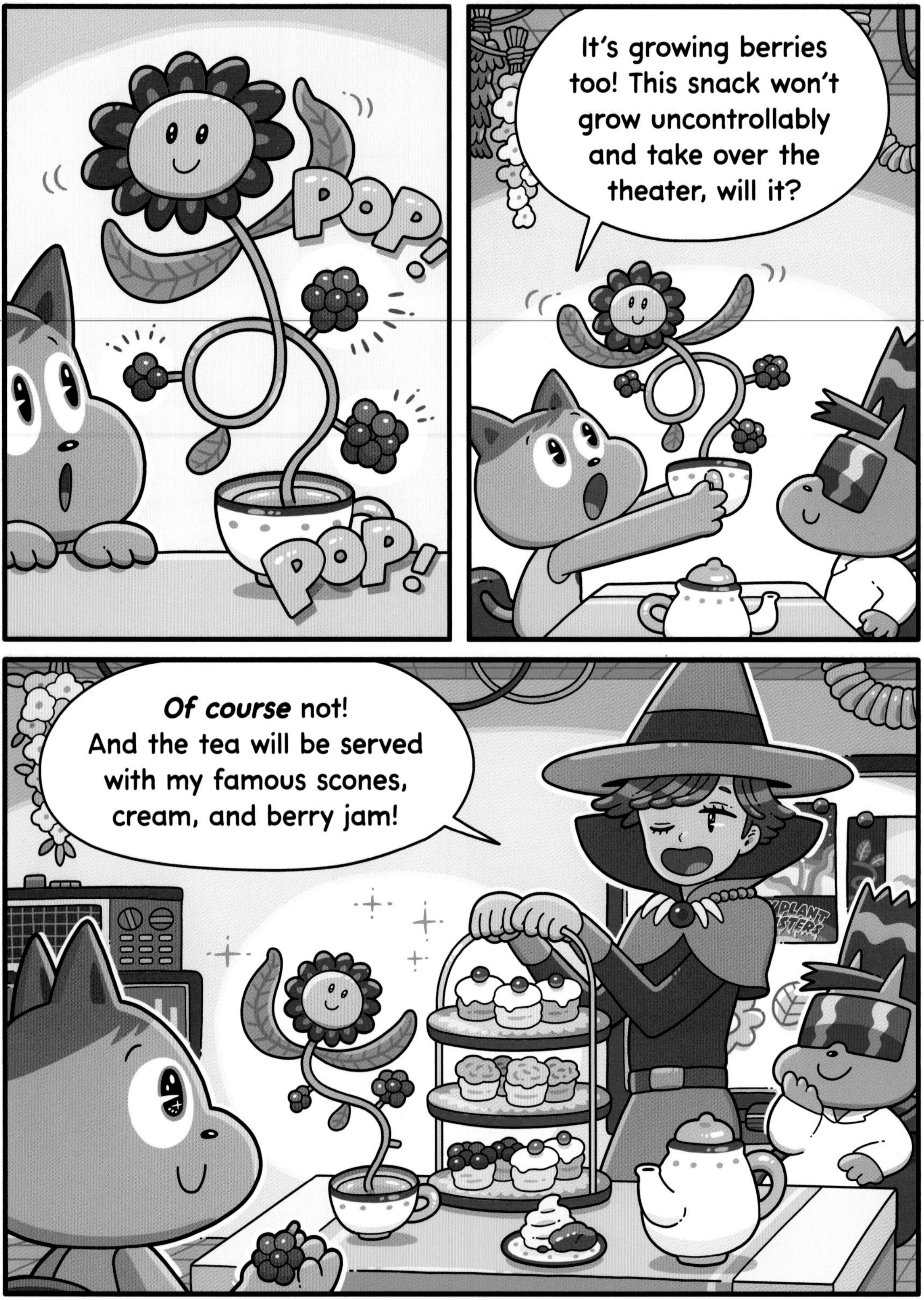

POP!
POP!
It's growing berries too! This snack won't grow uncontrollably and take over the theater, will it?
Of course not! And the tea will be served with my famous scones, cream, and berry jam!

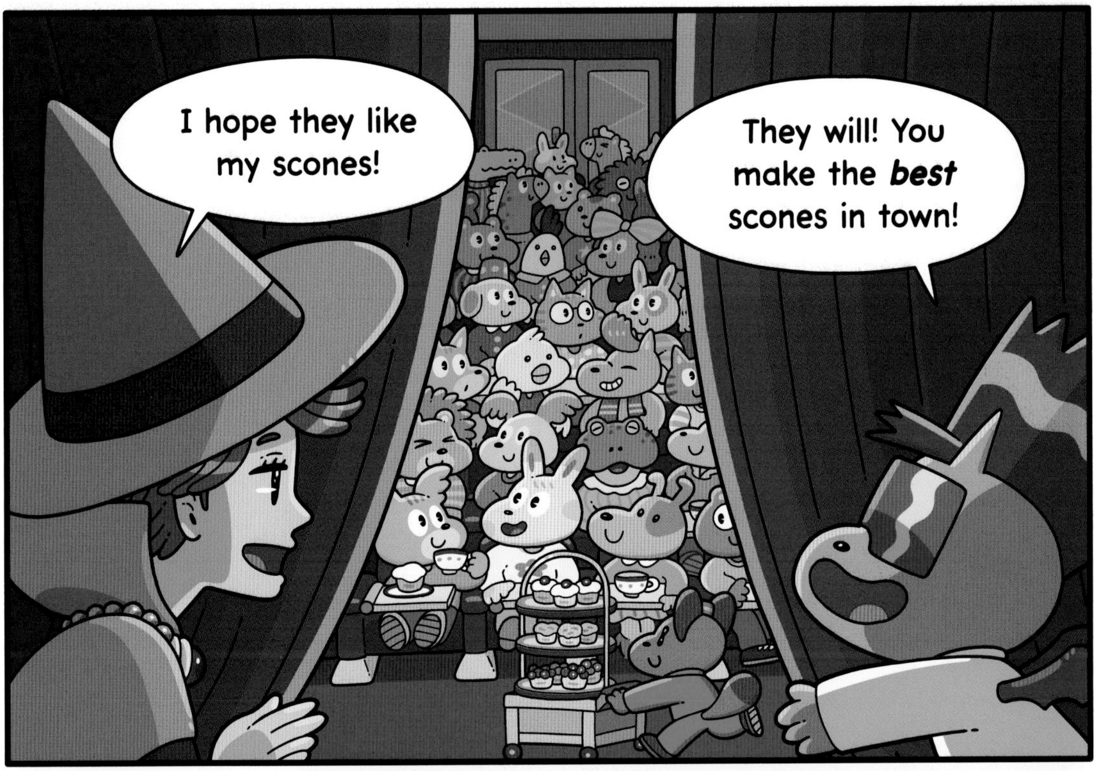
I hope they like my scones!
They will! You make the *best* scones in town!

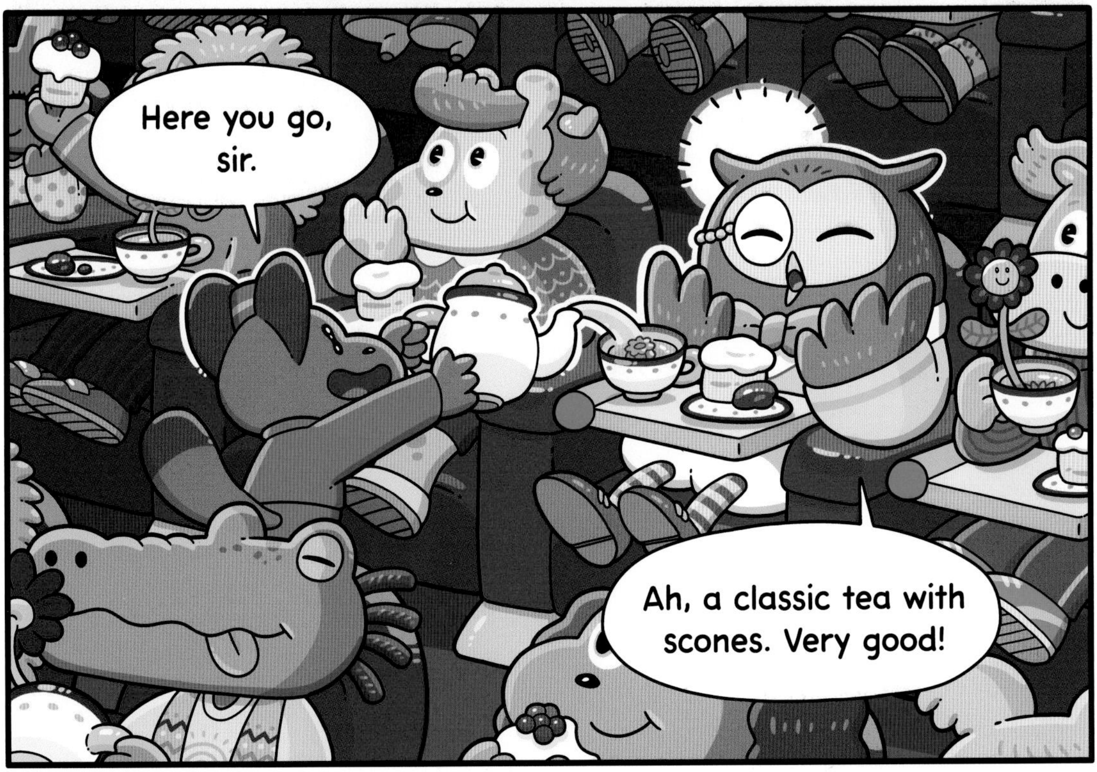
Here you go, sir.
Ah, a classic tea with scones. Very good!

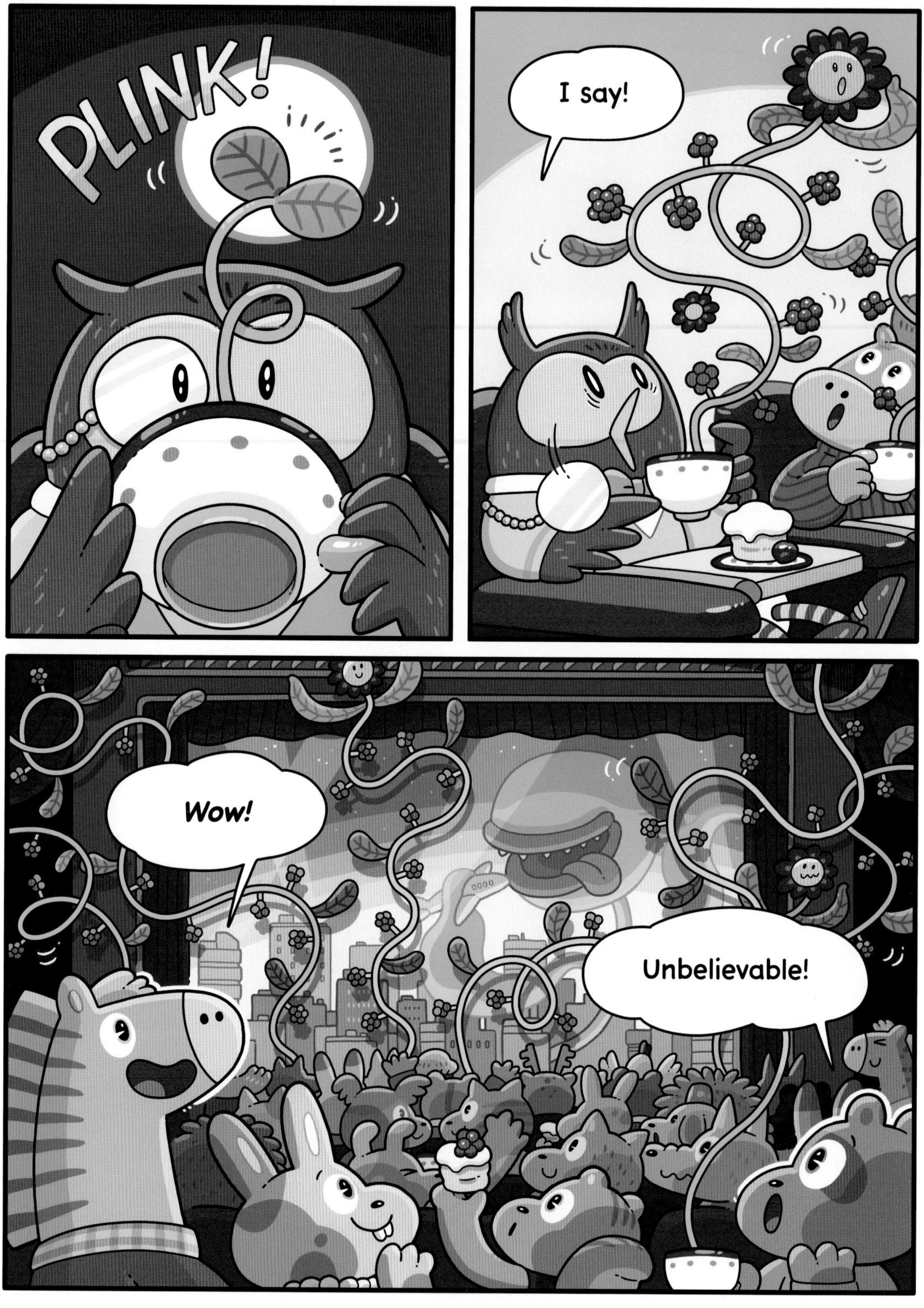
PLINK!
I say!
Wow!
Unbelievable!

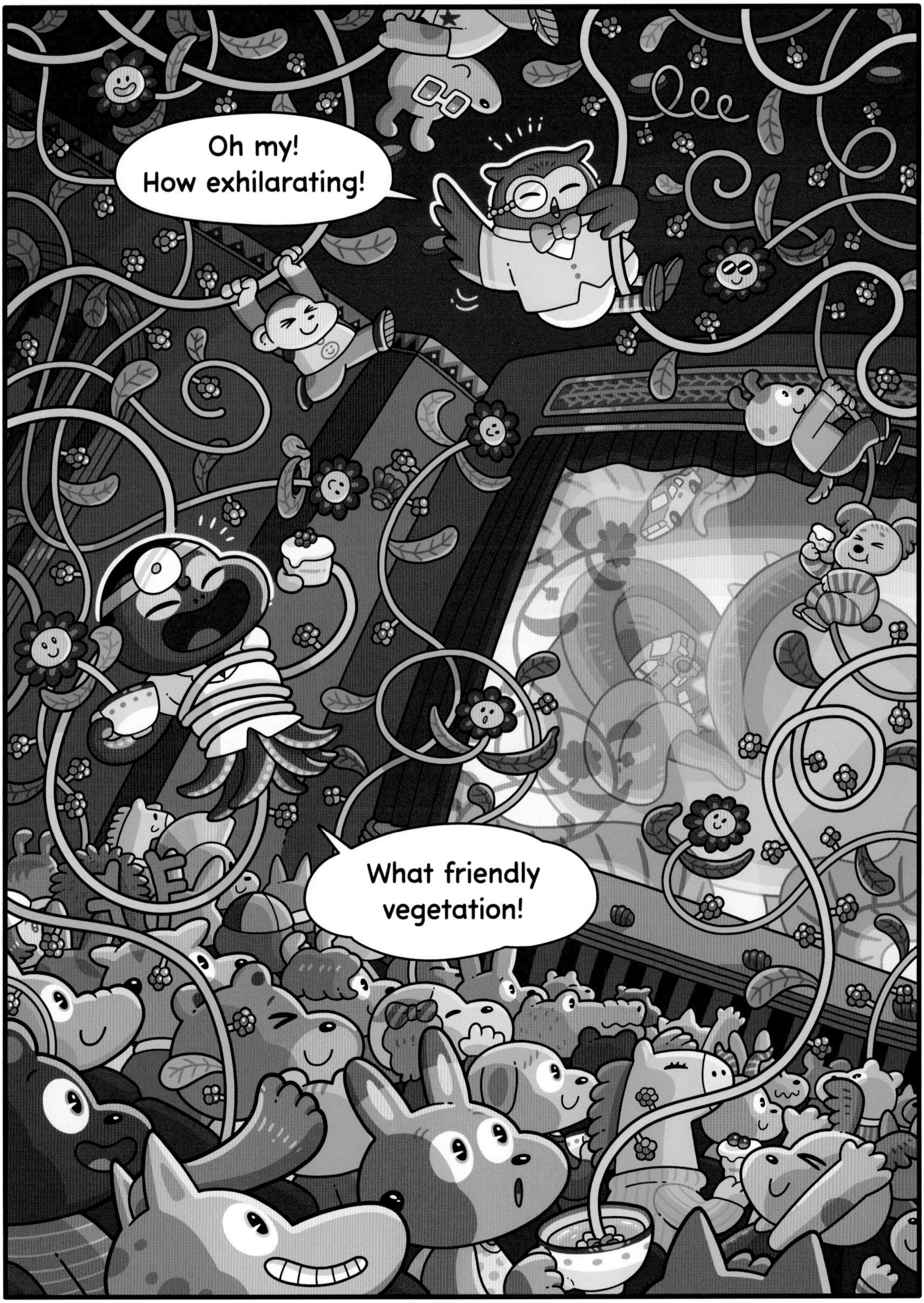
Oh my!
How exhilarating!
What friendly
vegetation!

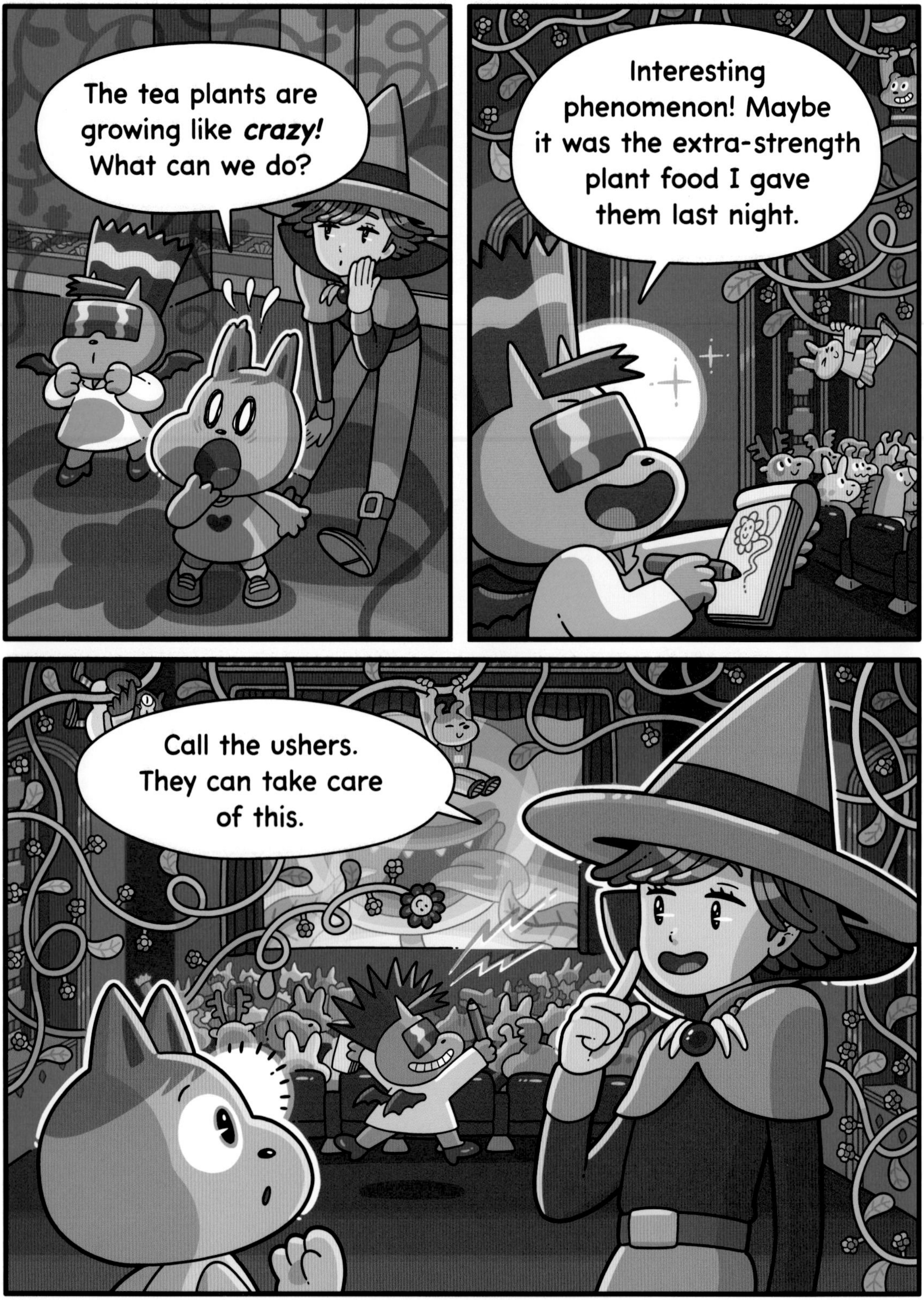
The tea plants are growing like *crazy!* What can we do?
Interesting phenomenon! Maybe it was the extra-strength plant food I gave them last night.
Call the ushers. They can take care of this.

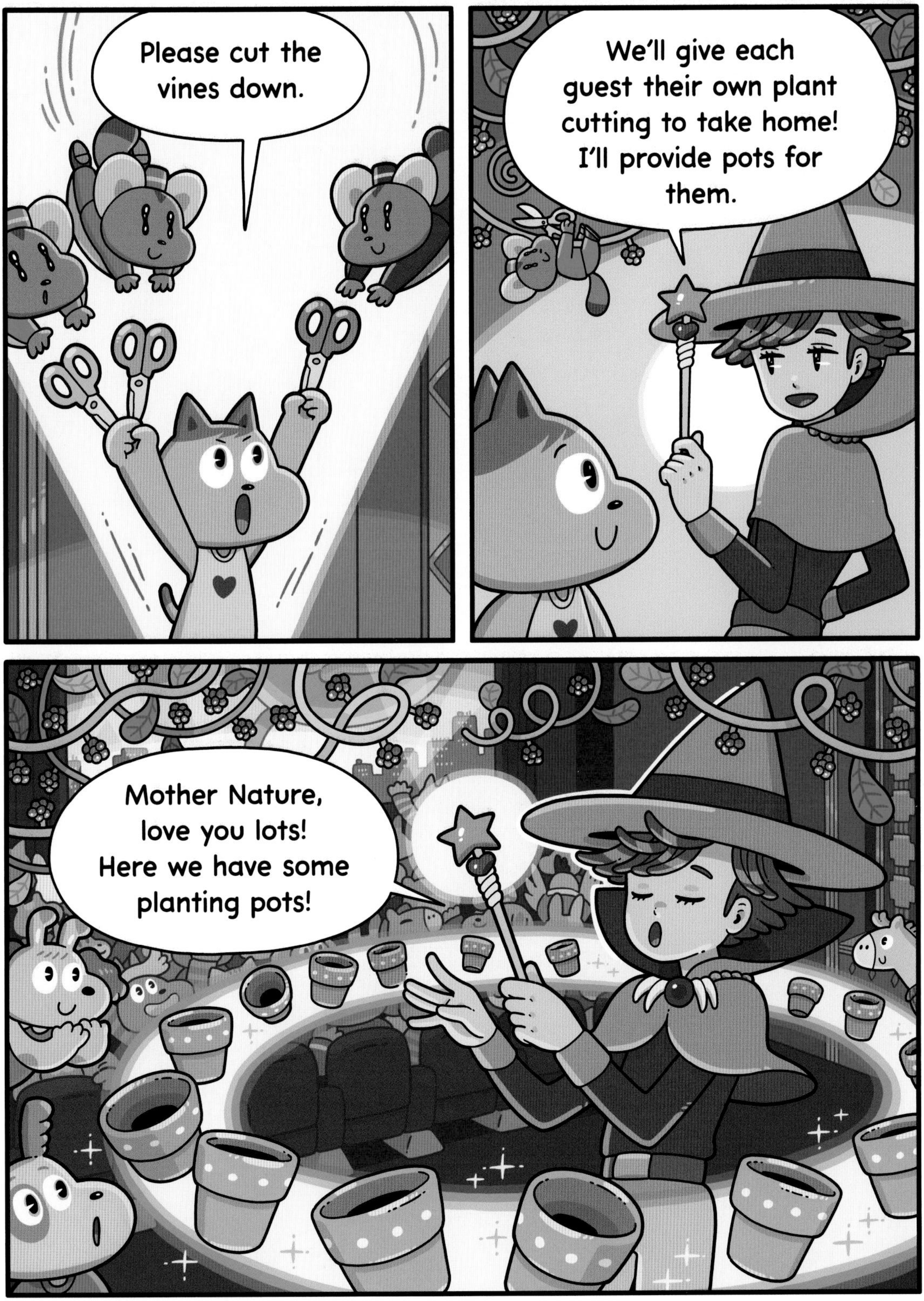
Please cut the vines down.
We'll give each guest their own plant cutting to take home! I'll provide pots for them.
Mother Nature, love you lots! Here we have some planting pots!

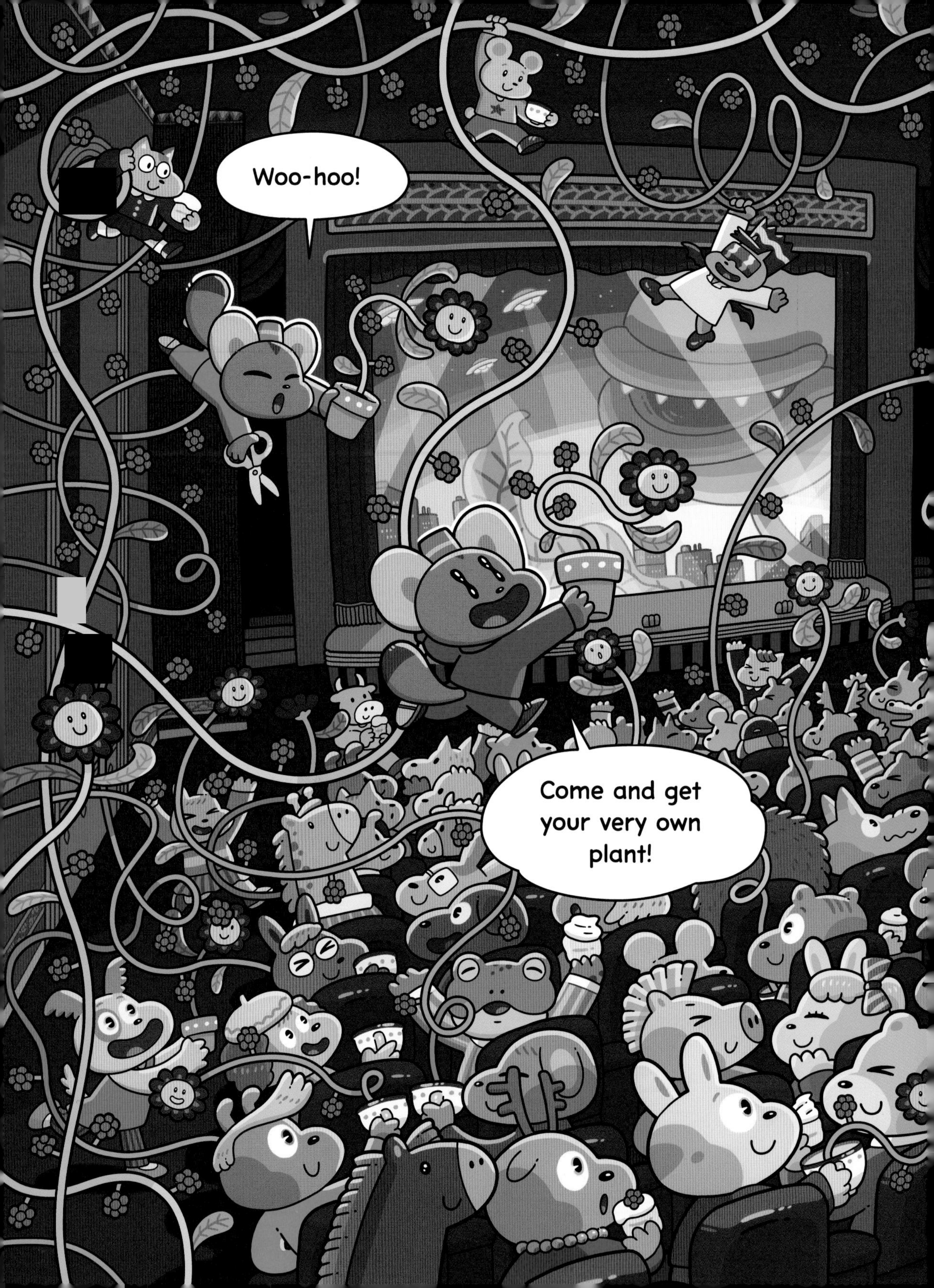
Woo-hoo!
Come and get your very own plant!

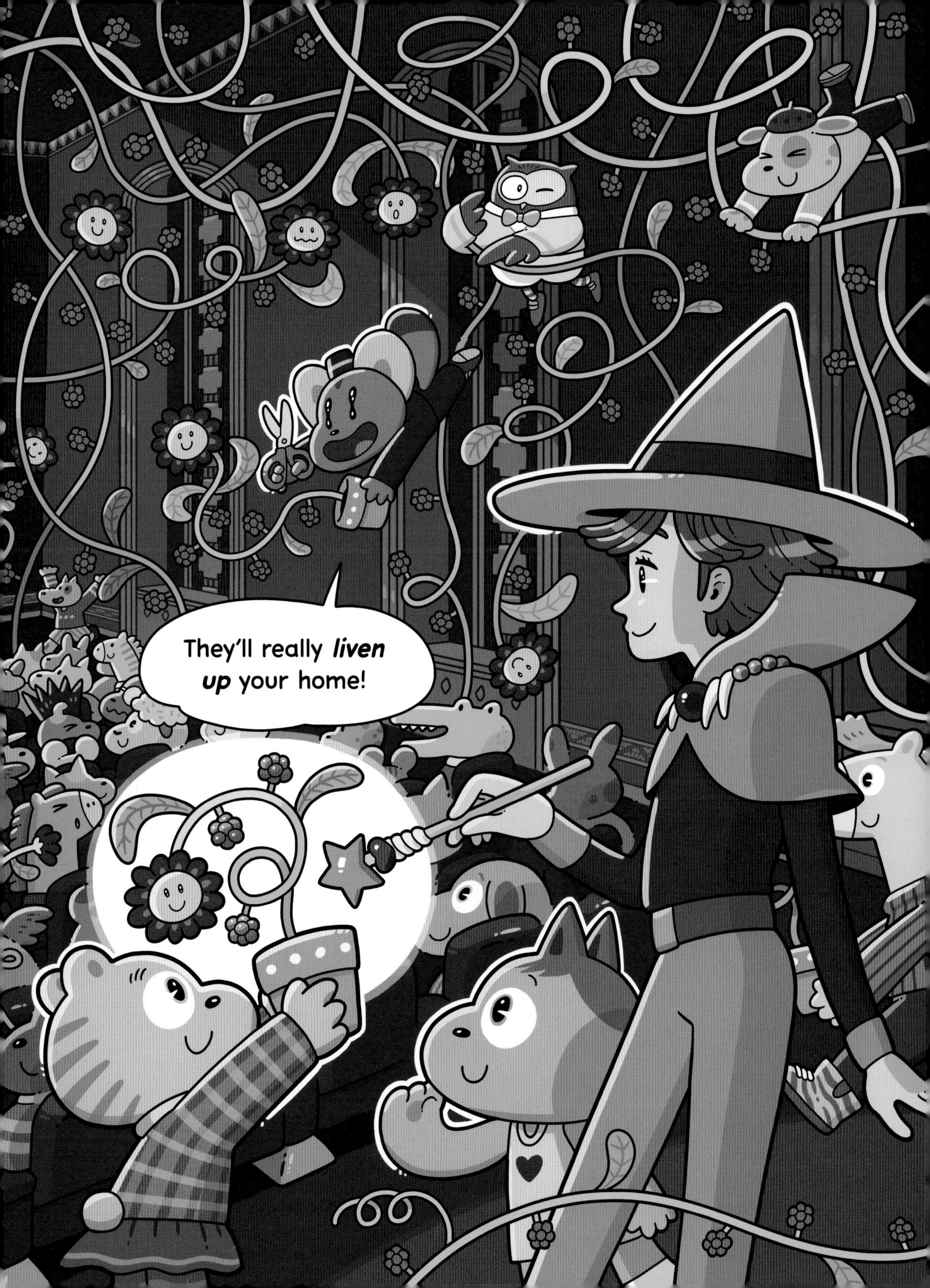
They'll really *liven up* your home!

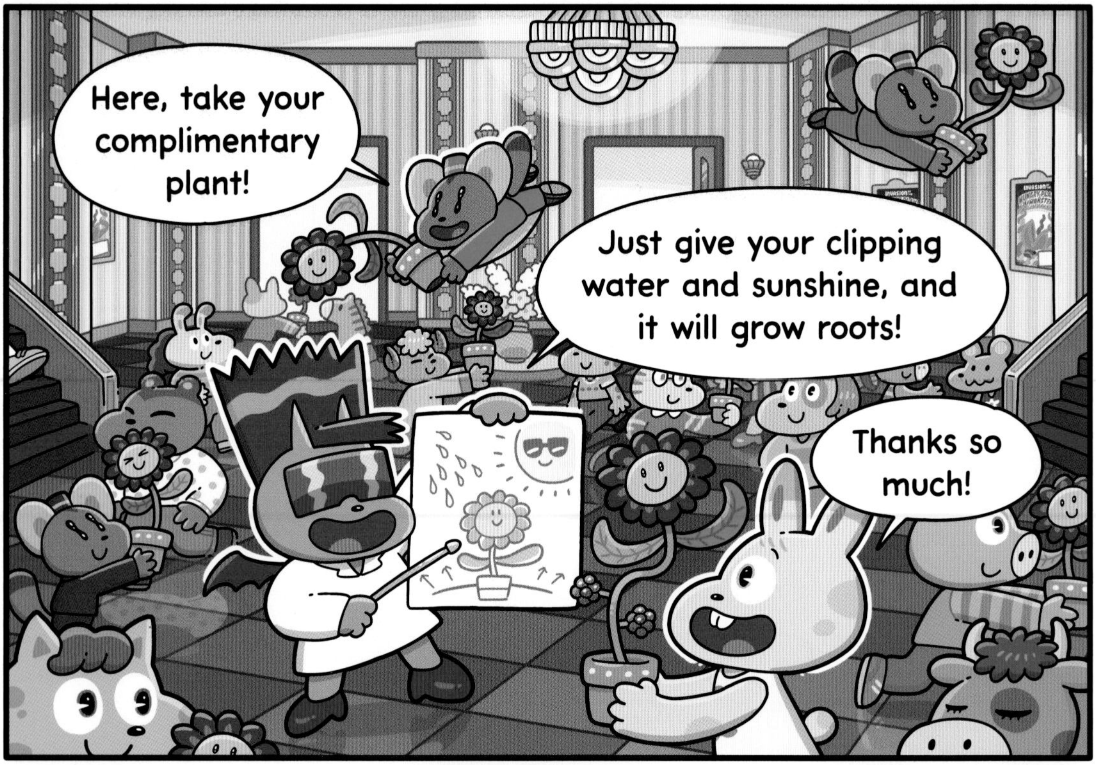
Here, take your complimentary plant!
Just give your clipping water and sunshine, and it will grow roots!
Thanks so much!

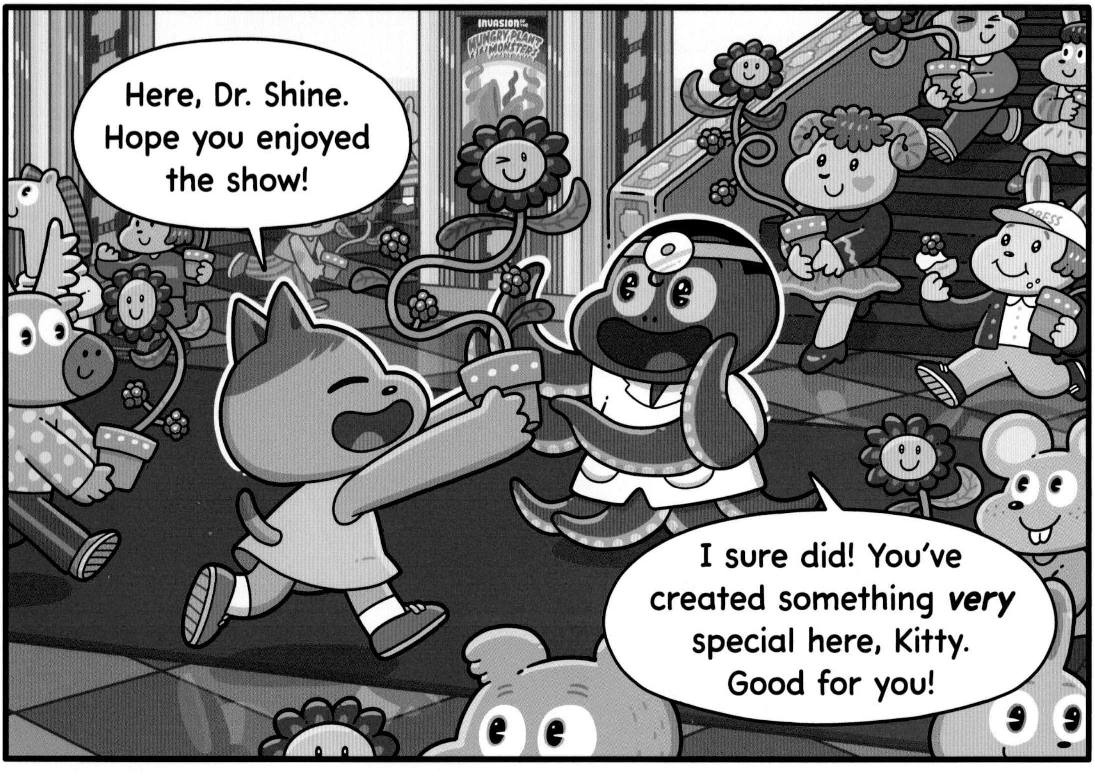
INVASION OF THE HUNGRY PLANT MONSTERS
Here, Dr. Shine. Hope you enjoyed the show!
I sure did! You've created something *very* special here, Kitty. Good for you!

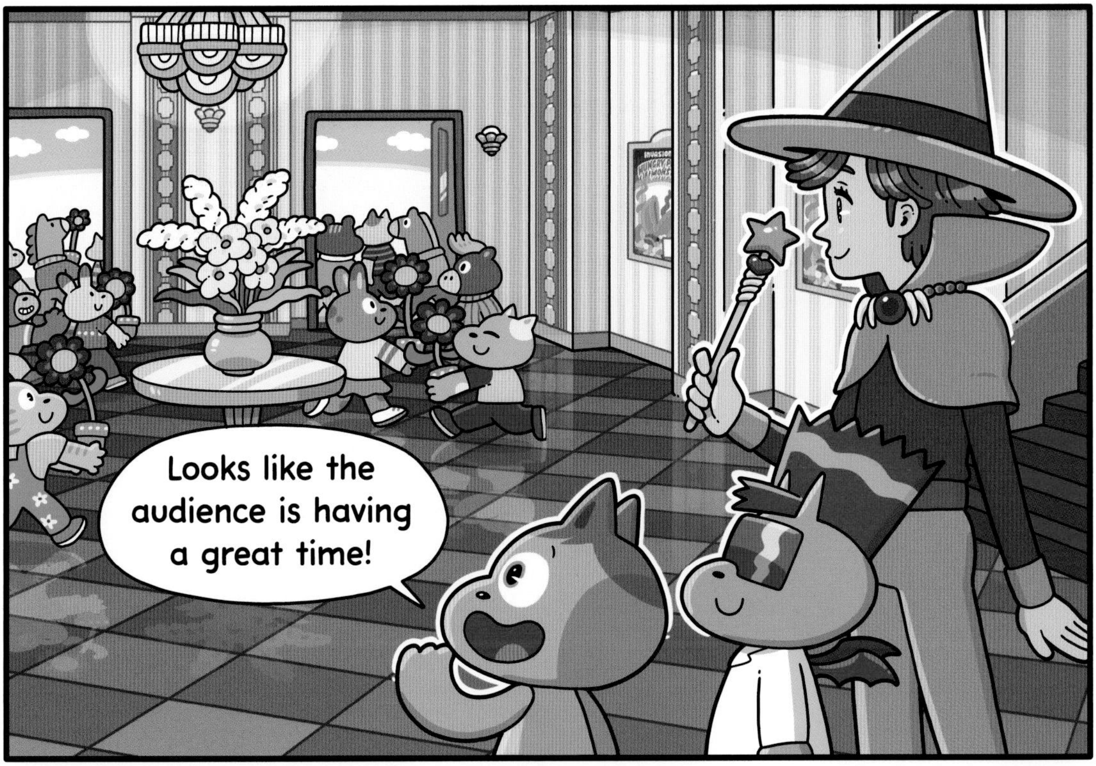
Looks like the audience is having a great time!

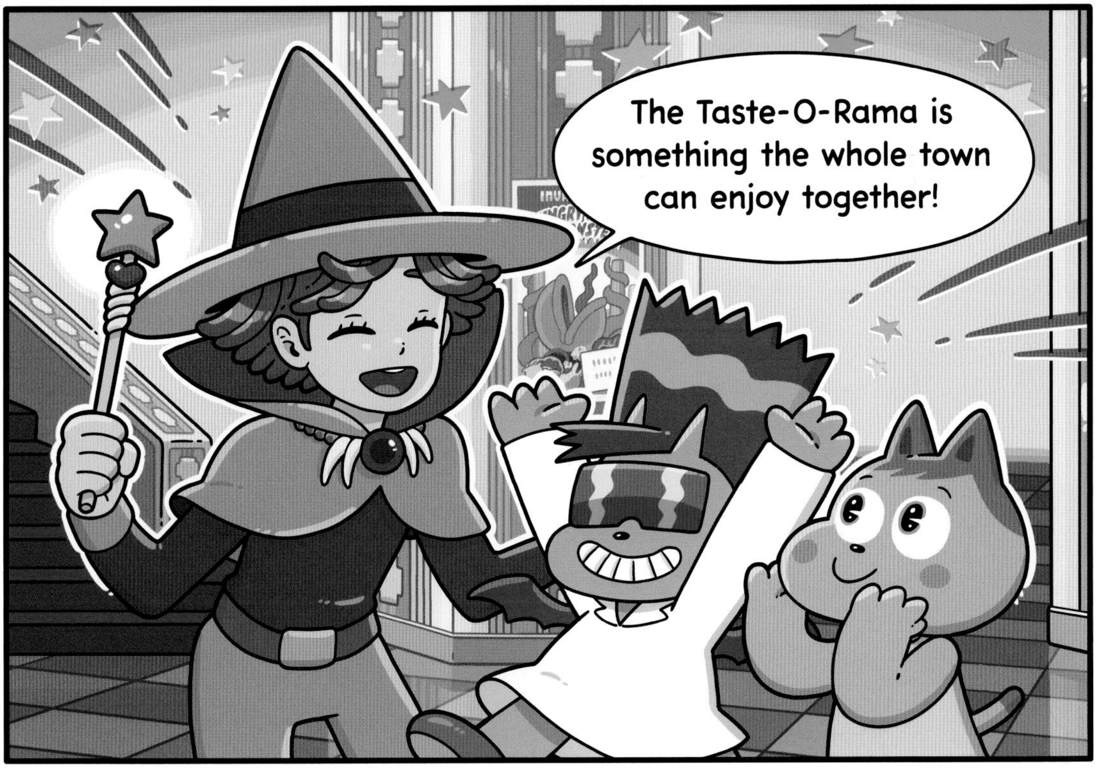
The Taste-O-Rama is something the whole town can enjoy together!

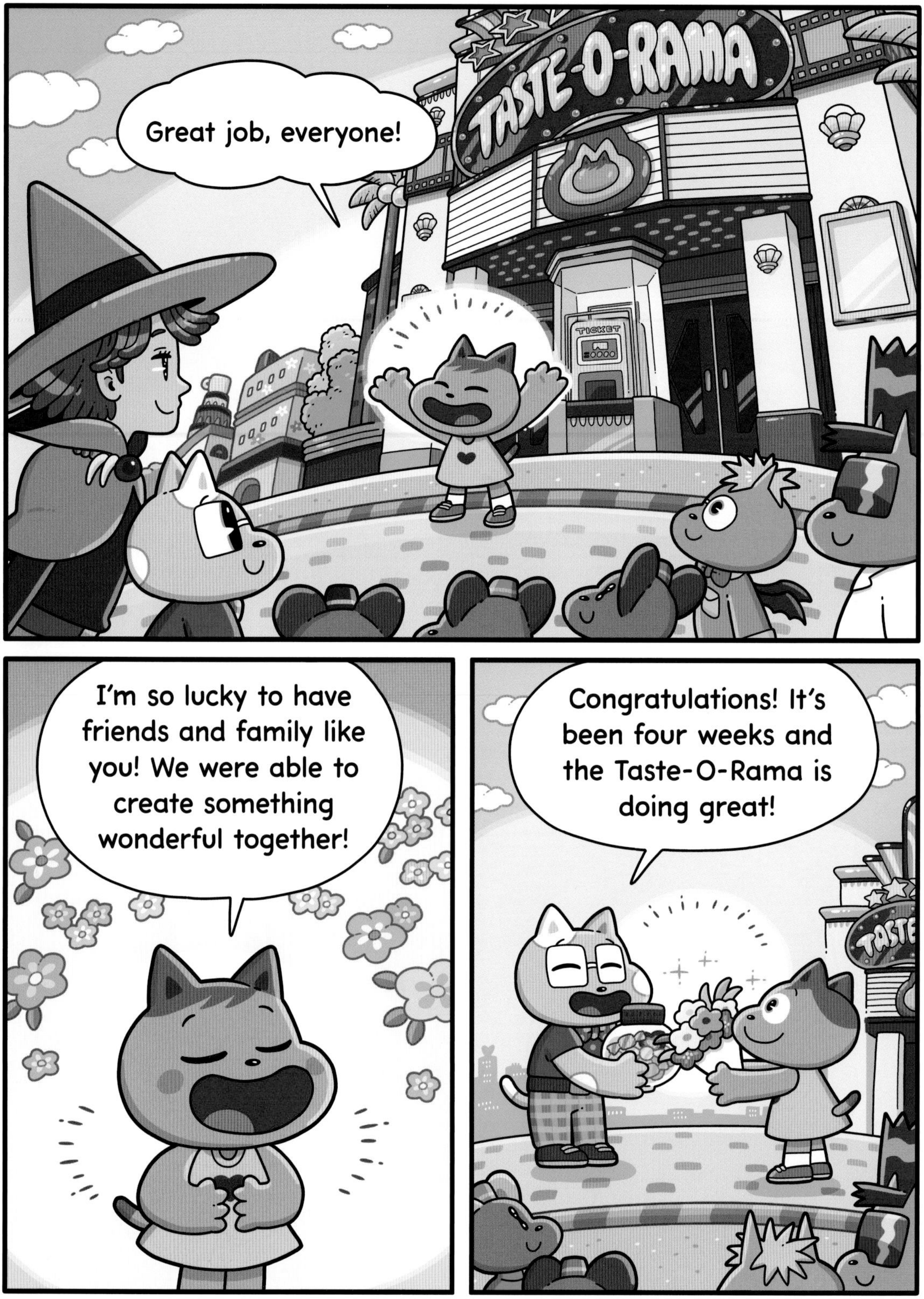
Great job, everyone!
TASTE-O-RAMA
TICKET
I'm so lucky to have friends and family like you! We were able to create something wonderful together!
Congratulations! It's been four weeks and the Taste-O-Rama is doing great!

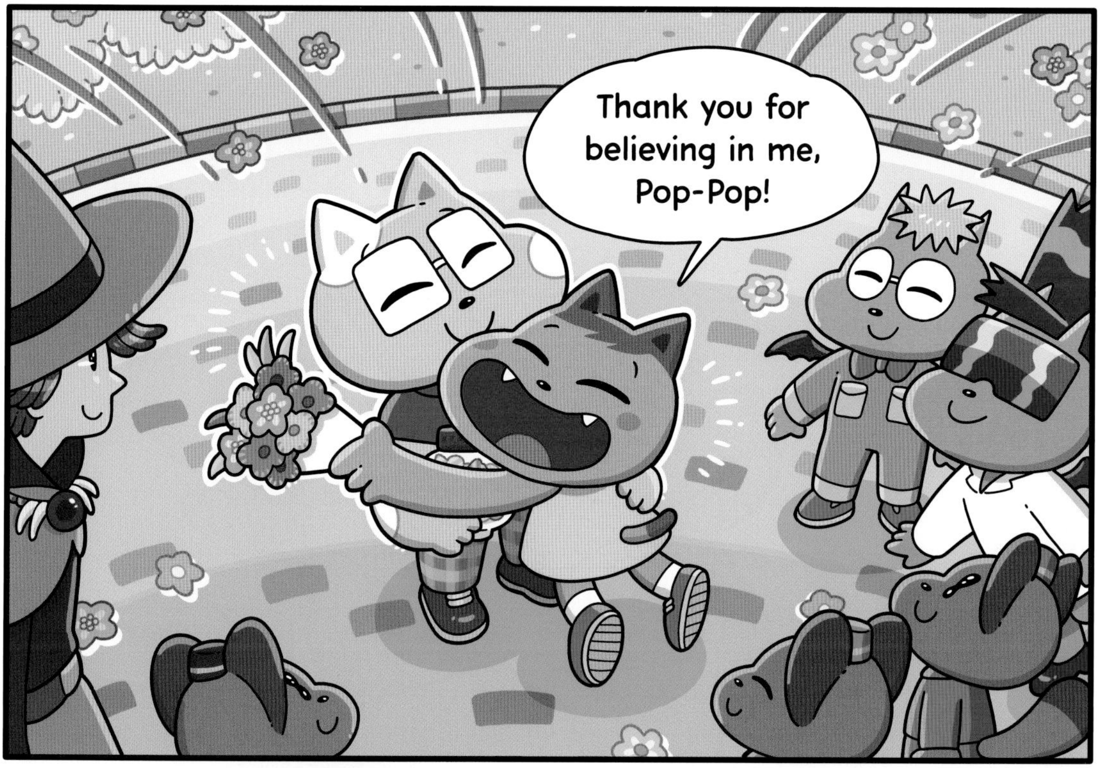
Thank you for believing in me, Pop-Pop!

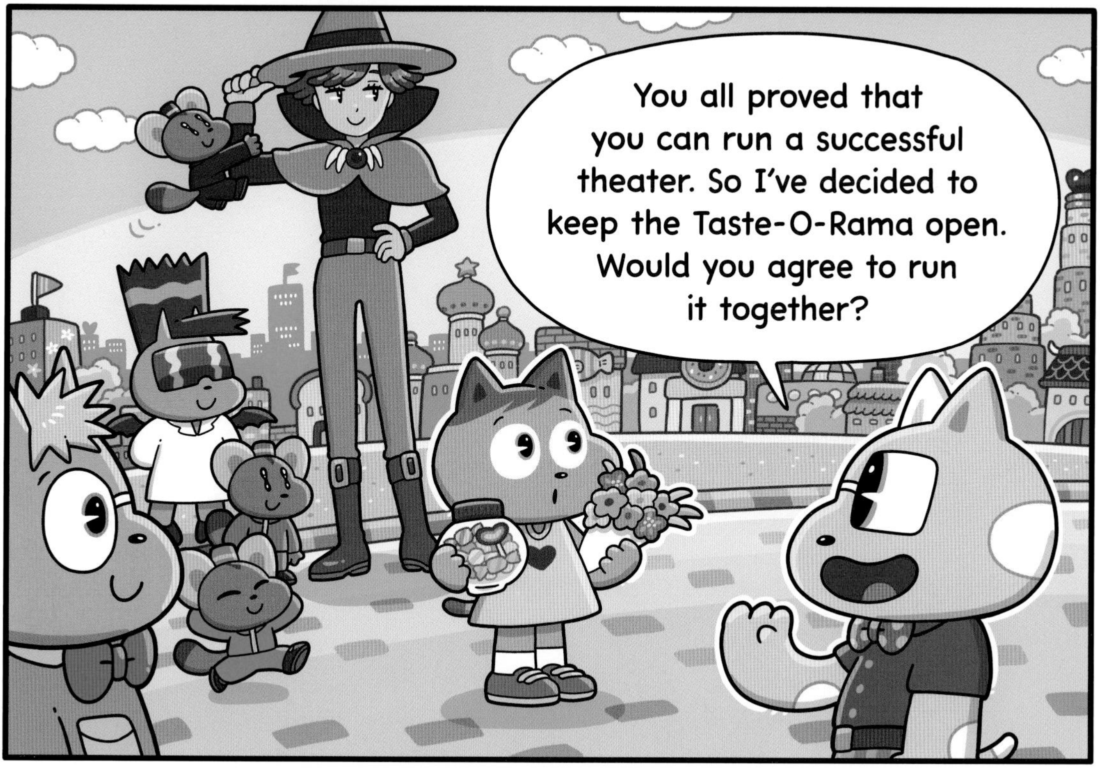
You all proved that you can run a successful theater. So I've decided to keep the Taste-O-Rama open. Would you agree to run it together?

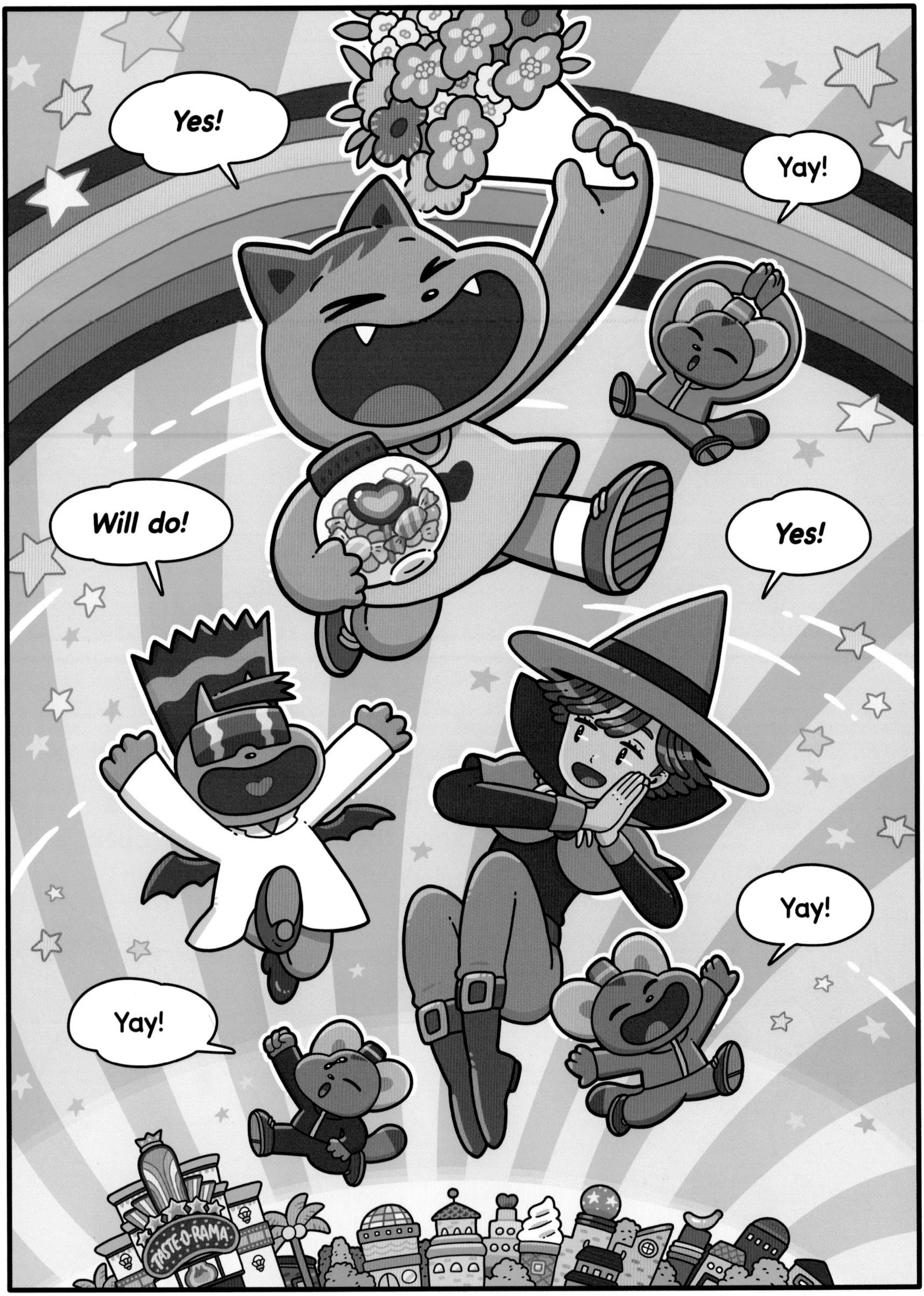
Yes!
Yay!
Will do!
Yes!
Yay!
Yay!
TASTE-O-RAMA

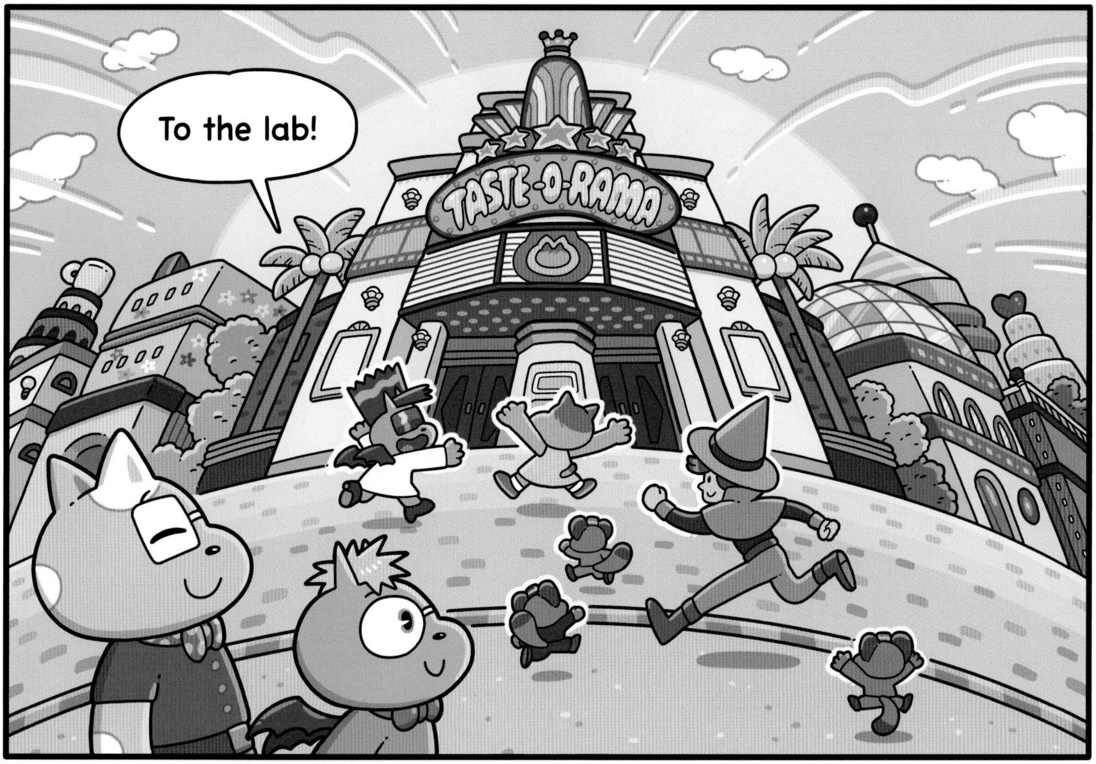
To the lab!
TASTE-O-RAMA

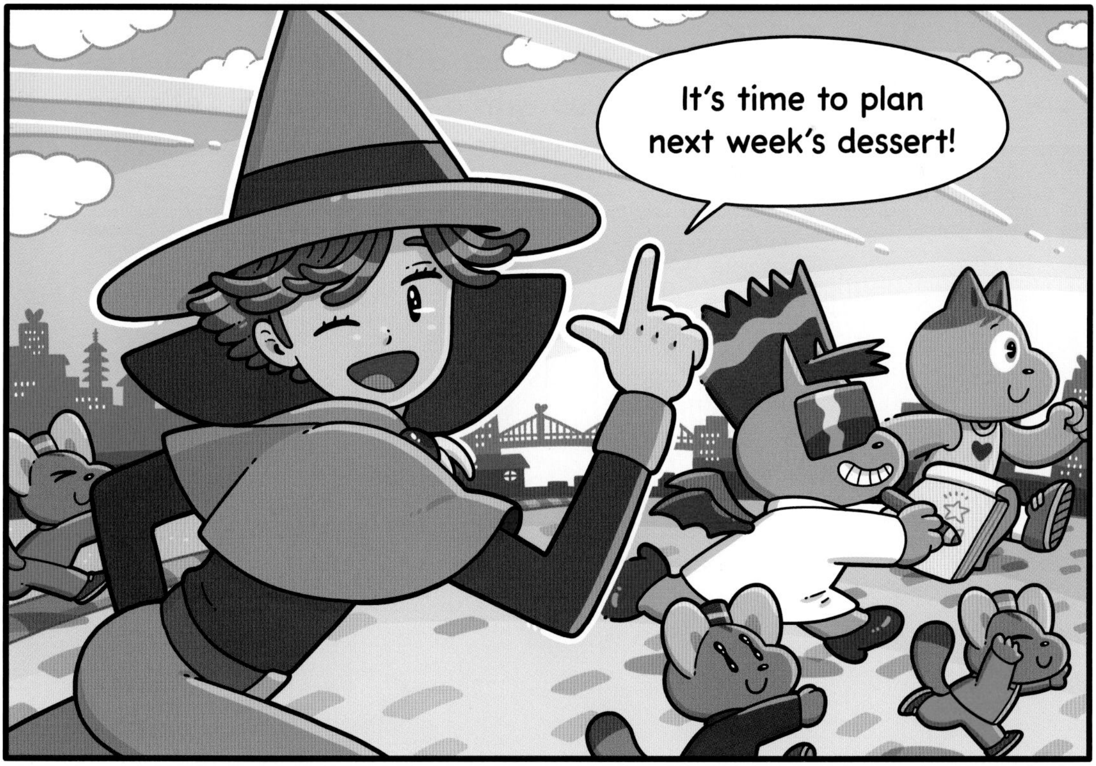
It's time to plan next week's dessert!

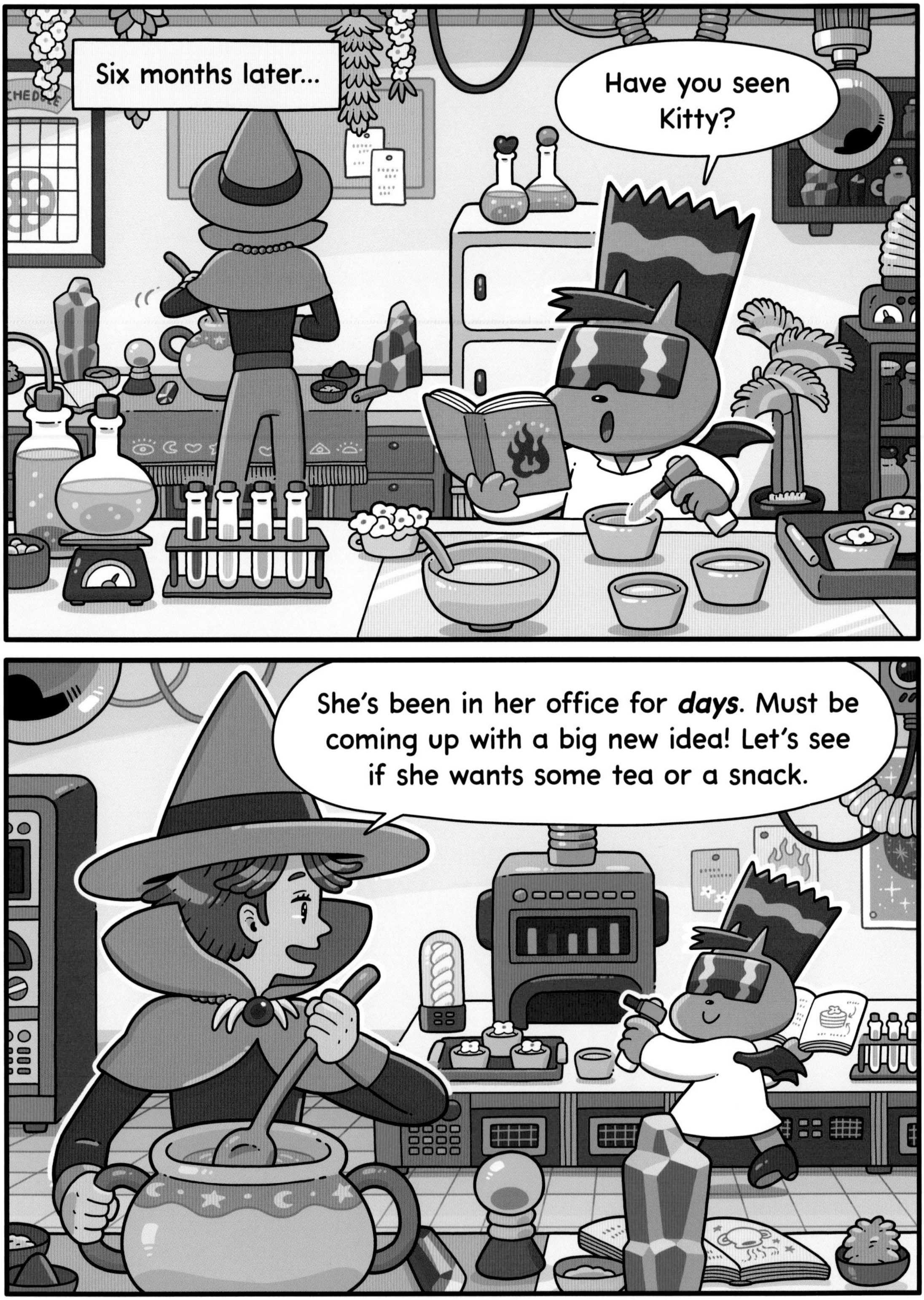
Six months later...
Have you seen Kitty?
She's been in her office for *days*. Must be coming up with a big new idea! Let's see if she wants some tea or a snack.

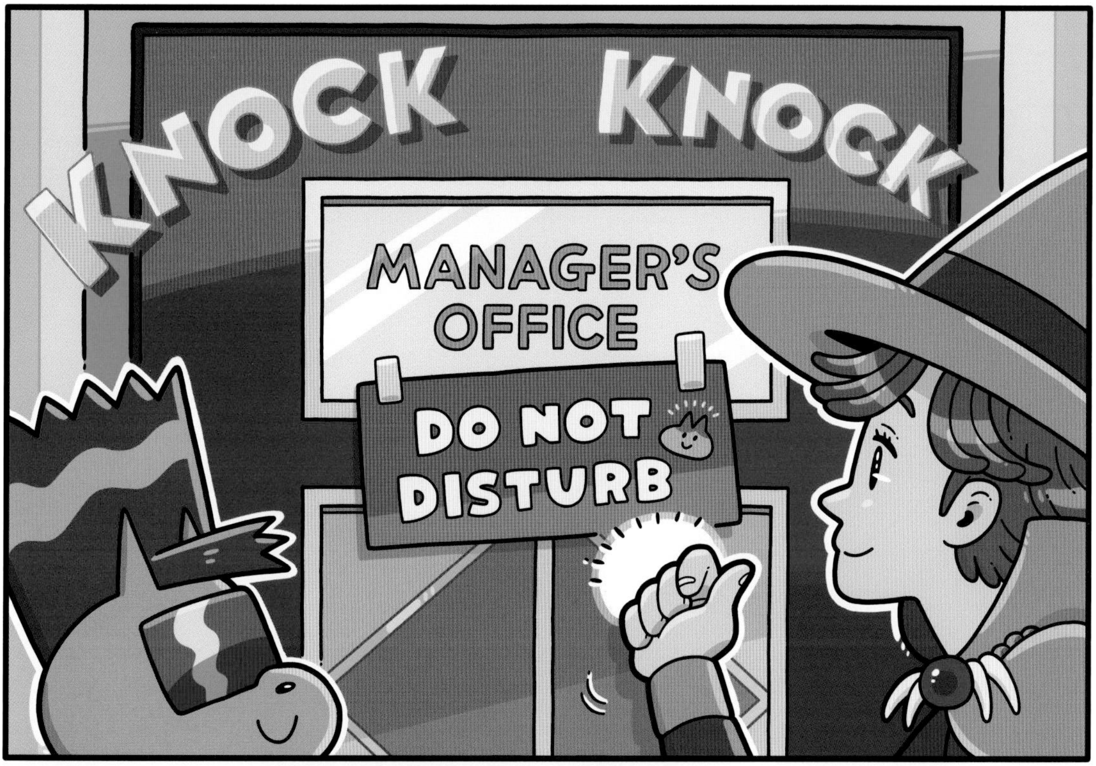
KNOCK KNOCK
MANAGER'S OFFICE
DO NOT DISTURB

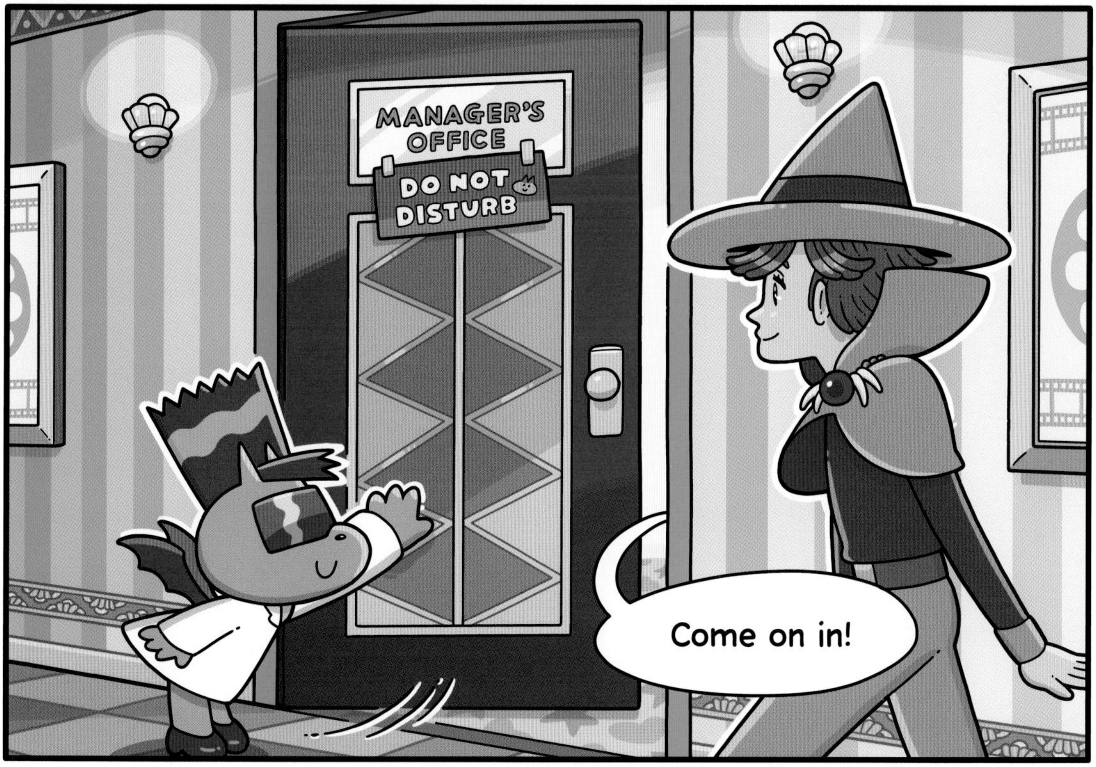
MANAGER'S OFFICE
DO NOT DISTURB
Come on in!

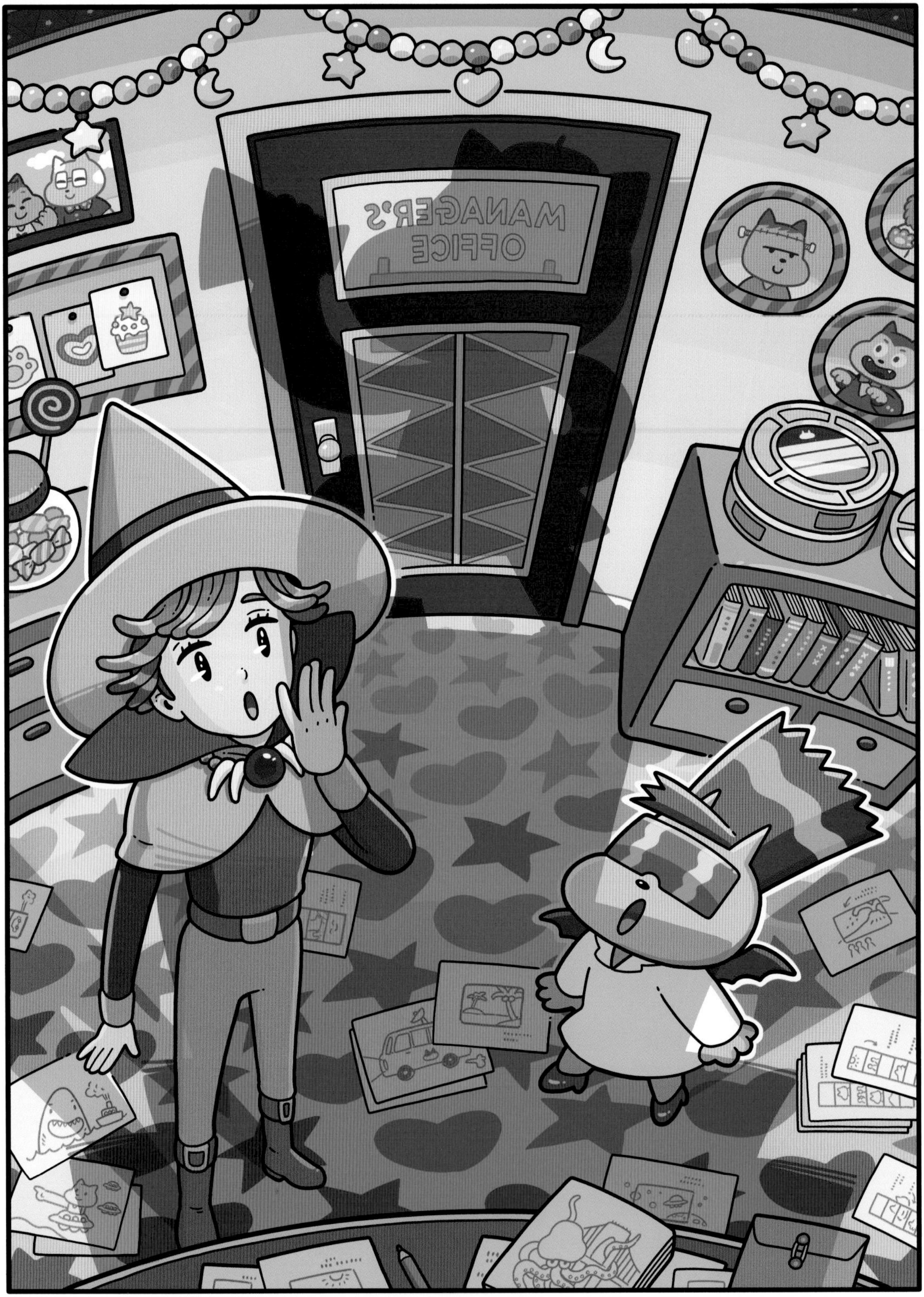
MANAGER'S
OFFICE

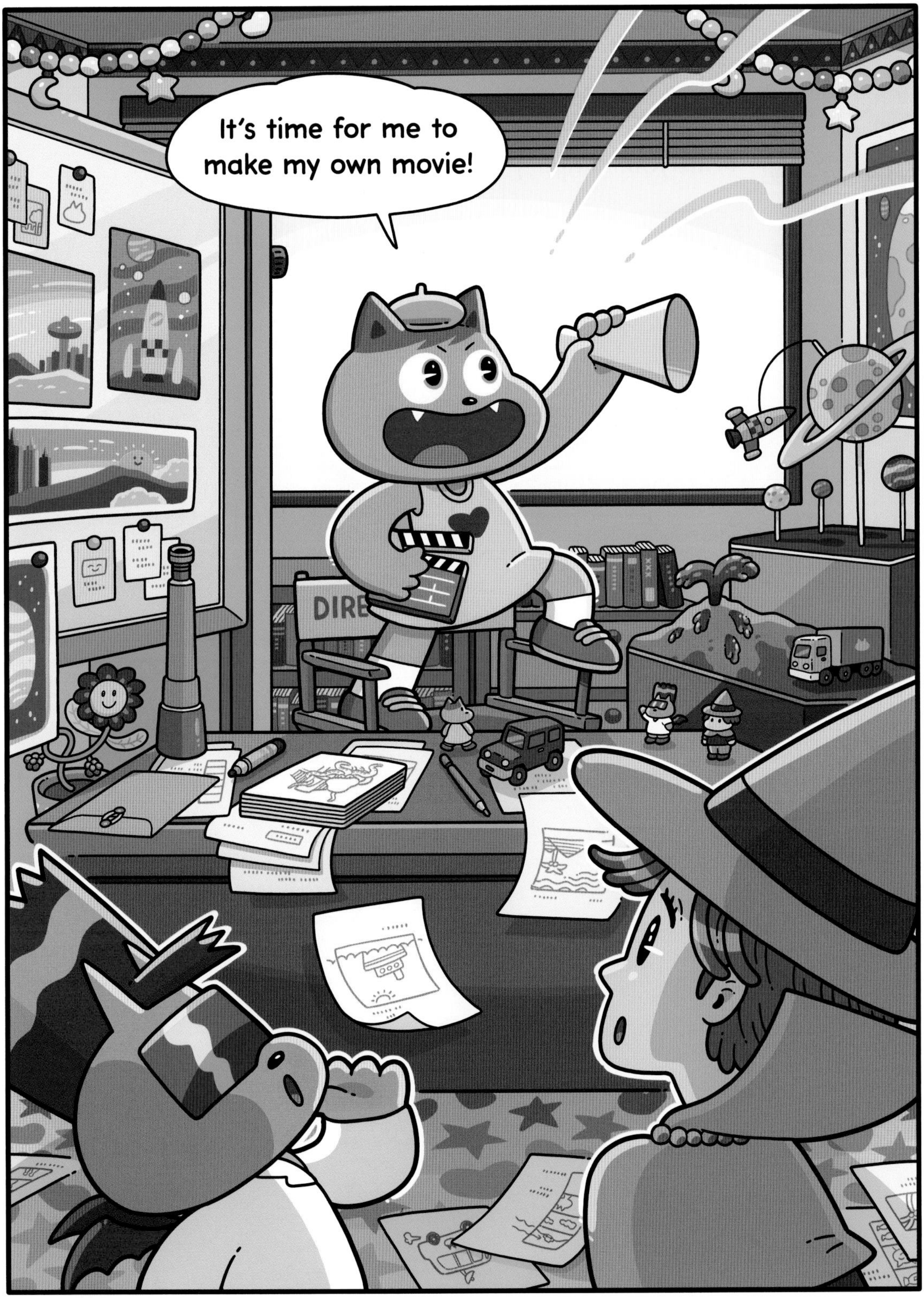
It's time for me to make my own movie!
DIRE

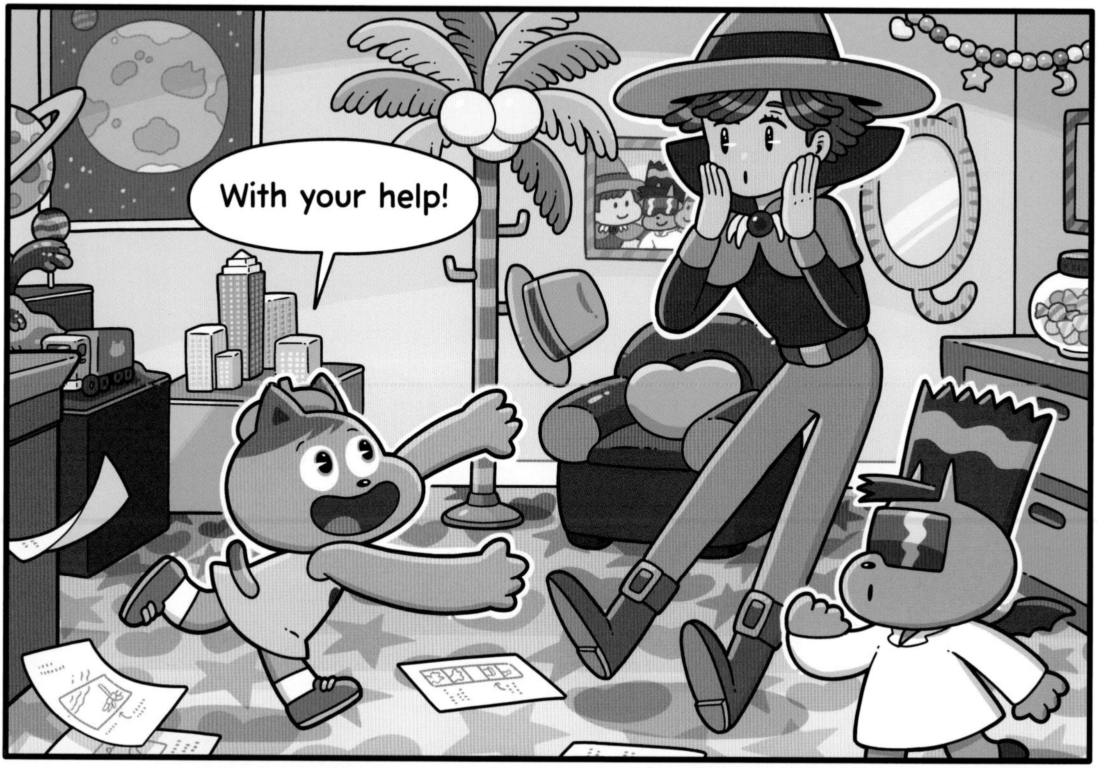
With your help!

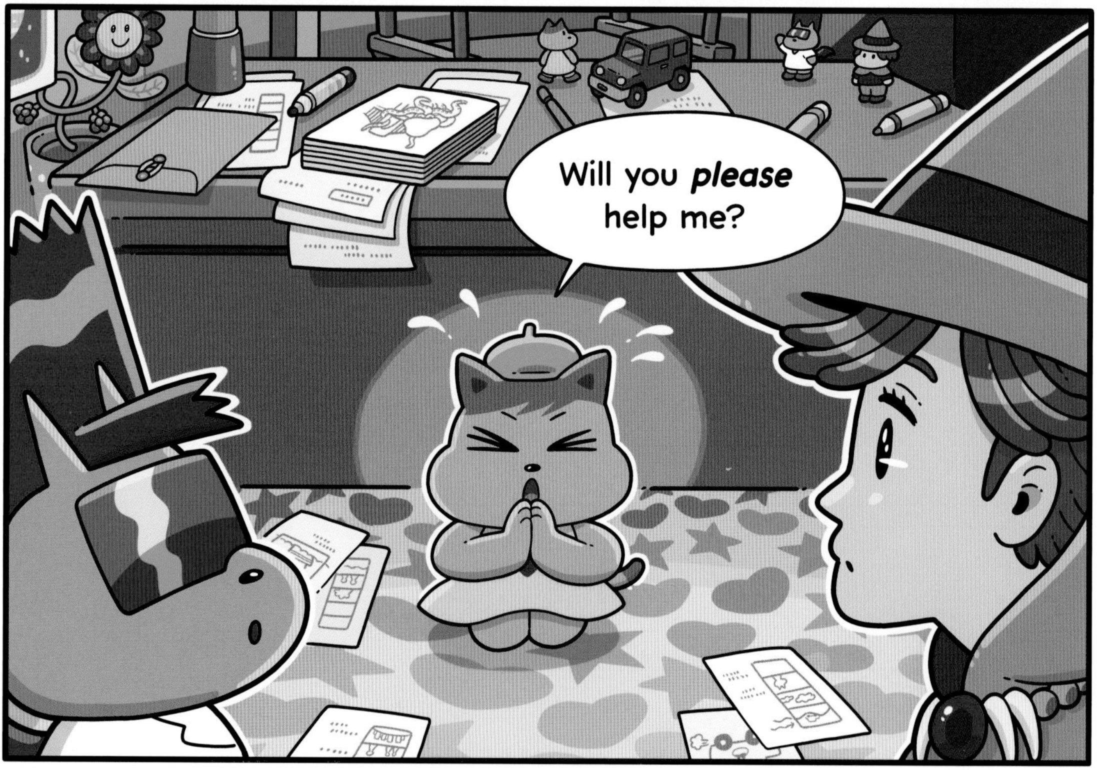
Will you *please* help me?

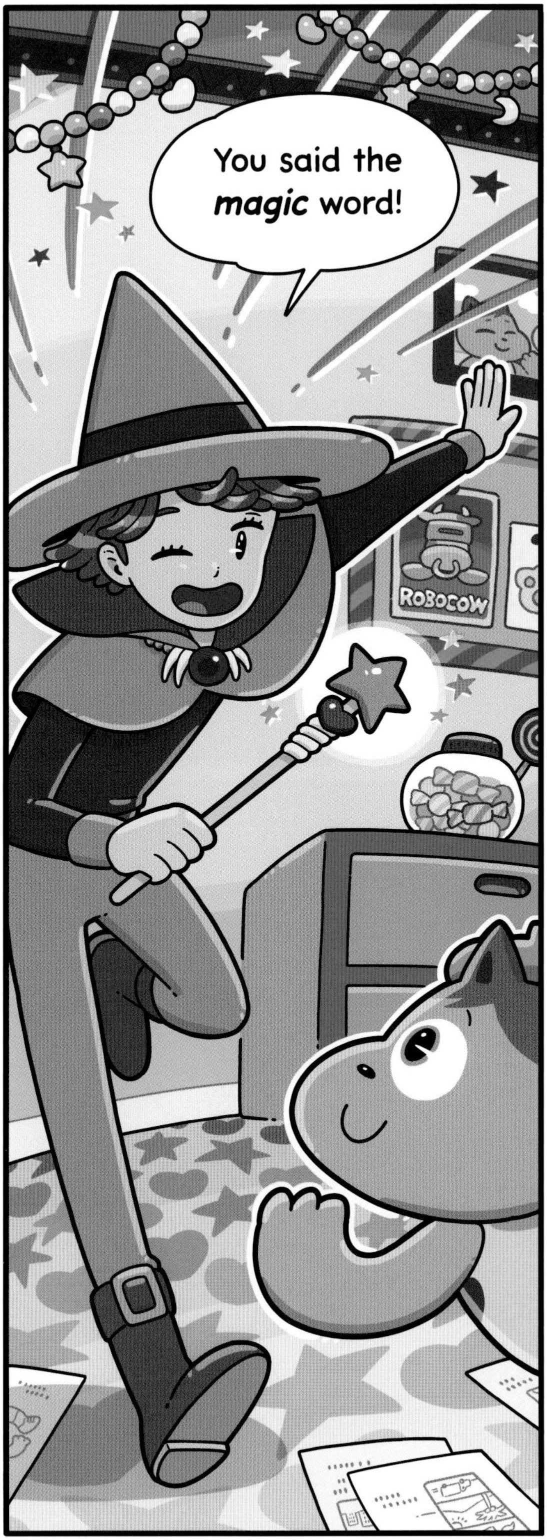
You said the *magic* word!
ROBOCOW

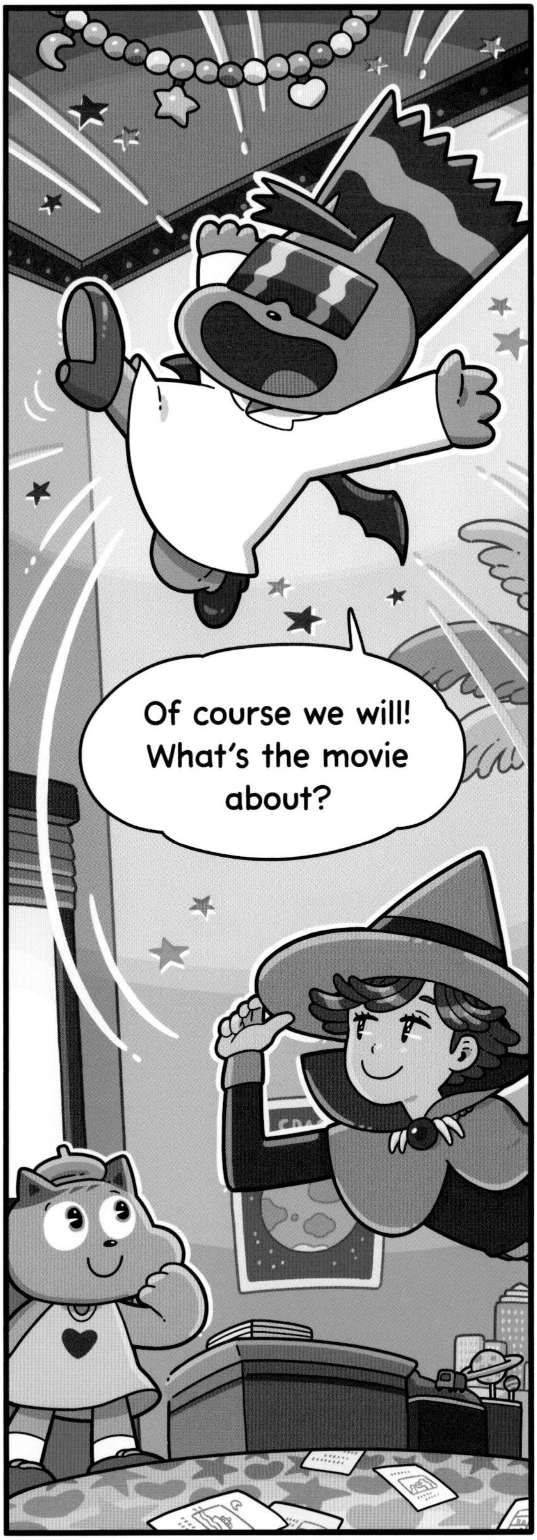
Of course we will! What's the movie about?

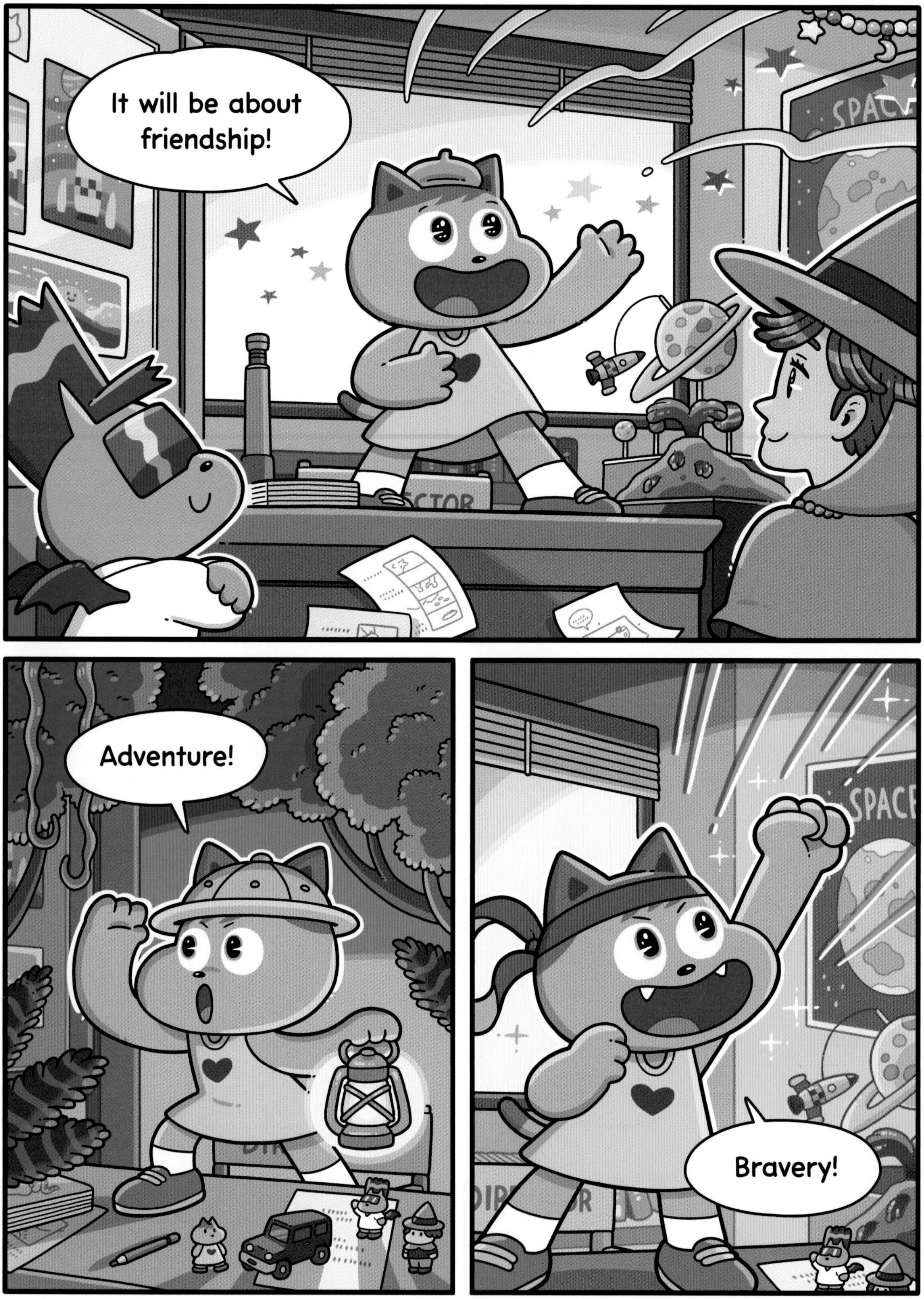
It will be about friendship!
Adventure!
Bravery!

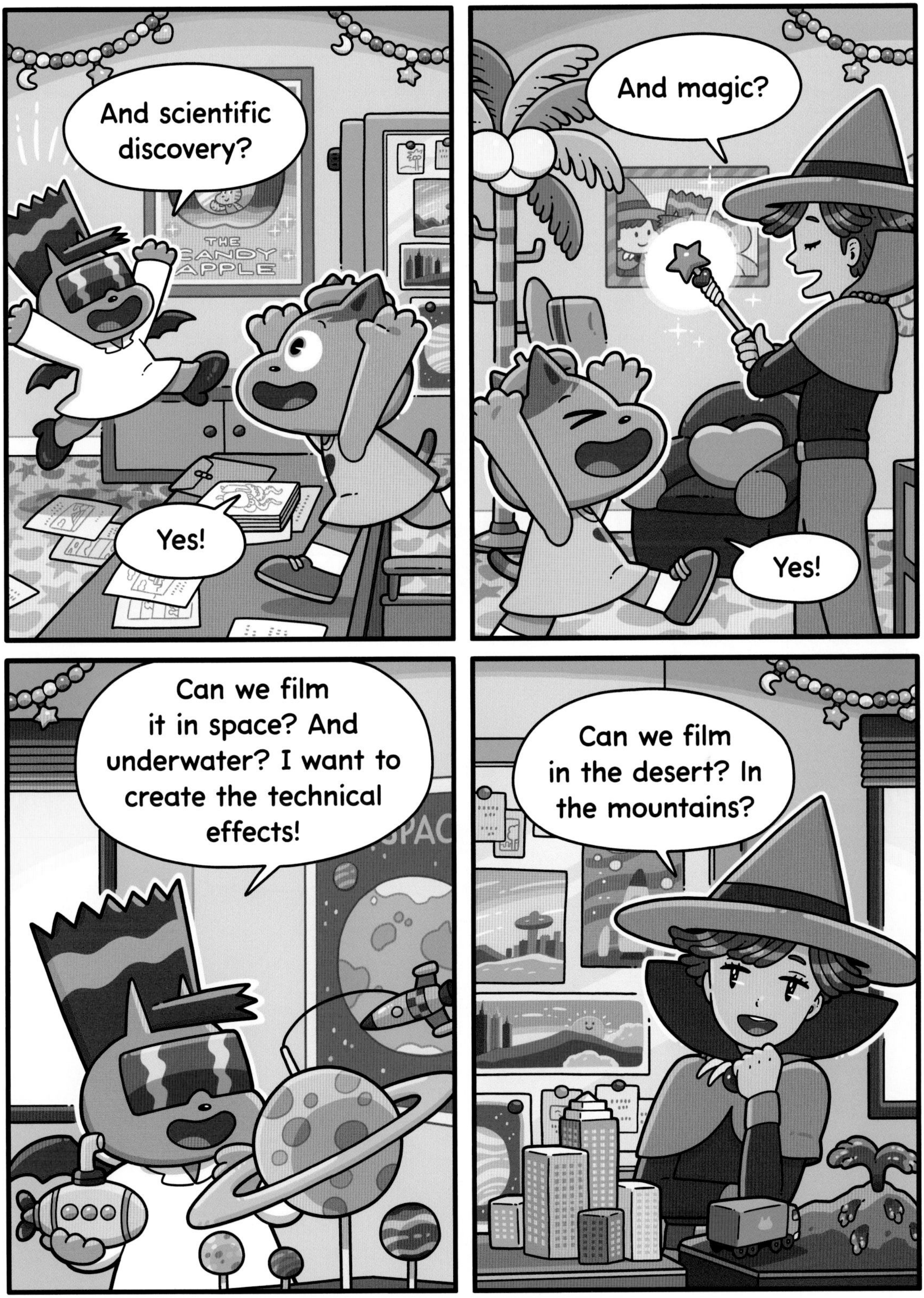
And scientific discovery?
THE CANDY APPLE
Yes!
And magic?
Yes!
Can we film it in space? And underwater? I want to create the technical effects!
Can we film in the desert? In the mountains?

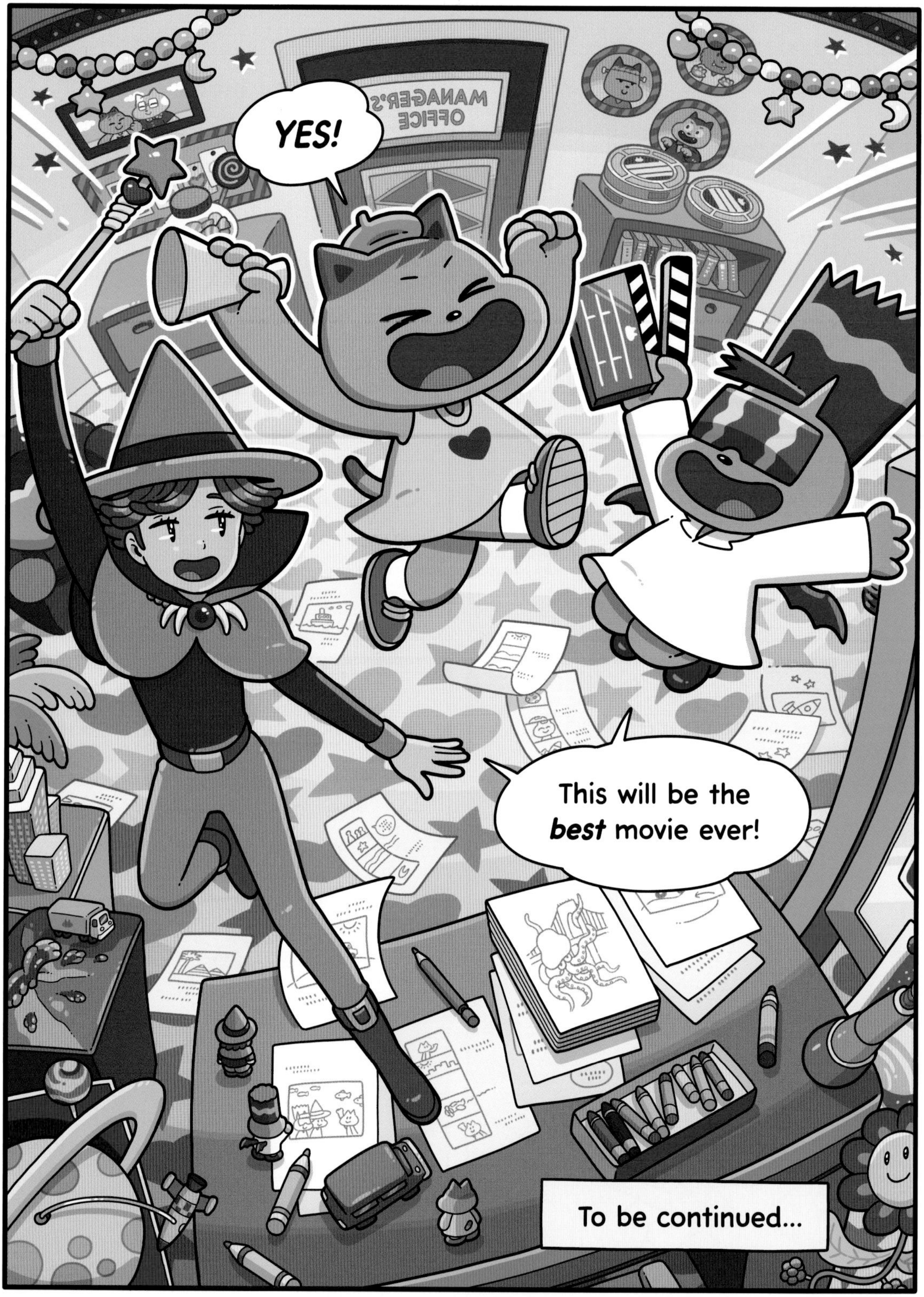
MANAGER'S OFFICE
YES!
This will be the *best* movie ever!
To be continued...

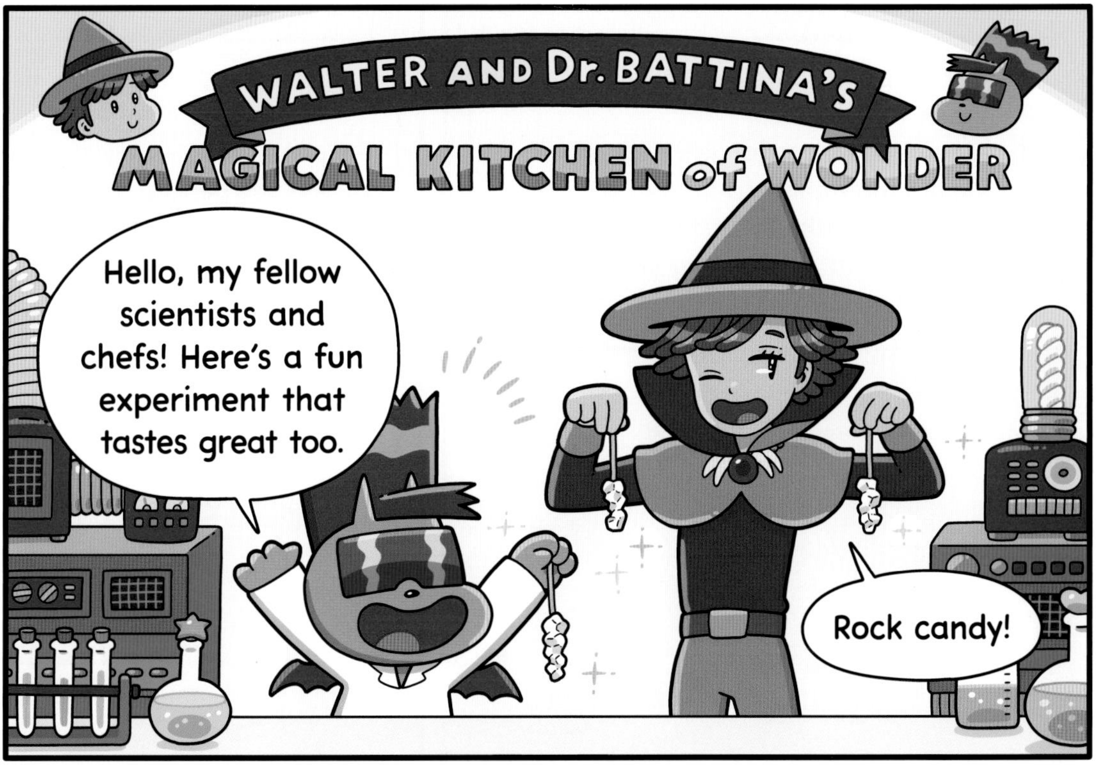
WALTER AND Dr. BATTINA'S
MAGICAL KITCHEN of WONDER
Hello, my fellow scientists and chefs! Here's a fun experiment that tastes great too.
Rock candy!

You will need these ingredients:

- 1 cup water
- 3 cups granulated sugar

You will also need two 8-ounce jars, a whisk or spoon, cotton string, a pair of scissors, two pencils, a butter knife or chopstick, and plastic wrap or paper towels.

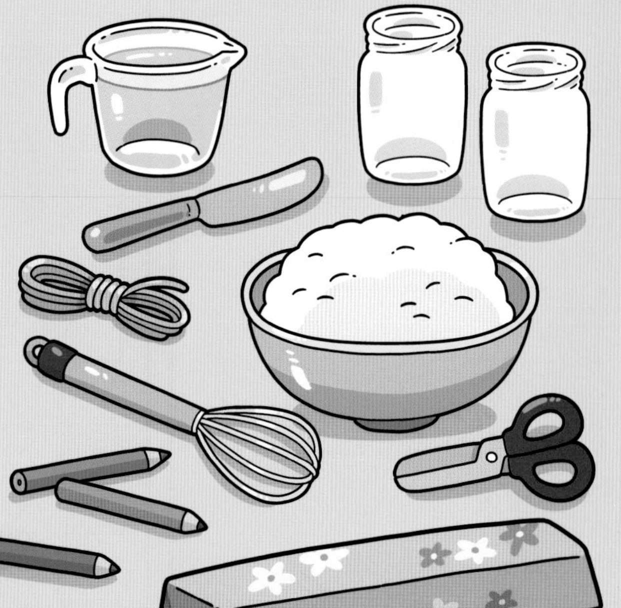

1. Get an adult to help you!
2. Wash your hands.
3. Clean each glass jar with hot water. Rinse thoroughly.
4. Cut two lengths of cotton string (one for each jar). Each string should be as long as the jar, plus a few inches.

5. Tie each string to the middle of a pencil.
6. Put the pencils across the openings of the jars. Trim the bottom of your string so there is one inch between it and the bottom of the jar.

7. Soak each string with water, and roll them in granulated sugar. Put them aside to dry while you prepare a sugar solution.

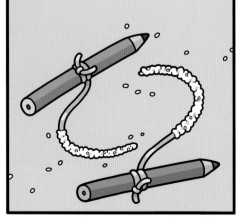

8. A grown-up needs to do this part! Hot sugar syrup can be dangerous! Place one cup of water in a medium-sized pot and bring it to a boil.
9. Add the sugar, one cup at a time, stirring as each cup is poured in. It will take longer for the sugar to dissolve after each cup you add.

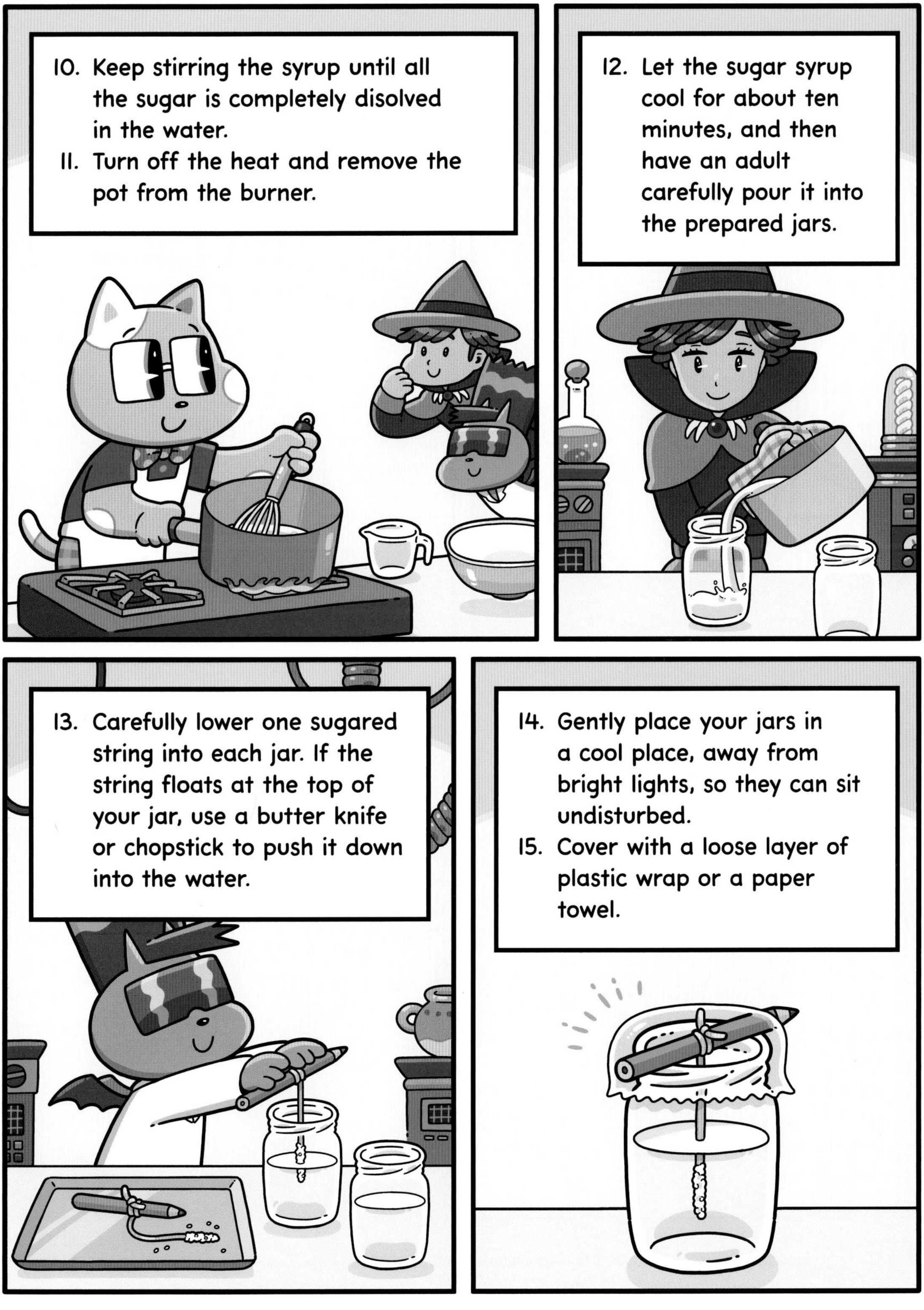
10. Keep stirring the syrup until all the sugar is completely disolved in the water.
11. Turn off the heat and remove the pot from the burner.
12. Let the sugar syrup cool for about ten minutes, and then have an adult carefully pour it into the prepared jars.
13. Carefully lower one sugared string into each jar. If the string floats at the top of your jar, use a butter knife or chopstick to push it down into the water.
14. Gently place your jars in a cool place, away from bright lights, so they can sit undisturbed.
15. Cover with a loose layer of plastic wrap or a paper towel.

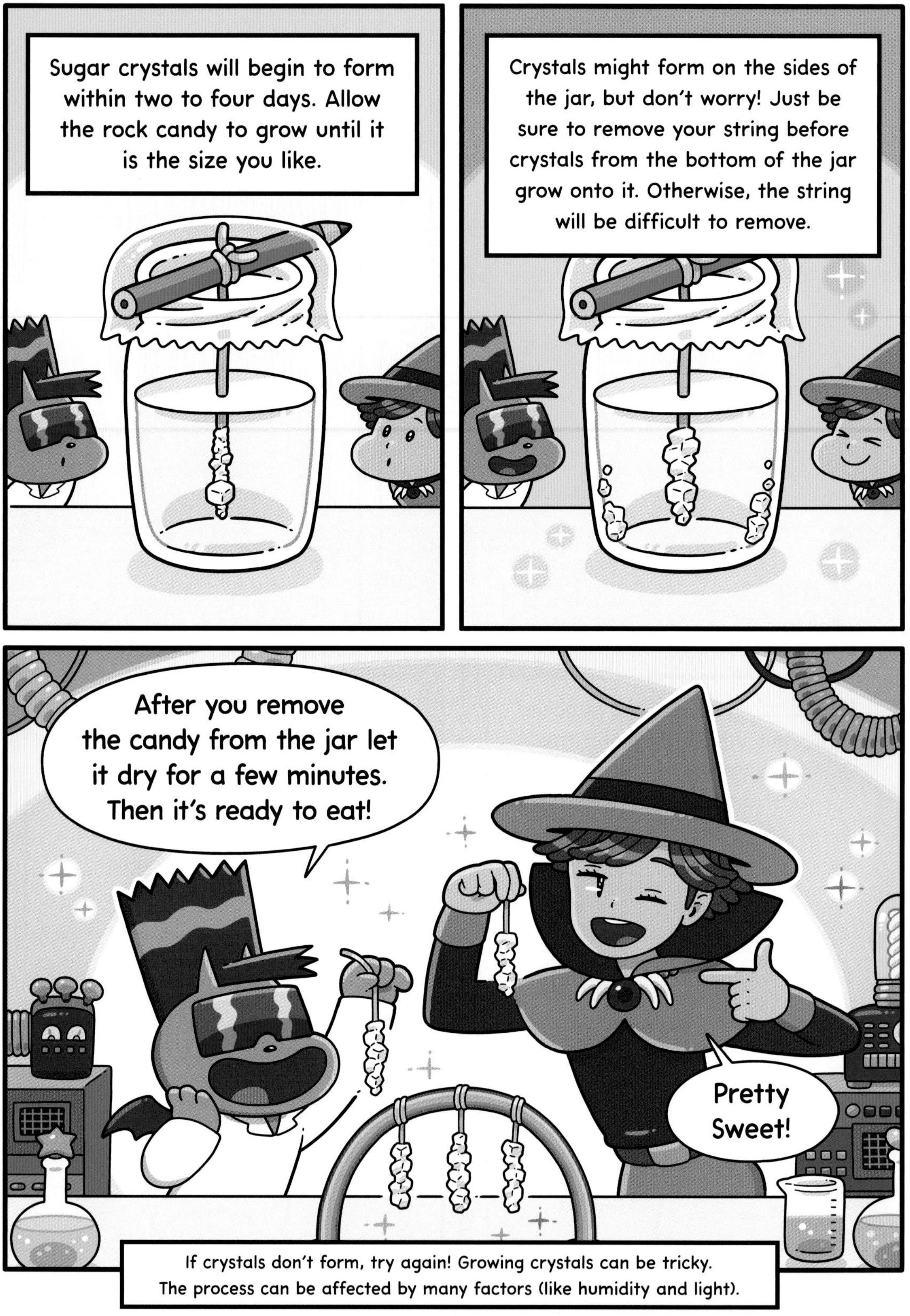

Sugar crystals will begin to form within two to four days. Allow the rock candy to grow until it is the size you like.
Crystals might form on the sides of the jar, but don't worry! Just be sure to remove your string before crystals from the bottom of the jar grow onto it. Otherwise, the string will be difficult to remove.
After you remove the candy from the jar let it dry for a few minutes. Then it's ready to eat!
Pretty Sweet!
If crystals don't form, try again! Growing crystals can be tricky. The process can be affected by many factors (like humidity and light).

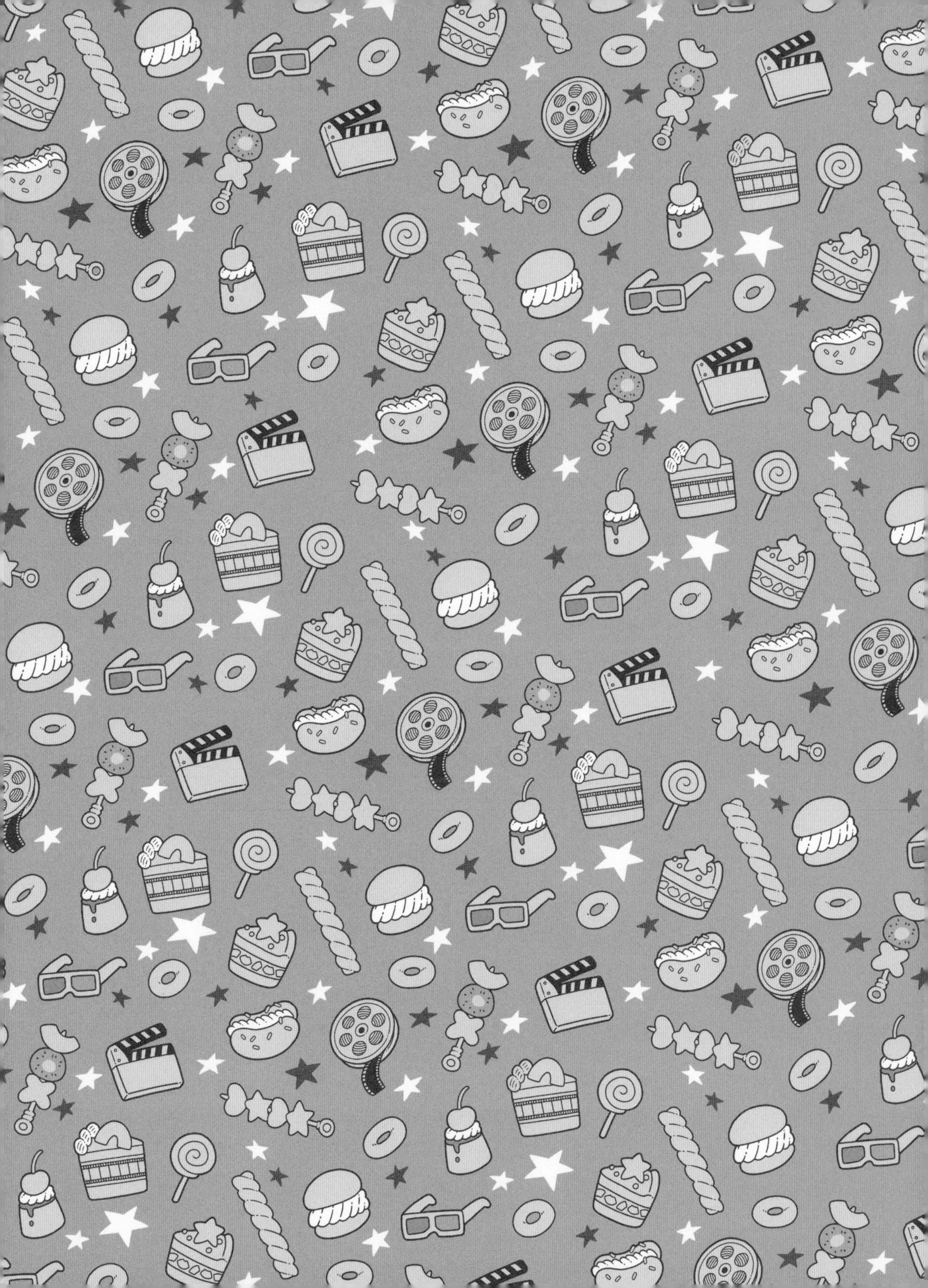

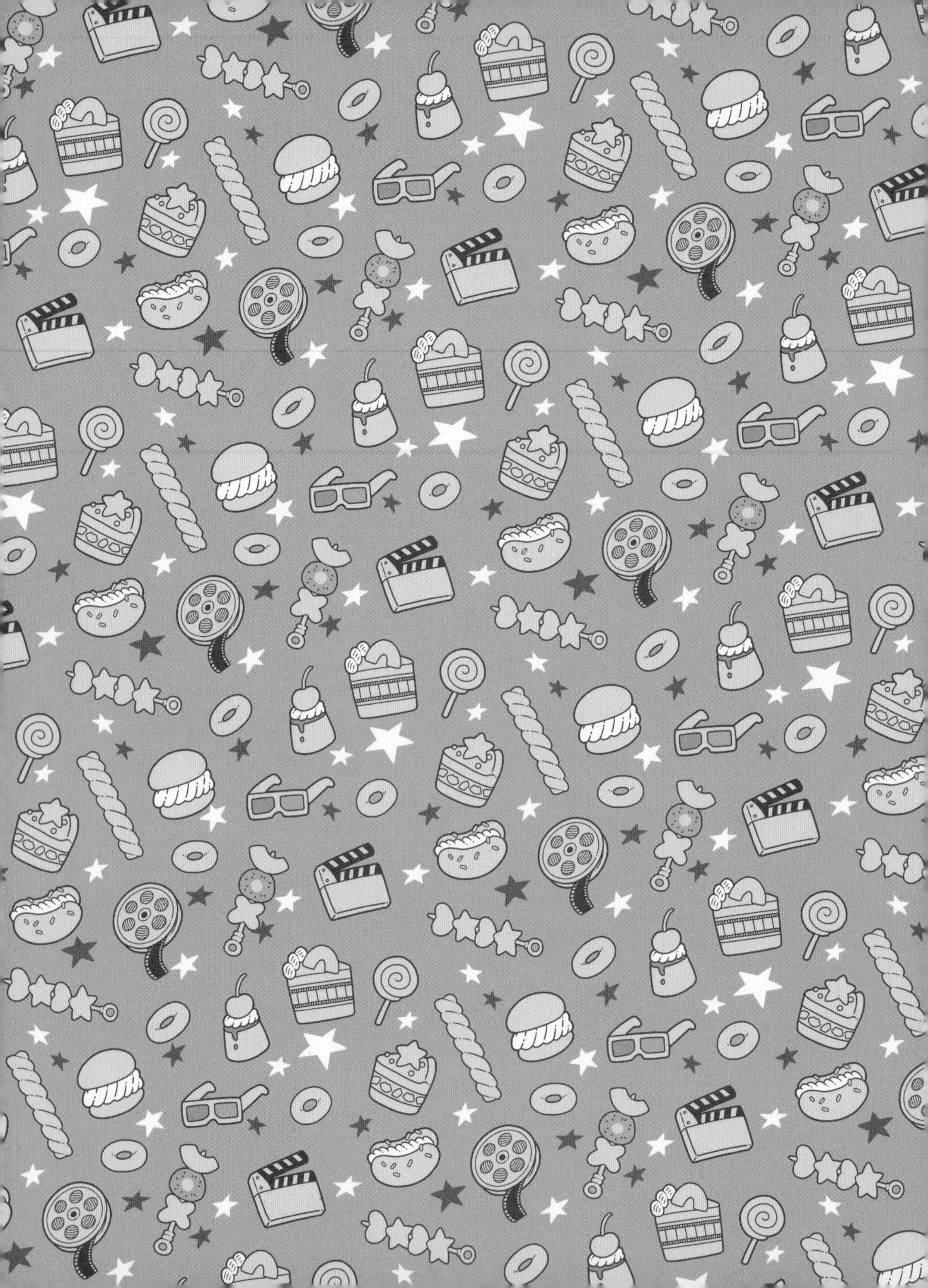